COVER MODEL

Devon Hartford

Want to get an email when Devon's next book is released and receive a FREE Bonus Story?

Sign up here: **http://eepurl.com/B7crf**

or go to **devonhartford.com**

and **click** the **blue SIGN UP button**

DEDICATION

To everyone who told me to get my ass to a romance convention, I decided to bring one to you.

COVER MODEL

They called him Connor HUGE.

Connor Hughes f**ked his way through every girl in my high school.

Except me.

We *hated* each other.

That arrogant a**hole insulted me, tormented me, and *ruined* me without ever laying a finger on me.

After graduating near the top of my class, I escaped to UCLA, got my degree, and threw myself into a career as a serious journalist. But I never forgot the damage Connor did.

At least I'll never have to see him again.

Until my editor at *Trending Magazine* tasks me with writing a tell-all article about Connor. Turns out my insufferable bad boy nemesis grew into the ultra-gorgeous model whose perfect body steams up the covers of half the romance novels on the bestseller lists.

Now I'm stuck shadowing him all weekend long at the world's largest Romance Convention. I'm forced to watch in disgust as 45,000 women throw themselves at him and worship his shirtless body while he taunts me incessantly.

We hate each other as much today as we did seven years ago. But I can't stop stealing glances at his perfect abs and perfect a**.

My better judgment tells me to drop everything and run, but **something deep inside me is dying to know if he's as HUGE as the rumors...**

Cover Model is a steamy standalone with an HEA

Prologue

ELECTRA

GRAD NIGHT, 2008.

"Not on your life," I chuckle, staring into the most beautiful blue eyes I've ever hated.

I stand toe to toe with Connor Hughes, the gorgeous young man I hate more than any other human being on the planet.

"You totally want me." He flashes his insolent grin, the one that makes all the girls in school drool over him and write his name in their notebooks and stalk his Facebook page in hopes that he'll mention them. "You've *always* wanted me."

My anger rises and I snort, "I've *never* wanted you. *Connor.*" I spit out his name like it's filthy. "You must think I'm pretty stupid if you think I'm going to let myself become yet another notch on your bedpost."

In the distance, a flickering rainbow of light beams from the grad night carnival set up behind our high school. All that frolic and fun seems a million miles away.

Ten hours ago, Connor and I walked separately across the stage in the North Valley High School gymnasium and got our diplomas from the principal. When Connor got his, he took a bow to an uproar of cheers and applause. Everybody loves Connor Hughes. Except me. When I took my diploma, nobody made a sound, not even the crickets.

Now it's four in the morning and I'm all alone with Connor under the starry night sky.

I fold my arms defensively across my chest and growl in his arrogant and undeniably handsome face. "The only reason you want me is because you never *had* me, Connor. We both know that if I was dumb enough to have sex with you, you'd get what you've wanted all along, and you'd move on. Just like you did with every other unsuspecting girl you've fucked. Tell me I'm wrong."

He opens his mouth to speak. A strained half syllable wheezes out but catches in his throat. "I—" He deflates, his muscled shoulders sagging.

"That's what I thought," I smirk. "I'm just another notch for you. But I've got news for you, Connor *Screws*. You will *never* catch me. I will *always* get away. After everything that you've done, I will *never* be one of your notches."

I turn on the heel of my brand new bowtie flats and stride across the damp grass field toward the main parking lot. I never look back, promising myself that I will *never* think about Connor Hughes *ever* again.

As far as I'm concerned, he is out of my life forever.

Good riddance.

Chapter 1

CONNOR

SEVEN YEARS LATER…

"Fuck, you're tight," I grunt as I push my dick deeper into her pussy. "And wet as fuck."

We're sprawled on the king-sized hotel bed where we've been fuckin since the sun came up.

Her eyes are clamped shut and her face is screwed up as tight as her pussy. "Ohhhh, yes, Connor, yes…" she moans. "I'm going to come again…"

They always do.

This will be her fourth orgasm this morning, and the seventh since last night when we stumbled up to my room.

I slam into her harder and harder. "Squeeze my dick, babe. Fuckin *squeeze* it… Yeah…"

Her mouth splits open and she cries out, *"Yes, yes, oh my god, yes!!"* Her nails claw my shoulders. This chick's a fuckin beast between the sheets.

I'm down with that. "Come on my dick, Juh—" I stop myself because I almost said Jasmine. She doesn't notice. I don't think this chick's name is Jasmine. Jasmine was Tuesday. At least I *think* it was Jasmine. Or was Jasmine on Wednesday and Siobhan was Tuesday?

Who knows.

I should just stick to calling all of them Babe.

The only thing I do remember about this chick is that she told me earlier she's half Chinese and half Brazilian. Exotic as hell. Long black hair, tanned caramel skin, perfect bod, killer tits. Crazy hot. You don't come across a chick like this every day, but I'm going to come inside her in a minute.

When she picked me up last night, she was easily the hottest chick in the club. I spotted her out of a sea of plastic Beverly Hills blondes immediately. I grew out of my blonde bimbo phase three years ago. They're usually shitty lays. But this chick around my dick is top shelf. Prime Grade. Just like that choice beef they serve down in the restaurants of Brazil. Or is that Argentina? I can't remember. For me, the month long jungle photo shoot I did down in South America was one big blur of exotic pussy, killer booze, and killer food. The steaks down there are unreal.

I nearly laugh out loud at the thought.

I can't believe I'm thinking about Argentinian beef while I'm fuckin this hottie, but I am. No matter how much I think I'm into a chick, my mind always ends up wandering during sex.

"I'm coming, Connor," she squeals as her pussy grabs my dick like a fist.

Yeah she is.

Time for me to let loose myself and get this over with. I've got shit to do today. I groan wordlessly as I pump harder and shoot a load into the condom. It's good but not great.

It's never great.

But it helps me forget about *her*.

For a minute, anyway.

The second I roll off Babe, or whatever her name is, and close my eyes, I see *her* face.

I fuckin *hate* that.

After seven years, I can't stop thinking about the last time I saw *her* face.

One of these years, I'm going to forget about Electra Warmoth.

Or not.

ELECTRA

I didn't spend four years at UCLA getting a degree in journalism for *this*. Writing an exposé on a male model who poses shirtless for romance novel book covers?

Please.

What about this assignment says serious journalism?

None of it.

Sleek modernist decor on the seventh floor surrounds me as I walk along the luxe patterned carpeting toward my destination. Early morning light shines through windows at the end of the long hallway, stabbing my eyes. I need coffee. It's way too early for this nonsense.

I'm beyond irritated about being here.

Why?

Late last night, Vince Pitts, my annoying ass of a Managing Editor over at *Trending Magazine,* insisted I cover this silly story if I wanted to keep getting work from him. I'm a freelancer, and only a junior contributor at that, which means I barely scrape by on what I earn. Considering I still owe a king's ransom on my student loans from getting my journalism degree at UCLA, I agreed. So here I am at Rom Com Con 2015, short for Romantic Comedy Convention, which takes place every summer at the sprawling Beverly Hills Resort and Convention Center.

Can you say waste of time?

I told Vince I didn't care that there will be over a hundred hot hard-bodied male cover models circulating throughout the convention for the next three days, signing autographs and showing off their flawless physiques. I reminded him that a few weeks ago, Hilary Clinton announced her candidacy for President. Whether I agree with her politics or not, I should be following *her* on the campaign trail, covering *her* story as she sets *her* sights on making feminist history. It's about time this country had a woman for president.

But *nooooo,* Vince insisted I spend my Fourth of July weekend here covering this trivial fluff piece. The only fireworks I'm going to see are the irritated ones shooting out of my ears.

Walking beside me in the hotel hallway is a guy named Romeo Fabiano. He's slightly shorter than I am, has olive skin, a coifed black faux-hawk, and a perpetual grin. As we walk, a slick black vinyl trench coat billows out behind him and a monocle bounces from a black string tied to one of his vest's many buckles. Emo chic. He and I met for the first time this morning. Margaret Lang, my media contact for the convention, introduced me to Romeo when I arrived at the resort. She instructed him to take me up to the interview.

"Are you excited to meet him?" Romeo titters. "I know *I* am."

"Excited?" I sigh. "Why should I be excited?"

"Because *no one* has ever seen *HIS* face."

"Maybe *HIS* face isn't worth seeing," I mock, picturing some random meathead gym rat with a dopey expression and a crooked nose whose only asset is his body.

"Surely you jest," Romeo says. "We're talking about *the* Connor. The hottest male model in the business. The man with the perfect body. The body by which all others are measured and found lacking."

The sour expression on my face says: *I don't care.* I could be reporting on the plight of displaced refugees in third world countries. Instead, I'm here at Rom Com Con covering *this*. Open disdain shows on my face. Poker is not my game. But I am a professional, so I try to think happy thoughts to smooth out my wrinkled brow. It doesn't work.

Romeo drives his point home. "A *Connor Cover*, as they're known in the industry, practically guarantees that a book will sell millions of copies and land a top ten slot on The New York Times best sellers list. His abs put washboards out of business. His chest makes granite statues weep with envy. His shoulders made Atlas shrug in defeat. And those tattooed arms? Mmm-mmm, girl. With a body like his, I can only imagine what his *heads* look like."

"You mean, 'head'," I correct.

"No, I mean *heads*. As in, plural. As in, both of them..." His eyes flicker impishly.

I refrain from rolling mine, but the urge is intense. "I hate to break it to you, but the logical conclusion why he's never shown his face is because it's not worth showing."

Romeo nods, "There's been endless speculation on the fan blogs about whether he's handsome or heinous."

"I vote heinous. He's probably a troll. With two troll heads growing from his shoulders."

"O, ye of little faith," Romeo snickers while pulling out a smart phone. He taps the screen and shows me an image. It's a shirtless and headless male torso on the cover of some random book called *Stepbrother Obsessed*. I have no idea what that is. Sounds pornographic. But there's no denying the perfection of the body I'm looking at. It's hard, cut, masculine, inked, and it makes something squirm between my legs, something I thought was either hibernating or flat out extinct.

"You're blush-*iiiing*," Romeo singsongs.

"No I'm not," I bark. I clear my throat and try to sound professional. Yes, I can appreciate a gorgeous body as much as the next woman or obviously gay man like Romeo. But I've always preferred brains over beefcake. "Who is this Connor guy again? Does he have a last name?"

"Nobody knows what it is. He's very protective of his anonymity. Some people believe Connor isn't his real first name at all."

That's no help. I sigh heavily, "Look, my editor literally gave me this assignment last night and I didn't have time to research Connor *Whoever*." The truth is, I didn't *want* to do any research because this is such a meaningless non-story. It's not like interviewing a headless male model with no last name at Rom Com Con 2015 is going to win me a Pulitzer. "So unfortunately I don't know the first thing about this guy. Can you fill me in?"

"Don't you *read*?" Romeo gasps. "Connor is *the* thing in the romance books business."

"I read the Wall Street Journal and Ms. Magazine. Not frivolous romance novels filled with gratuitous sex. I know about 50 Shades of Grey."

"Your loss," Romeo shrugs. "Sounds to me like you could use some frivolity and gratuity in your life."

"What's that supposed to mean?!" I bark.

"Here we *ARE-rreeee*!" Romeo sings, ignoring me.

We stand in front of room 714.

"Are you ready to meet him?" Romeo asks anxiously, his eyes shining gleefully. "I know I am."

"I guess." I fold my arms across my chest and shift my weight impatiently onto the heel of one pump.

"The man of my dreams is on the other side of that door." Romeo beams while he knocks. "Do you think he'll be wearing a mask? Like a sexy but mysterious professional wrestler?"

I didn't realize professional wrestlers were sexy. As before, I try to keep my confrontational comments to myself. I reach into my conservative purse and flick the power button on my mp3 voice recorder to make sure the battery is still good. It is. Distracted, I ask, "Why would he be wearing a mask?"

"Maybe he's horribly disfigured like *The Phantom of the Opera*. Yes, that's it! Once a dashing young man, he lost his looks in a tragic opera fire."

"Opera fire?" I ask doubtfully.

"Yes, bear with me," Romeo says seriously. "Now he's wounded, his heart damaged beyond repair. He yearns in secret for the love of a strong young woman to save him from his solitary misery!" Romeo's eyes light victoriously.

"You're hopeless, Romeo," I chuckle.

"I know, right?" he smiles and winks at me. "Now THE Connor is finally going to make his first *ever* public appearance this afternoon, mask and all, exclusively for Rom Com Con 2015!!!"

I arch an eyebrow.

"It's an historic event," he says seriously.

"*An* historic event?" I mock. *A woman president would be an historic event.*

"That's what I said. Did I misspeak?"

Misspeak? Romeo is definitely in a class by himself. I frown at him and nod toward the door. "Never mind. Let's get this over with. Let's meet *THE* Connor."

Romeo knocks on the door and we wait.

And wait.

Wait a second…

No way.

A jumble of loose thoughts suddenly straighten in my mind. It's just a coincidence, right? Thousands of men are named Connor. It seems highly unlikely that *this* Connor is…*him.*

Connor Hughes.

I haven't seen or heard from Connor in seven years. I haven't even thought about him…

Dark memories lasso my guts and cinch tight. I wince internally, forcing down nausea, not letting it show. I never let it show.

Keeping a straight face doesn't stop the distressed thoughts from pinballing around in my head.

It can't be him…

CONNOR

"I can't believe how good you are in bed, Connor," Babe, or whatever her name is, says breathlessly. "I've never had so many orgasms in one morning." Her lush lips spread into a grin.

Mine don't.

I stand naked at the foot of the bed having just dumped my condom in the bathroom trash.

Babe is a vision of caramel delight on the rumpled white confection of the hotel sheets.

I couldn't care less.

She runs her hands across her breasts, massaging them briefly before sliding her manicured fingers down her taut stomach and between her slick thighs, stroking herself invitingly. She locks eyes with me, hers half-hooded with naked desire for more. "Mmmmm, Connor. Do you have any idea how yummy you are?"

Yes. Some other chick called me yummy last week. Yummy turned into a chick cliché four years ago. I hear it all the time.

"Your cock is twitching. Does that mean you want to go again?" she purrs.

I'm always up for fuckin. Working out seven days a week makes me horny as fuck all the time. And I have to admit, Babe is fuckin hot. But hasn't she had enough of me? I've had enough of her. As hot as she is, she just didn't do it for me. They never do. I sigh, "I don't mean to be a dick, but I have an interview here in the room in a few minutes. I need to clean up before they get here."

"Interview? For what?"

"It's nothing. Some, uhhh, fitness thing," I lie. "Some guy's YouTube workout channel."

"That sounds exciting."

I always tell girls I'm a fitness model, but I never go into more detail than that. I hate talking about myself. "It's pretty boring. Kind of technical. Blood sugar levels, triglycerides, recovery intervals. Boring shit like that." Usually the technical talk turns them off.

"I don't mind," Babe purrs. "I'm sure I'll learn something."

Maybe this chick has potential…

She does that stripper thing where she sticks out the tip of her tongue and runs it across her top teeth. When that doesn't work, she tweaks one of her nipples with her fingers, lifts her tit to her mouth, and licks the nip.

…Then again, maybe not.

Why'd she have to go and ruin it?

"Trust me," I chuckle, "You'll be snoring inside of two minutes. And the guy is a nobody. I think his biggest video has like 700 views. I'm doing it as a favor for a friend." I'm making all of this up as I go along. Babe will never know.

"It's no big deal, Connor. I really don't mind."

This always happens. A girl like her has guys throwing themselves at her 24/7. I saw it at the club last night. Five hundred different guys talked to her, but she went back to the hotel with me. What should've been a one-nighter is suddenly turning into a pain in my ass. I don't know how to break it to her that I'm not interested. After fuckin them, I never am.

So, how to get rid of her?

Usually, I like the direct approach.

"You need to go," I grunt.

ELECTRA

Romeo leans his ear against the door, "I don't hear anyone inside. Do you have a drinking glass?"

"Why?"

"So I can hear better. Don't you watch spy movies?" he hisses.

"Not really."

"Which celebrity do you think he looks like?" Romeo muses gleefully, his ear still glued to the door.

"I have no idea." Nor do I care. My kind of man has a career path. Soft porn modeling is *not* a career path. Nothing gets me going like a suit and tie. Not that I've had anything going on in the boyfriend or the bedroom department since forever. I'm focused on being a journalist, not meaningless flings.

"Whatever he looks like," Romeo swoons, "I bet he's gorgeous. I'm picturing chiseled cheek bones, a brooding brow, smoldering eyes, and a rugged stubbled jaw."

I smirk, "That sounds like a caveman or a neanderthal. Does he wear a leopard skin for a loincloth and carry a club too?"

"I hope so," Romeo grins, his eyes dreamy. "Then he can pound me with his club, take me back to his cave, and pound me with his *human* club from behi—"

"Stop!" I bark.

"Never mind me," he giggles. "A serious woman like you is only interested in serious information, right?"

"What makes you think I'm serious?" I ask defensively.

His eyes sweep up and down my outfit. One of his eyebrows arches dramatically and his face says, *Have you looked in a mirror lately?* But his mouth says, "Please, girlfriend. Your outfit was on the cover of the latest issue of Business Matron's Monthly."

I hide my scowl as I look down my nose at him through my stylish eyeglasses. "That's not even a real magazine." My long auburn hair may be pinned up in a conservative bun, but I look good in my pumps, pencil skirt, and blouse. I always dress my best so people take me seriously.

"We'll work on tomorrow's look later," he smiles. "But we can do something about that uptight hair of yours." He reaches for my bun like he's going to fiddle with it, or worse, let it down completely. "Your hair bun is so tight it's giving you a facelift."

"Hands off!" I growl, pulling back defensively. He thinks he can give *me* fashion advice? He looks like a cartoon character. I resist the urge to kick his shins with my pointed pumps.

He drops his arm to his side, "Loosen up, girl. I'm just trying to help."

"What do you know about women's fashion? Look at *your* outfit! I didn't realize sci-fi emo was still a *thing*," I spit. "And what's with that stupid monocle?"

With practiced flair, he flips the monocle up with a flick of his wrist and squinches it in his cheek. He stares at me through it, the monocled eye comically magnified. "Perhaps you need a personality makeover, darling," he mutters before letting the monocle tumble free.

I'm about to give him a tongue lashing when I stop myself. I admit it. I'm very sensitive about my looks, my personality, everything. Let's face it. I'm just plain sensitive. I blame four years of high school torment from Connor Hughes. That asshole left me scarred.

That's when the hotel room door suddenly whips open and my chest locks down tight, stopping my breath.

It's him.

Connor Hughes.

No. Fucking. Way.

Chapter 2

CONNOR

Fuck me.

It's her.

Electra Warmoth.

Standing on my fuckin hotel doorstep, rockin the sexy librarian look with the hair bun and sexy glasses. And those fuckin legs? They go on for miles.

My dick is instantly hard.

Forget about Babe.

Electra Warmoth is in the fuckin house.

Damn.

When did she learn to dress like such a fox? All I remember is her funky thrift-store overalls and plaid shirts.

Where the hell has she been hiding for the last seven years? Electra was the girl who got away.

Memories blast up outta my past.

In high school, Electra had the sharpest tongue out of anyone, guy or girl. She had a goddamned mouth on her that could peel paint. When it came to me, Electra Warmoth spit venom on a daily basis.

Weird thing was, her mouth was also the sweetest thing I've ever seen. Her clunky braces never fooled me. To this day, she still has the best pair of lips on the planet. Now she has the braces off, they might be the best pair in the universe.

Not that I ever found out how those lips tasted.

Nobody in high school found out. Electra hated everybody.

I *wanted* to find out. I was *dying* to find out. I would've given my left nut to feel those sweet lips on mine, braces or not. But I never got to. Everybody said she'd die a virginal spinster. Believe me, I tried to save her from a lifetime of solitude, but nothing worked.

Electra never let down the brick wall she built around herself.

The harder I tried to get close to her, the harder I got thinking about her. I couldn't sleep because of her. Every night in my dreams, she gave it up like a porn star. You know a girl with a hot mouth like that is crazy as fuck in the sack.

During the day, Electra gave me nothing but grief. Dirty looks, harsh comments, insult after insult. She literally flipped me off every time she saw me. The chick hated me. She dubbed me The Con Man, Connor Rude, Connor the Stooge, Connor Brews, Connor Pukes, and countless others. Yeah, I drank way too much in high school. What can I say? I was a drunken fuck up back then. Arguably, I still am.

But I'm no idiot.

They say the definition of insanity is doing the same thing over and over and expecting different results. Believe me, I tried every angle I could with Electra. Early on, I realized pursuing her was pointless. When someone says no to you all the time, you realize you need to find someone else who'll say yes.

Plenty of girls were happy to say yes.

Let's face it.

In high school, I was Connor Huge.

Every girl who put out wanted to find out if the rumors were true.

They were.

I got more pussy than any high school kid deserved. I banged my way through every hottie in town. What do you expect? I'm a guy. The only downside was I got in plenty of fights for screwing other dudes' girls. I didn't care. I was always up for a fight.

Sad thing was, four years of fuckin and fighting didn't make any difference. I was still dying to taste Electra's sweet lips.

Both pairs.

If I want something bad enough, I'm gonna get it eventually. I'm fuckin persistent when I wanna be.

The night we graduated senior year, I gave it one last shot.

We were both at our school's on-campus grad night. Unlike some high schools, North Valley is huge and has plenty of money. So our grad night was off the hook. They closed off all the fields behind the school and turned it into a fuckin carnival. Literally. All kinds of cool roller coaster and gyro rides, a ferris wheel, a big ass bounce house, carnival games, cotton candy, caramel apples, popcorn, photo booths, fortune tellers, all that shit. People loved it. It was the perfect setup for me to make one last pass at Electra Warmoth.

How did it go?

Let's just say that after the shit that went down at four in the morning, I knew my chances with Electra were burnt fuckin toast. Down in flames. When she ran off that night, I thought she was outta my life forever.

Or so I thought.

Cause here she is.

Will wonders never fuckin cease?

<<<<<<<>>>>>>>

ELECTRA

"There's no way I'm doing this interview," I snarl, glaring into Connor's arrogant blue eyes. They glimmer at me from beneath his thick lashes. A smarmy smirk spreads across his face.

I'm instantly furious. Think nuclear.

It doesn't help my mood that the boy I hated more than any man in the history of men is all grown up and excruciatingly handsome. With nothing but a white bed sheet wrapped around his narrow waist, he may as well be naked. Nothing is left to my imagination. He is picture perfect, taller and better looking than I remember. Tan hard muscles, tattoos criss-crossing his broad shoulders and biceps, perfect abs that I hate more than I hate his azure eyes, the bulge beneath the bed sheet—no. What am I thinking? I'm not sure, but I'm not thinking about *that*. Because:

I.

HATE.

CONNOR.

HUGE.

I mean, HUGHES.

I always have, and I always will.

"Power Pole?" he chuckles in his oh so maddeningly familiar baritone drawl. "Is that you?"

Like a whipped dog, I cringe at the old high school nickname.

A younger version of Connor's voice echoes up from memory: *Check it out! It's Power Pole! She's a toothpick no matter which way you look at her! And what's with those throw-back clothes? Did you get them from a dumpster?* Followed by laughter from Connor and his fratty friends. Despite Connor's "Rebel May Care" persona, his chain-smoking, and his tattered leather jacket, he was friends with the jocks. They all loved to loathe me. For them, mocking me was a team sport, and Connor was their quarterback.

Power Pole.

One of Connor's many electrically themed insults. When my hippie parents named me Electra, I think they thought it would make me cool. Somehow, these things never work out the way they're supposed to. I was completely flat-chested in high school and naturally gangly. Believe me, being skinny is not necessarily a blessing. On me, it looked all wrong. Picture sticks and strings. Add to that the goofy glasses I used to wear, the braces, the second-hand clothes, my dorkish nervous energy, and you can see how Power Pole became the obvious insult of choice.

Other favorites included: High Tension (an accurate description of my usual mood caused by daily insults from Team Connor), Lightning *Dolt* (which I grew out of when people realized I made Honor Roll every semester), High *Vulvage* (because of my long legs), Benjamin *Skank*lin (I think one of the cheerleaders suggested it—it was eventually shortened to just *Skanklin*), and Brown Out (which somehow implied I pooped my pants when I got angry, and you better believe being called Brown Out all the time made me plenty angry, but I never pooped myself, not once).

I push away all the old memories and smash them down into my subconscious and slam the lid on it like the over-stuffed suitcase of past pain that it is.

Ignoring Connor's half-nakedness, I glare at my old nemesis. "Well, well, well," I snark, "if it isn't Connor Douche. In the flesh." Why did I have to say flesh? Maybe because that's all he's wearing.

Completely unaffected by my harsh words, Connor rubs his large palm across his rippled abs.

Why do guys with great bodies always have to touch their abs? Do they fear their abs don't draw enough attention to themselves already? Or are they touching them to make sure they're still there? Either way, it's a sign of shallow insecurity. I learned that tidbit at UCLA in one of my electives: Psych 127A *Abnormal Psychology*.

Connor snickers, pleased with himself. "It is you, isn't it, War *Mouth*?" He says it with his usual self-assured superiority. "Don't tell me you're here for my interview."

"Uh, *yeah*," I snort. "Why did you think I was here?" My skin crawls as his eyes slide across every inch of my body until they come to rest on my chest. "Don't answer that." I glare at him. "Can we get started already?" I want this over and done.

His eyes claw at my blouse.

It figures.

I turn up the disdain on my face. My expression says, *If you say one more nasty thing, if you call me Power Pole or High Tension or Benjamin Skanklin, I will peel every inch of skin off your body with a rusty paring knife then roll your skinless body in salt. Picture what happens when you pour salt on a slug, because a slug is all that you are, Connor Pukes.* The only sound I actually make is a short sharp snort.

Ignoring my ire, he rolls out a haphazard chuckle. "You grew breasts. I didn't think you had it in you." He leers with that same damn leer I learned to loathe in high school.

"I'm full of surprises," I smirk. Before I realize I'm doing it, I fold my arms protectively over my blouse. It's an old habit of mine. I'm an expert at defensive posturing, thanks to Connor. I thought I'd broken the habit. Despite Connor's leering stare, I drop my arms to my side. Not that there's much for him to see. Yes, there's more than there was in high school, but I'm sure my boobs are nothing compared to the over-inflated Barbie balloons he goes for.

He leans casually against the door frame, grinning at me. "Damn, War Mouth. I can't believe you went and got hot."

Is he being serious?

Of course he isn't.

I scowl a silent reply. I will not play into his usual games. I know he would love for me to take the bait and thank him and accept the compliment at face value. Knowing Connor, he has some witty retort lined up to make me look stupid. Something like *"No, I meant hot, as in sweaty, as in, you have huge pit stains. Did you forget your anti-perspirant this morning?"* or something worse. Connor was always a master at twisting my words so I looked like an idiot in front of everybody. That's why I resist the urge to glance at my armpits. I *did* put on anti-perspirant this morning, didn't I? Wondering about it makes my body temperature spike thirty degrees.

Damn it, it took less than a minute for him to get me flustered.

Romeo nudges against my arm and whispers, "Why does he keep calling you War Mouth?"

"Because my last name is Warmoth," I hiss.

"Luv it," Romeo giggles.

I slap him with a hateful glare. My dirty looks are dangerous. I got really good at them in high school, again thanks to Connor. Sometimes a hateful look is easier than coming up with a witty retort on the fly.

Romeo winces nervously. "I mean, *hate* it. Worst nickname ev-*er*. So, ummm… may I presume you two know each other?"

"I went to high school with this limp dick stick," I grumble.

Romeo's eyes explode in awe. He gasps, "You know *THE* Connor?"

"Unfortunately," I mumble.

Romeo titters, "Someone get me a fainting couch! I'm about to expire!"

Sudden chaos erupts from behind Connor.

A beautiful young caramel-skinned woman in a disheveled emerald cocktail dress and heels barges out of the room. When she sees me, she stops abruptly and her eyes headlight. "Who are *you*?" She hisses at me, "Are you the *fitness* interview?"

I'm too stunned to answer.

"I should've known," she seethes. Then she turns to glare at Connor. "I faked all my orgasms, asshole!!!"

"Sure you did," Connor chuckles.

Her face wrinkles with disgust. "Fuck you!" She grabs the bed sheet and yanks it from his waist before wadding it and throwing it in his face. "You piece of shit!"

The sheet tumbles to the ground as the woman saunters down the hotel hallway. It's the most hateful Walk Of Shame I've ever seen.

Despite the drama, Connor still leans casually against the doorframe like nothing happened.

Except he's completely naked.

I'm staring right at his huge—

"Can I have this?" Romeo asks, squatting to the ground at Connor's feet while reaching tentatively for the crumpled bed sheet. "No, seriously, can I have this?" He stares up at Connor and his—

I didn't think it would be THAT big...

"Be my guest." Connor says casually to Romeo. But his eyes never leave mine.

Romeo grabs the sheet and twirls it into a ball which he hugs to his chest like it's a wad of thousand dollar bills.

Meanwhile, my rage has gone super nova.

Screw my professionalism.

I don't care. I'm not interviewing Connor Hughes. No matter *how* big of a—

Never mind.

I swore if I ever saw him again I'd shoot him in the face. Since I don't have a gun handy, I decide the polite thing to do is walk away before I claw his eyes out.

"I'm outta here." I turn and march down the long hallway toward the elevators.

I can't wait to hear what Vince Pitts has to say when I tell him he needs to find someone else to do this useless interview.

CONNOR

"I'll go get her," the short goth dude with Electra says before jogging off.

I was sorta hoping for a cat fight. Oh well.

Sitting on the bed, I wait around for a while with the door open. They never come back. My jeans are crumpled on the floor in the corner. I grab my phone from the pocket and check my voicemail. I've had the ringer off since I brought Babe back to the room last night.

"Connor, this is your dad."

I smile to myself. Like I can't recognize his voice.

"We just want you to know we're having a great time on our trip. The air in Denver really is thinner. Your mom and I went up the steps of the capitol building to that mile high medallion. We were both huffing and puffing like a couple of old farts."

"*You* were huffing and puffing," Mom laughs. "I jog, remember? And you smoke!"

"She was huffing and puffing," Dad chuckles into the phone. "Anyway, I should focus on driving—"

"Gimme that!" Noises as Mom takes the phone and giggles, "Yes, your father should focus on driving. Connor, we just wanted to call to say we're having a great time and we wish you were here."

"No we don't! He's old enough to take care of himself. When are you going to cut the apron strings, Kelly? Connor's his own man. Right, son?" There's a pause and Dad chuckles. "What am I thinking? This is a voicemail! You can't answer. Oh! Did I mention we're going to stop at Mt. Rushmore? Your mom doesn't wanna go but I told her it's educational and maybe she'll learn something."

"I know plenty, Finn. If it wasn't for me, you'd be eating hot dogs for dinner every night."

"I like hot dogs!" Dad laughs. "Anyway, I've always wanted to find out if Rushmore really does look smaller in person."

"Compared to *your* giant head," Mom snickers, "*everything* is smaller."

"Which one?"

"Finn!" She's laughing. "You're such a bad influence. Connor, promise me you'll never be an egotistical ass like your father."

"It's too late for that," Dad chuckles. "Anyway, kid, we just stopped for lunch. We'll call you again soon."

"Bye, Connor!" Mom cheers. "We miss you!"

The message ends and I look out the window of the room and stare at the Pacific Ocean, smiling to myself.

ELECTRA

"Have you lost your god damned mind, Warmoth?!" Vince yells.

Wincing, I hold my phone away from my ear. With my free hand I grab clean wet clothes from the laundry cart and throw them into one of the big dryers at the Lucy's Laundromat around the corner from my tiny apartment. Since I bailed on the whole Connor interview thing, I decided today was a good day to do laundry. I hate having to drive here, but I don't have a choice. I can't afford to live in a nicer apartment complex that actually has an on-site laundry facility. "I can't believe you set me up on this story, Vince! A male model tell-all? It's ridiculous!"

"What's the problem, Warmoth? Guy get your panties in a wad?"

A thousand megapixel image flashes through my mind of the bed sheet crumpled on the floor beneath Connor's enormous junk. I growl into the phone, "That's sexist, Vince." While his comment *might* be true, it's still sexist.

"So what the hell is the problem? You got a thing for this guy?"

I snort, "You couldn't be any more off the mark if you were on the moon, Vince!" I hurl a pair of wet jeans into the dryer and they thud against the back wall with a metallic echo. "There's no way I'm doing this interview!"

"I'm sorry," Vince says with feigned politeness, "did I hear you right? I think there's a bad connection."

"You heard me," I seethe, grabbing a fistful of wet leggings from the laundry basket.

"That's odd, because I could've sworn you said you were all over this story because you want to keep getting work from me, and the last thing you want to do is piss me off to the point that I lose your phone number."

I squeeze my smart phone so hard I think I'm going to crack the screen. When that doesn't happen, I consider throwing it into the dryer with my clothes.

"You picking up what I'm putting down, Warmoth?"

"Yes!"

The truth is, if it wasn't for Vince, I wouldn't have enough work to make rent every month. Paid work as a journalist is very hard to find. The last thing I want to do is move back in with my parents. I swore to myself I'd never get that desperate. If I wasn't already short on rent for next month, I'd seriously consider telling Vince to stick this story so far up his ass that he could read it with his eyes closed.

I sigh to myself.

Everybody knows that adulthood means from time to time you have to bend over for your boss whether you want to or not. The image of sweaty Vince Pitts with his stringy comb-over flopping against his forehead while he bends me over his glass desk at the *Trending* offices makes me want to throw up all over my laundry. I swallow down my disgust. I don't want to run this load of darks again.

"What's it gonna be, Warmoth? Am I calling Audrey to handle what you can't?"

Audrey Fisher is a senior contributor for *Trending Magazine*. She's a kiss ass and a job hog who would love to take my paycheck.

But I hardly care about her.

I care about my reputation.

Never in my career have I balked at an assignment. I'm the go-to girl. I get stuff done. I'm up for *any* assignment, no matter how much I might dislike the subject. I've interviewed drug dealers, embezzlers, corporate criminals, and human rights abusers. I always get the story, no matter how much the subject turns my stomach. But this is different. This is personal.

"Well, Warmoth?"

I grit my teeth. "Fine. I'll do it."

"Good. Remember, your interview copy goes live to-*day*. Austin will meet you in the lobby at the hotel at noon to take pictures."

"I thought we weren't getting an exclusive on the photos."

"We're not. The agreement with Rom Com Con and Connor's agent is that nobody gets any pictures until the live reveal. They've gone out of their way to keep this Connor guy's face a secret. Why, I have no idea. But I want to go live with your article the *second* Austin has pics. Otherwise *TMZ* will break the story before we do. So drop whatever you're doing and get your ass back to that hotel and finish that fucking interview! You hearing me, Warmoth?!"

"Yes!!" I scream into the phone.

The few people doing their laundry this early in the morning all stop what they're doing and stare at me.

"Sorry," I mutter to the room. *Not sorry.*

"I don't want to hear sorry, Warmoth! Get your ass in gear!'

"I was talking to the—"

Vince hangs up before I can finish my sentence.

While cursing Vince under my breath to the high heavens, I yank my wet laundry out of the dryer and stuff it in my basket. Then I stop one of the many washing machines in the laundromat with a violent twist, nearly snapping the knob off the control panel. I pull my unfinished load of soapy towels out and drop them sopping into my basket. I carry the dripping mess to my car. I don't even bother to drive home and drop it off.

My clothes are going to have to sit in my trunk until this evening. I hope they don't get all mildewy between now and then.

It is my sincerest wish that Vince Pitts dies a slow and painful death at the hands of an epileptic dentist who forgot to take his meds.

No offense to epileptics, of course.

Or dentists.

Unless they deserve it. Like Vince Pitts.

Damn him!

Chapter 3

CONNOR

"How did the interview go?" It's my agent on the phone, Gloria Powers. She's been repping me for five years. Her voice is all smiles.

I chuckle, kicking back on the unmade bed in my hotel room. "It didn't happen."

"What?" Now her voice could cut glass.

"She bailed," I say casually.

"*Who* bailed?"

"The reporter from *Trending Magazine*. She left before the interview started."

"Ugh. Why did she leave?"

"I may have pissed her off."

"You didn't try to get her into bed, did you?"

I chuckle. "Jealous?"

"Fuck you, Connor. Did you try to screw her or not?"

"You sound jealous to me." I grin to myself.

"Damn it, Connor. Do you know how many favors I had to call in to set up this interview?"

"All of them," I say sarcastically. "Look, I don't fuckin know what happened, G. But I didn't try to fuck her." Not yet, anyway. If I can track Electra down, I just might. I can't believe War Mouth dropped back into my life today.

"You sure? No flirting? No grab-assing?"

"No, Gloria. I told you. I didn't do anything. She just flipped out." I realize how stupid this sounds. "I think she had a screw loose. For all I know, she needed to take a huge shit and didn't want to do it in my room and stink up the place."

"That's disgusting, Connor."

"What do you want me to tell you? She left. No explanation."

She groans. "As long as you didn't try to sleep with her."

"I swear, I didn't."

"Good. Because the last thing we need is *Trending* printing an article about you sexually harassing their reporter."

"That might actually be a good story. You know what they say about bad press…"

"That might work for Caitlyn Jenner and the Kardashians, but you're still a nobody, Connor. You're unknown. You know what they say about first impressions."

I run my hand through my hair. "I didn't do anything, G."

"If I hear otherwise when I talk to my contact at *Trending,* you better hope I never find you because I *will* cut your dick off and soak the stump in rubbing alcohol."

I wince. "You wouldn't want to do that to your favorite dick, would you?"

"Don't test me, Connor. I have a business to run. You're not my only client." She sighs heavily. "I'll make some calls. Stay where you are. I'll see if I can rebuild the bridge you just burnt."

I toss the phone on the mattress.

Fuck her and her bridges.

I don't need this shit.

I don't even want to be here for this ridiculous reveal. It was all Gloria's fuckin idea. I would've been happy to remain anonymous. But Gloria is dead set on building my brand.

I guess her fifteen percent of my take home isn't enough. So she has to make up for it by getting me more exposure which supposedly leads to bigger and better paying gigs and starring roles and all that shit. I don't know what's wrong with making just enough cash to cover rent and food and gas for my bike every month. What more do you need? I mean, besides pussy? And that shit's free.

—*scream*—

I shudder.

Maybe *I* need to bail on this whole fuckin convention reveal bullshit. I can think of a thousand things I'd rather be doing.

Top on the list is fuckin Electra Warmoth, which isn't gonna cost me a dime.

<<<<<<<<>>>>>>>

ELECTRA

"Just my luck," Connor chuckles. He stands fully naked in the doorway of room 714.

"Put some clothes on or I'm leaving," I snap. It's an empty threat but he doesn't know that. "I don't need to be here."

"You're right. You being here is a privilege."

"You wish," I spit.

"Really? My agent has been hounding me to do a big interview like this for months. We already turned down *People*, *US*, *GQ*, and *Esquire*."

"You're lying."

"Nope. Everybody wants me, War Mouth. But you already knew that."

How does he make it *so* easy to despise him? He's truly talented. "Okay, if that's true, Connor *Lewd*, why did you pick *Trending Magazine*? *Trending* is still the up-and-comer. Those other magazines are well established." Although I'm truly curious, mainly I don't want to think about how *naked* he is right now. And the fact that we're all alone.

"Because I *am* the trend," Connor says, cocky as ever.

Cock.

I snort, "You're still full of yourself after all these years, aren't you?"

"Of course I am. Admit it, War Mouth. You like what you see."

"I do not." It's not like I haven't seen Connor nearly naked before. He was always one of those guys who took his shirt off at the drop of a hat so he could parade his abs around for the girls. This is no different, except he's taller and more muscular and I can see his... I close my eyes with obvious irritation. I'm not going to stare. "Can I ask you a serious question?"

"What?"

I glare at him. "Do you know what it feels like to be kicked in the balls by a woman wearing pointed pumps?"

"Nope."

I smirk, "If you don't put some clothes on so we can start this interview, you're about to find out."

"You're bluffing," he says, amused. He really doesn't care that he's standing naked in the hotel hallway.

I sigh with irritation. "Get a towel from the bathroom or something. Let's get this interview over with. I have a deadline and I'm not about to miss it because you're playing games." I shoulder past him into the room and stride toward the round table by the picture window. The hotel room is standard but classy, with a king size bed and stylish dark wood furniture.

The room door closes solidly behind me.

One might say ominously.

A large, muscled, naked model of a man stands somewhere behind me.

Am I going to regret this?

No. I can take care of myself. I've been in far more dangerous situations than this. I know how to deal with Connor Hughes. He's a man-child. An authoritative tone ought to be enough to keep him in line.

Connor's voice tickles my ears, "Do you have any idea how incredible your ass looks in that skirt?"

If Connor was a co-worker, I'd threaten him with a sexual harassment lawsuit. But he's not. There's nothing I can do but ignore it. It's not like he means it.

"I haven't seen an ass that good since..." He sounds lost in thought. "Since the last time I saw you, War Mouth." He chuckles to himself.

Maybe he means it? No, he's just trying to irritate me. We both know it's not true.

"Fuck, woman. Your hips won't fuckin quit." The tone in his voice is blatantly sleazy. I can feel his eyes crawling all over my ass. "What I wouldn't do to bend you over that table and fuck you from behind while we both enjoy the view."

I swallow hard.

I haven't had a man talk to me this way since...

Ever.

But that's not why I'm here. And speaking of views, the view out the window is very nice. I can see the Pacific Ocean. That's the view he was referring to, right? Who am I kidding. This is Connor Hughes. Pursing my lips for my own benefit, I shake my head. "Can it, Connor. Either we're doing this interview or—"

"I'm doing you. Take your pick."

"That's not what I said. And stop talking like a rapist. Not every woman on this planet wants to have sex with you, you know."

"You do. But you won't admit it."

"Ha! I wouldn't have sex with you if you were the last man on earth."

"Speaking of sex—"

"No, Connor!"

"—when was the last time you had any?"

I swallow hard again. It's been years. But I won't admit that to him or anybody else. Nor will I admit that I can't help but wonder what it would feel like to have him inside me, bent over this chair, squirming as he takes me from behind and an orgasm rips through me...

"And I don't mean throw-away sex, War Mouth. I mean the kind of sex that is so good you call all your girlfriends and brag about it for months."

Not that I have many girlfriends to call. My career leaves me little time for friends. I make a lot of acquaintances on the job, but I wouldn't call those people friends.

He continues, "The kind of sex where you're soaking fuckin wet and your pussy lips are swollen because it goes on all night long, the kind where you come so hard you see stars, the kind where you're afraid to come one more time because you think it might kill you but you do it anyway. The kind of sex where your pussy aches the next morning but all you can think about is doing it again. And again. And *again*. And—"

"Stop! I get it!"

Am I panting?

I think I was panting.

One thing's for sure, my panties are—

"I bet you're wet right now just thinking about it."

Damn him.

He's right.

My back still to him, I steady myself by grabbing the top of the chair in front of me. My eyes are closed and my head is spinning and I'm about to fall over.

Jesus.

"What you need right now is for me to throw you on that table, hike up that tight skirt of yours, tear your panties off, and devour your pussy until you come all over my face. *Then* I'll fuck you until you can't see straight."

Not what I was just thinking, but close enough. My knees are literally wobbling.

He chuckles throatily. "I'm right. You are *dyin* for a good fuck." It's a statement of fact.

And he is right. If he was somebody else.

Power Pole. High Tension. Lightning Dolt. Benjamin Skanklin. High Vulvage. Brown Out. Those names represent the history of my misery. Why in the world would I want to have sex with an asshole like Connor Hughes? I won't let him make a mockery of me. I don't care how sexy he *thinks* he is. I grit my teeth. "Connor, I'm here to do an interview." I spin around. "I really *wuh*—" The feral power of Connor's nakedness stops me short. I lock eyes with him because it's the only safe place for me to rest my gaze.

"Want me to do you," he finishes my sentence. Again.

"That's not what I was going to say!"

"But it's what you *want* to say." The grin on his face is rakish and sexy as hell.

I hate it.

"Wow, Warmoth. You are *red*. Did you just come?"

"No!" That's when I realize I'm boiling. I want to fan my face or take a cold shower, but I'm not going to let it show. I break eye contact with him and suddenly find myself staring at his cock.

It's fully erect.

Oh my god.

It's large and in charge.

I'm sopping wet and horny as hell myself. My lady parts are literally spasming in anticipation of a toe-curling orgasm. And surprise, there's a gorgeous able-bodied man standing right in front of me with his gorgeous able-bodied cock pointing straight at me.

But he is my arch nemesis Connor Huge.

I mean, Connor *Hughes*.

Oh, shit.

What am I going to do?

ELECTRA

"Shall we?" Connor smirks, showing off his perfect teeth.

At the sight of those even white teeth, another aspect of my painful past comes crashing instantly back. I try not to snarl. Unlike me, *Connor* never needed braces in high school. Before I got braces, *my* teeth looked like a graveyard full of tombstones after a tornado hit. *His* teeth were naturally perfect. But I do believe he whitens them. Smoker's teeth don't come in that shade of fluorescent. Not that the brilliant white looks bad against his tan skin and stubble. It looks quite—what am I thinking! I have work to do. I'm a journalist, not one of his rabid groupies. "Shall we what?" I growl. "Start the interview already? Sounds like a great idea."

"I wasn't talking about the interview…"

I follow his gaze to the disheveled king size bed. The sheets are everywhere, revealing the plush pillow top mattress.

That breaks the spell. A firestorm of rage explodes inside my chest. "Can I get you a cigarette?" I ask.

"Huh?"

"Don't you, you know—" I motion toward the bed with my chin, sounding friendly and sarcastic at the same time, "—want to take a moment to maybe enjoy a few puffs on a Marlboro? I know you liked to smoke in high school, and I imagine you'd want a cigarette *AFTER YOU JUST FUCKED SOME RANDOM SKANK IN THAT BED!!!*"

After a long silence, Connor breaks into a self-satisfied laugh.

"Jesus, Connor! Did you seriously think I'd have sex with you *right after* you had sex with someone else? In the *same* bed?! I was standing right there when she walked out! How long is your memory?"

"Not half as long as my dick," he smirks.

It's long all right, and still a throbbing hot rod that is noticeably twitching in time with his heartbeat. Looking away, I shake my head in awe. "I can't believe your audacity, Connor! Are you still trying to get me to have sex with you?"

He lifts his eyebrows, grinning from ear to ear.

"Gosh, Connor. Maybe I should take a number first." I stride to the hotel room door.

"Where are you going?"

I whip the door open and twist my head from side to side, looking back and forth along the empty hotel hallway. "Just checking to see how long the line of bimbos is."

He laughs like this is all some big joke.

Maybe it is.

I slam the door closed and stare him down over my glasses, my fists on my hips. "News flash, Connor. I have a job to do. If I don't get this interview, I will not get paid. If I don't get paid, I can't make rent. Someone like you probably has no idea what that even means." I scowl at him like he's a steaming mound of toxic waste.

He stares at me, blank faced.

I hike my eyebrows. "Well? Do you have anything to say for yourself?"

"Damn, Warmoth. I forgot how gorgeous you are when you're mad."

I blink several times. "What the hell are you talking about, Connor?"

"Look in a mirror. Most girls go ugly the second they lose their cool. Their faces bunch up like a paper sack. Yours doesn't."

Although there's a huge mirror mounted to the wall over the low chest of drawers, I refuse to look at it. "Grow up, Connor. I'm here for your interview. That's it."

"How much?"

"What?!" I gasp. Then I figure it out. "I'm not a *hooker*, Connor! I'm a reporter! Jesus! You never quit!"

"Nope. Never." He grins smugly. "Anyway, how much are they paying you?"

I shake my head, totally lost. "What are you—?"

"For the interview? How much are they paying you to do this interview?"

"That's none of your business, Connor!"

"All I'm saying is, if they don't pay you, I'll cover it."

"What?! Why?!" I sound like I'm losing my mind. The truth is, I'm so confused right now I really am starting to lose it. Connor *always* did this to me. He literally makes me insane.

He shrugs. "I don't know. I guess because I wouldn't want you to miss your rent payment. Getting evicted is a bitch." His words are soft and sincere.

I'm taken aback. "Um, *thanks*?"

He smiles instantly. "Any time. So, about this interview?"

There's a knock at the hotel door.

"What?!" I shout as I yank it open.

ELECTRA

"Did we come at a bad time?" Romeo asks.

He's flanked by two people: a man with camera bags and lighting equipment, and a woman with what looks like makeup cases.

I lean toward Romeo and mutter, "I thought there weren't supposed to be any photographs until the unveiling?" I'm thinking about what Vince told me on the phone earlier, but if it's okay to snap photos of Connor's secret face, I'll whip out my smart phone and take a bunch of candids and upload them to Vince with a headline inside of sixty seconds.

MYSTERIOUS HEARTTHROB CONNOR HUGHES FINALLY COMES CLEAN. Exclusive Exposé to follow...

I don't want anyone beating us to the punch.

"They're with the convention," Romeo says, motioning to the people with him. "Margaret asked me to escort them up here."

Great. I haven't even started my interview. I need a settled room if I'm going to do it right. These people will be a distraction. Interview subjects aren't apt to reveal the kind of sensitive information that makes for a juicy Q&A if they aren't relaxed. This is a disaster. If I have any hope of uploading my article before my deadline runs out, I need everybody out of here.

Romeo strides into the room like he's on a mission. He stumbles to a stop when he sees naked Connor standing by the bed. He gasps, "What have you two been *doing* in here?!"

"Nothing," I grunt. Am I surprised that Connor's cock is still half erect? No. And how does it make me look being in the room with him naked? At least I'm dressed, which gives me plausible deniability. I don't intend to be a part of Connor's steamy story. I'm just the reporter.

"Did you shoot video?" Romeo demands. "I'd pay good money to watch your sex tape."

"We didn't do anything," I grumble.

Romeo's eyes dart between me and Connor.

Connor shrugs, "I tried. Couldn't get her chastity belt off."

"Do you need a key?" Romeo pulls a massive jingling keyring out of his black vinyl trench coat. "I have plenty."

"What are all those for?" I marvel.

"Chastity belts. Handcuffs. Padlocked bondage outfits and ball gags." He shrugs. "The usual. You never know when you might get stuck and need a key."

"What was your name again?" Connor laughs.

Romeo twirls his hand in the air and does a low courtly bow. "Romeo Fabiano, at your *dis*service," he says impishly. "I always aim to *tease*."

"Where should we set up?" the guy with the camera bags asks as he shoulders into the room lugging his gear, followed by the woman with the makeup cases.

The makeup woman stops in her tracks when she sees Connor and his cock. "Ahhhh… should we come back later?"

The photographer is all business, already setting up his gear. "We can shoot him from the waist up. It's fine."

"But I have to put his makeup on first," the woman says. Her own makeup is conservative but artful. She gives me a nervous glance. "I'm Beverly. You can call me Bev. Pleased to meet you."

We shake hands.

"Nice to meet you." Now she has an ally. I can tell she's uncomfortable being in the room with naked Connor and the photographer. The photographer has scraggly long hair, a blurry tattoo of a naked woman on his pale upper arm, and those yellow tinted shooting sunglasses. He reminds me of a sketchy gun-toting anarchist.

What woman wouldn't be nervous in this situation? It's not like Romeo is going to pull a laser rifle out of his Matrix trench coat and save Bev and I if the men get out of hand. I smile at her, "My name is Electra."

"That's a nice name," she says warmly before setting her makeup cases on the low chest of drawers along the wall. She starts unpacking them with practiced skill.

"I'm Ted," the photographer says to me, offering his hand. His jagged smile says he's trying to flirt.

Ted? Like, Ted Bundy? The serial killer?

"Nice to meet you," I say politely, withholding my name even though he probably heard me give it to Bev. I've dealt with crazies on assignment in the past, but Ted seriously skeeves me out, and I don't skeeve easily. I briefly shake his hand, which is rough and calloused. He seems like the kind of guy who likes to tie women up and lock them in his filthy roach-infested sex bunker. His hands are probably calloused from tightening all his itchy sex bunker ropes. Poor women. I repress a shiver.

I notice Connor's eyes are pinned on Ted. He's watching the guy like a hawk. What's that about?

Ted says to me, "So, why are you here again?"

"I'm doing the interview."

"Oh? Who do you work for?"

Why do Ted's questions make me feel like he's invading my privacy? "Uh, *Trending Magazine*?" It's not like telling him that reveals anything important about me.

"Do you have your own blog or Facebook or something? Where you post your articles?"

"Um, no," I lie. Ted is making me increasingly uncomfortable.

"Do you have a card? I do a lot of freelance photography for other journalists. Maybe we could exchange emails and—" *I could tie you up in my smelly sex bunker and lick your face with my filthy tongue* "—work together some time?"

A deep voice booms behind Ted. "You sure ask a lot of questions for a photographer, Ted," Connor says ominously. He's a mountain of muscle towering over the smaller man.

Ted nearly jumps when he notices how close Connor is standing. The fact that Connor is *very* naked and standing mere inches behind Ted adds a certain Jailhouse Justice vibe to the moment. Ted gulps audibly.

Connor says to him, "Maybe you should get to work setting up. *Ted.*"

Relief washes over me. I turn my head to the side, repressing a grin.

"Yeah, yeah," Ted grumbles nervously as he retreats to the far corner of the room. He starts snapping together a lighting tripod while shooting dirty looks at Connor's back.

Wow, I can't believe Connor stood up for me. That's a first. I didn't think he had a nice bone in his body.

Bev turns to Connor, "Do you mind if I start your makeup?"

"Sure. Where do you want me?" Connor grabs a pair of black boxer briefs off the floor and steps into them.

Bev relaxes noticeably now that Connor's privates are covered. "How about by the window where the light is good?"

"Sounds great." Connor sits on the table top.

Bev goes to work applying foundation with a foam wedge.

Connor glances at me. "Why don't you start with your questions, Warmoth. I've got nothing but time."

CONNOR

"First question," Electra says, facing me in a chair by the window.

"Shoot—" *my load all over that pretty mouth of yours,* my mind finishes. Electra is crazy fuckin hot. I can't stop staring at her sweet-ass lips. I would kill to have her wrap that fiery mouth of hers around my cock and go to town. My dick is raging in my boxer briefs. It's pointing straight at her. I may have fucked Babe What's Her Name an hour ago, but I'd do anything to have Electra hike up her skirt and sit on my dick. Then I'd grab those perfect hips of hers while she rode me like a horse at a merry-go-round. I want to come inside her so bad right now I can't think straight.

Fuck.

I'm going nuts.

Speaking of nuts, thanks to my hard on, my boxers are all bound up and digging into my balls. I shift on the table, trying to get some relief. I feel bad for Bev, but she's a trooper. She ignores my giant rager and applies my makeup like this is business as usual. Who knows? Maybe it is. Maybe she does makeup for porn.

"How did you get started as a cover model?" Electra asks. "Were you discovered? I'm sure your fans would love to know."

I smirk to myself.

Being a model seems great until you know why I became one. Then you wouldn't wish my life on your worst enemy. But nobody wants to hear that sad shit. They want a glory story. How I got discovered surfing or base jumping, or shit, while I was working at a gas station. And how everything was golden after that: money, bitches, mansions, blah blah blah.

People want to hear about rags to riches.

Not rags to shit.

Nobody wants to believe that being any kind of celebrity is weird and twisted and so much bullshit I avoid like the plague.

"Well?" Electra prompts.

"My agent saw me in a club on Sunset. Told me she wanted to represent me." It's true enough. Five years ago, Gloria Powers took one look at me in that club and drove me back to her place where we fucked until morning. *Then* she offered to rep me. I didn't even know she was an agent. She was hot. I wanted to fuck her. End of story. It turned out she was a bitch in bed, which I liked. Seemed like she'd be a good agent. So why the fuck not?

"Is that it? Just, 'Here's my card, Connor, call me for representation'?" Electra sounds amused.

"Pretty much." Like I said, the truth is uglier than fiction, and people want the fiction.

"That sounds boring, Connor. Maybe you'd like to embellish it a bit? For your fans?"

Damn, when did Electra develop fuckin mind-reading radar? "What do you want, Warmoth? My life story? You already know it. We grew up together."

"I don't know you, Connor. Just because we went to the same high school doesn't mean I know the first thing about you."

"Whaddya mean? We talked practically every damn day at North Valley."

"You *harassed* me every day, Connor. I'd hardly call it talking."

"True." Thinking back, I sort of feel like a dick. I was hard on her, but I didn't know how else to get through her thick skin. She never opened up to anybody that I knew of. I don't think she had friends. Not *real* friends. Shit, neither did I. Most of those fuckin jocks were just good time buddies. Just because you talk to the same people every day doesn't mean they're your friends. As sappy as it sounds, there was something about Electra that made me think maybe me and her could relate on a deeper level. We were both cut off from everybody. Maybe I was wrong. Who knows. I was a dumb kid back then.

"Back to the question. How did your career start? Was it book covers from the beginning?"

"Yeah, pretty much. My agent knows people in publishing. She sent out my body shots and I was doing my first photo shoot three days later with one of the Big 6 houses back east. They flew me out to New York and put me up for the weekend. Easiest money I ever made. Been working steadily ever since." That part is all true.

"So you just fell into cover modeling?"

"Pretty much."

"Sounds like the Connor I remember. You never did anything that was hard."

I grin, "I'm all about doing things the hard way…" My dick's only at half mast now, but I'll be full sail the second the opportunity presents itself.

"Moving on. Why don't you show your face?"

"I'm gonna show it to 45,000 screaming fans today."

"But why *haven't* you shown it until now?"

I don't answer.

"Connor?"

"Next question."

"Knowing you, Connor, it's probably because you don't want your face on America's Most Wanted. Someone's liable to recognize you and call in a tip which'll put you in jail."

She's trying to get a rise out of me. It's not gonna work. "Not too worried about that," I chuckle. "I'm a nobody from the neck up. But you're right. A wanted poster would make a better story than the truth."

"So tell me the truth. I'm sure your fans want to know." She says it like we're best friends gossiping about whatever the fuck.

You ask me, she smells blood. Time for me to deflect. "Once they see my face, they won't care why I hid it." I flash my cocky smile.

"You're kidding, right? Women will want to know all about a handsome *mysterious* guy like you. Believe me."

I smirk, "Do *they* want to know, Warmoth, or do *you*?"

Frustrated, she frowns. "Yes, I'm curious. Even if I didn't *sort of* know you, I'd still wonder why you've stayed out of the limelight for so long. There's something romantic about a mysterious man with a mysterious past, don't you think?"

Man, when did she get so relentless? She needs an answer with some meat or she's never gonna quit. I smear my palm across my mouth thoughtfully. "Here's the deal. If I showed my face on every cover, they'd stop hiring me. By cutting off my face, every book publisher can use me. Put makeup on my tattoos as needed, Photoshop new tattoos as needed or leave them out. It allows me to keep working.

It's just a business strategy. There's nothing romantic about it."

It's the truth. Part of it, anyway. Nobody knows all of it. Except me. And I'll take that shit with me to the grave...

—*screa*—

"But that's not the only reason, is it, Connor?"

—*screamscrea*—

I shudder. "Sorry, what?"

Her eyes narrow like a predator but her voice is all soothing songbird. "What were you thinking about just now?"

"Nothing." I pin her eyes with mine. "What was your question again?"

"I was wondering if there was some other reason why you hid your face for so long?"

—*scream-scream-scream-scream*—

"Connor?"

I clench one fist so hard the knuckles pop. I really want to punch something right now. Ted the photographer looks like a good option. That guy bugs the fuck out of me. But his back is to me and he's busy doing whatever the fuck with his camera gear. I level my gaze at Electra. "I told you already," I growl, losing more cool than I intended. "I hid my face for business reasons. That's. It."

"Sore subject?" Her voice is all sugar and spice.

"*Next* subject," I snort.

She's digging way too close to the bone.

There is something dangerous about this older and wiser (and hotter) Electra Warmoth. She's not the same innocent little girl I last saw on grad night seven years ago. She's a gorgeous siren trying to get me to crash my ship into the rocks.

Good luck with that.

"All done," Bev says, finished with the makeup.

All done is right. I'm ready for this interview to be over.

Chapter 4

ELECTRA

We ride the elevator down to the lobby.

It's just me, Connor, and Romeo. Romeo is escorting us to the convention hall.

Ted and Beverly are gone. After Ted finished with his photos, both of them left. Unfortunately, I didn't get anything else out of Connor that I can use for my article. Once Ted started snapping photos, Connor ignored me completely. At the rate my interview is going, I won't have anything substantial to upload before my deadline. Vince is going to skin me alive and hang me out to dry.

And I won't get paid.

"Here are your badges," Romeo says as the elevator descends, handing Rom Com Con 2015 plastic badges to Connor and I. Both hang from pink lanyards and both say STAFF. "These will grant you access anywhere in the convention halls. Don't lose them. The security here is worse than the Olympics." We both thank him and hang the badges around our necks. "Are you guys ready for the insanity?"

Connor wears tight ripped jeans, a tight black T-shirt, and motorcycle boots. Incredibly, he's even sexier dressed than when he was naked. His ass looks amazing in his jeans. He pulls a black L.A. Dodgers baseball cap out of his back pocket and screws it on his head. Then he slides on a pair of coffee-tinted aviator sunglasses. "I'm ready. You ready, Warmoth?"

"Uh, yeah. Will you have time for more questions in the convention hall?"

"Anything for you, Lex," he grins.

Lex? Did he just call me Lex? Nobody has ever called me Lex, not even my parents. What's that about?

Before I can say anything, we reach the ground floor and

commotion explodes through the elevator doors.

The lobby is mobbed. There must be hundreds, if not thousands, of people crammed shoulder to shoulder inside. The crowd is 99% women. No surprise there. Many wear pink Rom Com Con T-shirts. Most carry identical Rom Com Con swag bags at their sides. The chaos of conversation is so loud, I can barely hear myself think.

This is way crazier than I imagined.

"Where we going?" Connor hollers in Romeo's ear.

"There's a side exit in the spa. This way." Romeo leads us around the perimeter of the crowd and down a long corridor. At the end of it is a spa waiting room with a Zen vibe.

A girl behind the desk dressed in white sees us. "I'm sorry, the spa is only open to hotel guests. *Not* convention attendees." She looks disgusted at the mention of the convention.

"We're staff," Romeo says.

When the woman gets a good look at Connor, she stands up from behind the desk. "I'm Jocelyn." She holds out her hand to shake, her eyes all over Connor. He shakes her hand, but seems distracted. He keeps glancing back up the corridor toward the commotion in the lobby.

"We should go," I mutter.

Romeo leads Connor and I out a side door.

Outside, we pass by a huge luxurious pool, tennis courts, and a golf course off in the distance.

"Anyone for tennis?" Romeo quips.

"Where are we going?" I ask as we walk.

"We can get into the convention hall from the back entrance. If we go that way, there's a bunch of meeting rooms where you and Connor can wait until his reveal."

"Are they private?" I ask.

"What," Connor says, "you wanna get me alone and have your way with me, Warmoth?"

I frown, "You wish." Then I smirk, "But if I can get you to finish your interview before the reveal, maybe I'll blow you."

Connor stops in his tracks on the cement walkway. "Really?" He sounds genuinely surprised.

"No!" I laugh. I hope he didn't think I was serious. I slow to a stop and turn to lock eyes with him. A moment passes between us that feels different. For once, it's not the same old minefield that has existed between Connor and I since day one. Part of me wants to reach out to him with an open heart. The other part of me wishes I'd never mentioned the blow job.

"I'll blow him if you won't," Romeo offers, breaking the tension.

Connor chuckles and steps in front of Romeo. He places his huge palms on Romeo's shoulders and grins down at him. Compared to Romeo, Connor looks like a giant.

Romeo gulps nervously. In a tiny voice he says, "Daddy?"

I wince, "Why does that sound *so* wrong coming from you?"

"And yet *so* right," Romeo titters.

"Look, Romeo," Connor says. "I like you."

Romeo brightens hopefully.

"But I don't *like you* like you."

Romeo slumps, heartbroken.

Connor pats him on the shoulder. "But the second I go gay, I'll let you know."

"Will you?" Romeo gasps.

Connor chuckles. "Yeah."

"Can we go?" I plead.

"Hush," Romeo mutters. "We're having a moment."

Connor breaks into laughter.

ELECTRA

After showing our badges to security, which in this case is a half-asleep middle-aged woman in a red Rom Com Con STAFF polo shirt, Romeo takes us up to a meeting room in the back of the convention hall on the second floor. He opens the door to the empty room.

"Here we are!" Romeo's smart phone rings and he pulls it from one of his many pockets. "Romeo Fabiano's office, how may I direct your call? Yes... Who may I say is calling? Yes... One moment, please..." He mutes his phone and says to Connor and I, "It's always good for people to think you have your own personal assistant. People take you more seriously."

I don't know how Romeo could possibly think *anyone* would take him seriously.

Romeo turns his attention back to his phone. "This is Romeo. How can I help you? ... Yes ... Yes, I've taken them to meeting room G ... Yes... I'll be right there..." Romeo gives me a sheepish grin. "Duty calls. You two are on your own. Or do you need me to stay and, um, help?" Hope shines from his eyes.

Connor snickers to himself.

I smile at Romeo. "We'll be fine. Thanks."

"My pleasure..." his face darkens devilishly. "...and hopefully yours. Don't do anything I wouldn't do, you two!" he coos.

I snicker, "Something tells me there's ten million things *you* would do that *no* one would ever do."

"So true," he grins. "You have my number. Call me if you need me to rescue you. Or join the fun..." He winks and makes a tee-hee sound. "Gotta go! Toodles!" He waves over his shoulder as he hustles down the hallway.

The modern meeting room contains a long wood table with a bunch of leather chairs around it. A package of unopened water bottles sits on the center of the table. Windows along one wall overlook the golf course.

Connor closes the door.

I jump ever so slightly. Or is that just my heart thudding in my chest? It's not like Connor is naked this time, so there's no reason for me to be nervous.

"It's just me and you, Lex. What're we gonna do now?"

"Not what you're thinking, sleazeball," I laugh and walk to the far end of the long table and sit down. "Pull up a chair. We can get through some more questions while we wait. How long do we have until your *BIG reveal*?" I ask sarcastically, then pull my notepad and mp3 recorder out of my purse.

"At least an hour. Is that *long* enough for you?" He plops into a chair at the far end of the table and drops his boots on the tabletop like he owns the place.

"Is everything about sex with you, Connor?"

He peels his shades off his face and locks eyes with me. "Most of the time."

I groan, breaking eye contact. "Can we get back to the interview already?"

"Why don't I interview you?"

"No, Connor. I don't have time."

"I'll make you a deal. For every question you ask me, you have to answer one of mine."

I grimace. "Why does this feel like Truth Or Dare?"

"We can play it that way if you want. I always preferred the dares anyway. Way more fun."

I sigh. "I need information, Connor. I can't print your dares in my article."

"Why not? Call the article something like *Truth or Dare: How I got the dirt on Connor Hughes.*

I smile, "Hey, that's pretty good."

"Isn't it?"

"Okay. We can play your way. But we need some ground rules."

"Like what?"

"Nothing involving you and me doing anything physically intimate."

He shakes his head, "No dice. We go Y.O.L.O. or we don't play at all."

"This isn't a game, Connor. It's my job."

"Don't you live dangerously as a reporter?"

"Sometimes," I sigh.

"What's the most dangerous thing you ever did on a job?"

"I don't know," I say thoughtfully. "Let me think... One time I was interviewing some Mexican gang bangers when their safe house got tear gassed by the cops."

"No shit?"

I nod. "Tear gas is the worst. I stumbled out the back door of the house before it got really bad, but I could barely see, my eyes were burning so bad. And I was puking my guts out all afternoon while I tried to explain to the cops I was just there doing a story. I mean, what about me says *chola*? Anyway, after that, I couldn't smell spicy food for a month without wanting to throw up."

"Damn, Lex. That shit happened?"

There he goes calling me Lex again. I nod proudly. "It sure did."

Connor laughs, "And you're worried about *me*? Fuck, Warmoth, you're crazy."

"Maybe *thiiiiis* much," I say in a high voice while holding my finger and thumb a half-inch apart.

Connor stares at me for a long time, a mellow grin on his face.

"What?" I ask bashfully.

"What the hell have you been up to for the last seven years, Warmoth?"

I shrug. "College. Working. Not much else. That was *two* questions, by the way. Now you have to answer two of mine."

"Two? What two?"

"Living dangerously as a reporter and what I've been doing the last seven years."

"You always were good at keeping track of shit. I'm surprised you didn't become an accountant."

"Thought about it. But an office job isn't my speed. Back to my question."

"Go for it."

"What's the strangest thing you've ever done as a model?"

He nods, "Good question. Hmmm. Oh yeah. I was a human sushi platter at a gay banquet."

"What?!" I laugh. "Is that even true?"

"Is that another question?"

"No. But you know I'm going to print that," I warn with a giggle.

"Go ahead." He smiles confidently.

"I think you're lying."

"Print it. I don't care."

"So, wait. Were people like… eating sushi off of you? Were you naked?"

"That's two questions."

"Never mind."

"Fine. My turn. Are you single?"

"Yes." I'm about to ask him why he cares, but that would be another question. We both know he just wants sex anyway. That's all Connor has ever wanted from any woman. "My turn. Why did you become a model?"

"I told you. My agent discovered me at a club."

"No, that's the *how*. I want to know the *why*."

He grits his teeth, his jaw muscles dancing.

He's hiding something. I lean forward in my seat. I can smell paydirt. This should be good.

"I needed the money," he grunts.

I snort, "That's no answer, Connor. Everybody needs to earn money. Why modeling?"

"It was easy."

"You have to give me more than that, Connor."

"Why? Lots of people pick jobs that are easy. Look at me. Being a model is the obvious career path." His smarmy smirk returns as he holds up his tattooed muscled arms.

They are *very* muscley.

I lean back in my chair. He's obviously covering something up. I need to come at it from a different angle later on. There's a story here. If I can find it, I might have something that will impress Vince.

"My turn," he says. "Why did you break up with your last boyfriend?"

My breath stops short. This is one question I don't want to answer. "How do you know I had a boyfriend to break up with? Maybe I've never had one."

"I'm assuming someone as beautiful as you has had at least *one* boyfriend in the last seven years. Either way, I only want to know about the last one."

My hands start to shake so I fold them in my lap. "Um…"

"I'm waiting."

"Let's just say there's not much to say."

He snorts, "That's not an answer."

"You didn't give me one. *Because modeling is easy*?" I'm mimicking his earlier words. "That's not an answer either."

He waves his hand in the air impatiently. "So make something up for your article, Warmoth. I'm sure you'll come up with something better than the truth."

What does that mean? His expression says he's not going to say a thing. Hmm. I *could* make something up about why he got into modeling, something plausible and entertaining that won't cause him to launch a libel lawsuit, but fabricating facts is unthinkable for a serious journalist like myself. I've never done it and I never will.

"Back to my question about your breakup," he prods. "Why did things end?"

"Do you really want to know this?"

"Yes."

I take a deep breath, considering. No, there's no way I'm going into it. Even after four years, the topic of Dylan Montgomery is an open wound for me. And since he's the only real boyfriend I've ever had, I don't have anyone else I can talk about. And I'm not going to lie. "Do we have to do this, Connor?"

"You want your interview, don't you?"

"Why do you always have to be so difficult?"

His brows knit. "Modeling is my job, Warmoth. What you print in your story will have an impact on my brand. If I say the wrong thing, or you take my words out of context, it could come back to bite me in the ass. So you'll excuse me if I'm careful with what I say to you."

"But I thought you said earlier I could make up anything I wanted about why you got into modeling?"

"Forget I said that. Answer my question about your last boyfriend or we can be done here. Or… you can take a dare."

"Fine. Dare."

He slowly smiles. "You sure?"

Exasperated, I sigh, "Yes, Connor. Dare."

"Kiss me."

"No! I said no physical intimacy!"

"Then answer the question."

I huff. "No, Connor."

"Then kiss me. How bad can it be?"

"The words *foul* and *terrible* come to mind."

He chuckles, "What about me seems foul and terrible?"

"Besides the obvious?" I giggle. "Let's see…Have you brushed your teeth today? I don't remember you scouring out your mouth or gargling with bleach since that girl left your room this morning. What was her name again?"

He raises an eyebrow.

"You don't know her name, do you?!" I'm appalled.

"Asia. Her name's Asia."

"That's not her name! You made that up! You're such a player, Connor!"

"Would it make you feel any better if I told you I never kissed her?"

"No! You *fucked* her, Connor! I'm sure you and her swapped spit and every other possible bodily fluid."

"I'm like a hooker. No kissing. Only fucking. And I used a condom. No spit or bodily fluids were exchanged at any time."

"Bullshit," I chuckle. "You expect me to believe that?"

He shrugs. "All I know is you called dare and now you have to kiss me. Those are the rules. And I brushed my teeth before we left my room. *And* I have mints, in case you have bad breath."

"Me?" I huff.

He pulls a pack of mints from his pocket and tosses it on the table top. It slides toward me across the polished wood, the mints inside the pack rattling a challenge.

I stare at the pack.

Why am I even considering this? I don't have to play along. Then again, I need this interview. Connor is too clever to just give up information for free. I shift in my seat. I wish my hair wasn't in a bun right now. I'd like to hide behind it because Connor is drilling me with those stupid blue eyes of his. Why does he have to be so damn handsome? And why do his lips have to be so full and luscious?

Damn him!

"Fine," I groan. I get up and trudge to his end of the table.

He sits up, an expectant look on his face. His blue eyes flash. Up this close, they glow. Or maybe that's just the sky light pouring in through the wall of windows reflecting off his azure irises.

I lean forward, grimacing, and… kiss his forehead.

I skip back to my seat, giggling. I stop on the way and grab a water bottle and the mints.

"Hey! What the fuck kind of kiss was that?"

"You never specified!" I drop into my seat, unscrewing the water bottle. I drink a swig and swish it around like I'm rinsing. Then I pop a mint in my mouth and make a sour face. "Nasty," I hiss.

"Your lips weren't even on my forehead long enough to taste anything," he chuckles.

"Says you. Next question."

He rolls his eyes. "Fuckin Power Pole."

"Hey!" I snap. "Don't call me that."

'You're right. You do have nice breasts."

"Next question! Ahem. Stay on point, Connor."

"I'm on point right now." He stands up and walks toward me.

The first place I look is his crotch, which isn't pitching a pointy tent like I'd expected. "What are you doing?"

"I'm coming to get my kiss."

"No you're not!"

He swaggers toward me. "Yes I am."

"Sit down, Connor! I'm warning you!" I shake my open water bottle like I'm going to splash water in his face. "You already got your kiss."

"No I didn't." He takes my water bottle and sets it on the table. Then he leans toward me, resting his big hands on the armrests of my chair.

We are nose to nose.

I can smell his skin. It's magnificent. I mean awful. I wince. "Get away, you smell."

He smirks. "That's pheromones."

"Smells like farts to me," I giggle.

"You wish."

He's right. He smells like a cowboy or something. He leans forward so far that I have to lean all the way back in my chair until my bun hits the back of it. I'm trapped. No place to go. "Go away, Connor."

"Not till I get a real kiss."

"Stop being such a rapist."

"I'm not raping."

"Could've fooled me." His lips are a quarter inch from mine. I stare at them. They need to be nibbled or licked, but not by me.

"I can wait all day. War Mouth. You know you want it."

"No I don't."

He smiles. Masculine energy pours off of him.

It's intoxicating. I haven't had a man this close to me in forever. In the past two years, I've been on a date or three, and there has been some limited kissing, but nothing worth mentioning. At the moment, I could write a book about what Connor's proximity is doing to me. My bra feels two sizes too small and my nipples are hard. My panties are too tight and straining deliciously against my clit. A flush rushes up my neck and heat flows down my chest beneath my blouse, pooling between my legs. And he hasn't even kissed me.

I look into his eyes. My voice is choked when I say, "Okay, maybe just a quick peck."

Connor reaches up and removes my glasses.

"What are you doing?" I demand.

"I don't want them getting broken." He sets them on the table.

"It's just a quick peck—"

His mouth crashes into mine.

Our tongues fight like cobras, twisting together in a swollen embrace. Pleasure sprays up from my core like a hot fountain of desire.

I grab Connor's T-shirt in my fists and pull him toward me. The office chair suddenly rolls back, slamming into the wall. Our lips never separate.

I am kissing Connor Hughes and it is the hottest thing ever.

Why did I wait so long?

Without warning, his huge hands scoop underneath my ass and he lifts me into the air. He stands up and I try to wrap my legs around his waist, but I can't. My fitted skirt is too restrictive. I end up bending at the waist and wrapping my knees around his ribs as he folds me against him, positioning me so that my wetness presses against his crotch. His hardness strains against me through his jeans. It's clumsy and it leaves me feeling wide open. It's like we're dry fucking with my knees around my ears but we're standing up and fully clothed.

I don't know if that's a good thing or a bad thing.

He breaks the kiss.

I don't want him to. My mouth is empty without his tongue in it. I want his lips back!

He hisses, "Fuck, Lex. I need to be inside you right fuckin now…"

If he had called me War Mouth or Power Pole or anything else, it would've ruined the moment. But this Lex thing keeps catching me off guard. "I—"

"Give me the word and I'll rip your clothes off and fuck you on this table. I want to feel your wet pussy all over my cock. Damn it, Lex, I need to fuck you…"

"I—"

Click!

Romeo leans his head through the door of the meeting room. "I may be gayer than a Pride Parade, but even I'm a little bit turned on right now…"

"Oh, shit!" I scream. If Connor didn't have such a good grip on my ass, I would've landed flat on the floor and broken my tail bone. Ouch!

Connor chuckles, still holding me up in the air.

Romeo grins at both of us.

Wow, this is awkward. Socially and physically. I try to lower my legs but I'm trapped by my skirt. "Put me down!" I bark.

"I'll give you two a minute," Romeo giggles while withdrawing his head from the room and closing the door.

"I'm gonna need more than a minute," Connor growls into my ear. "It's gonna take at least an hour to fuck you right..."

The sound of his deep voice melts my brain and any remaining good sense I have dribbles out my ears.

CONNOR

I breathe into Electra's ear, skimming the curve of it with my tongue.

"Ohhhhhh," she shivers, squeezing her quivering thighs around my ribs. She drops her weight down so her pussy pushes against my dick through my jeans.

I grind up against it. "I need to fuck you, Lex. I know you're fuckin wet right now. I can smell it. I know you want this as bad as I do."

For a moment, she's seriously considering it. She's breathing hard, her face buried in my shoulder.

"Say the word, Lex, and I'll make you come harder than you've ever fuckin come..."

She whimpers, "Romeo is right outside. Don't you have a reveal for your fans? Your first public appearance?"

She isn't letting go.

"Fuck all that noise," I growl. "All I can think about right now is you. Until I come inside you, I can't think about anything else."

I can feel her heart pounding in her chest.

Then her arms and legs go slack. "We need to stop, Connor. Please put me down."

I set her ass gently on the table top.

Her arms still hang loose around my neck. She hangs her head. "We shouldn't have done that."

Why am I not surprised she said that? "Yeah. This was a bad idea." My monster hard on says otherwise.

Her head tilts up and her eyes search mine.

There's a second where I think maybe she's hurt. But that can't be right. Warmoth has skin thicker than a mule.

"This was *your* idea, Connor," she scowls.

Same old Warmoth. Always fuckin angry at me. As always, it drives me up the fuckin wall. "What the fuck, Warmoth? You were all over *me*."

"After you forced me!"

"I didn't force anything."

"Bullshit, Connor! The kiss was *your* idea. Truth or Dare was *your* idea. Trading questions was *your* idea. How was any of this *my* idea? If you'd've done this interview like I'd asked, like you and your people *wanted*, none of this would've happened!"

"Was it *that* bad, Warmoth?"

"What?"

"The fuckin kiss!"

"Yes! No! I don't know!" She glares at me, her eyes on fire.

"Fuck, Warmoth! Maybe if you'd relax and let that fuckin uptight hair bun of yours down for five seconds, you might actually enjoy yourself for once! Do you even know how to have fun? Or is everything for you WORK FUCKIN WORK?!"

"NO!!"

I shake my head. "There's a reason I started calling you High Tension in high school, and this is it."

"Don't call me that!"

"Why not? It fits, doesn't it?"

"Fuck you, Connor *Screws*! Do you ever think about anything other than sex sex sex?"

I snort, "What else is there in life?"

"Lots! If you stopped thinking with your dick for more than five seconds, you might find out! Did you actually *graduate* from high school, or did they just kick you out?"

"Fuck you, War Mouth. I graduated." Barely. But I walked and got my diploma, just like she did.

"Fat lot of good it did you," she grumbles. She grabs her purse off the table and jams her notepad and digital recorder inside. "Find someone else to write your stupid fluff piece, because that's all you want. Better yet, have your PR person just send a press release to *The National Enquirer*. I'm sure they'll be happy to print whatever the hell you tell them!" She sweeps the pack of mints off the table then realizes they're not hers. She throws them back on the table and the case pops open, spilling a bouncing spray of mints that *tick tick ticks* all over the wood. She scowls, "There's your… *mints*."

She yanks the door open and storms out of the meeting room.

Romeo stands in the hallway, staring at me with wide eyes.

I shout out the door, "Fuck you too, War Mouth!"

ELECTRA

Damn him!

I march down the hallway, ready to explode.

What was I thinking letting Connor Douche kiss me? I never should've played stupid Truth Or Dare with him. How professional was that? I have no one to blame but myself for this disaster of an assignment. I didn't *have* to come back here. I should've told Vince Pitts and *Trending Magazine* to go fuck themselves. There's other magazines in the world. This whole day was one huge cluster fuck from the begin—

"Lex!"

Connor's voice squeezes my heart.

I stumble to a stop in the hallway.

"Lex, wait…"

I don't turn around. I'm afraid to turn around.

There's a softness to his voice that I'm not used to. He sounds almost… apologetic. I barely recognize the tone. Considering he's never been anything but a first class ass since the day we met in high school, I don't know what to do.

My entire body has gone from quivering rage to… quivering *something*. I'm shaking with… what, I don't know.

My chest flutters as I slowly turn around.

Connor stands in the hallway next to Romeo. They're both staring at me. Romeo looks shocked. Connor looks… incredibly handsome. His face is *friendly*, which I barely believe. I'm not used to seeing him this way.

A powerful sense of hope warms my entire body from head to toe.

Connor holds something up. I can't quite make out what it is without my—

"You forgot your glasses," he mutters.

My body wilts with disappointment. Disgust quickly replaces it. I stride grimly toward Connor, my eyes glued to his hand. The second I get my glasses, I am outta here.

Two steps away, I reach out for them…

"Lex, I'm—"

Our eyes meet.

Hope floods my veins.

"There he is!" A woman's voice rings out from behind Connor. It's Margaret Lang, the media relations contact for Rom Com Con. She's flanked by four other people, two in red Rom Com Con STAFF polo shirts and the other two in business casual. All of them wear STAFF badges on lanyards. "The man of the hour," Margaret beams as she shakes hands vigorously with Connor.

While the four women surround him, he hands me my eyeglasses as an afterthought. The women fawn over him like he's, well, like he's as handsome and manly as he actually is.

I'm sure he's loving every minute of it.

His head turns back and forth between me and them. "Lex, I'm—"

Margaret cuts him off, "It's almost time for your highly anticipated reveal, Connor. Are you as excited as we are?"

Connor gives me a final look.

"Oh, hello, ah…" Margaret notices me at last. "Electra, right?"

"Yeah." Gritting my teeth, I smile at her, "Good to see you, Margaret."

Margaret then proceeds to introduce everybody to everybody. I can barely keep track of the names.

"How did your interview go?" Margaret asks me.

I give Connor a horrified glance. I try to smile through it, but my face is strained. "Great," I lie.

"Excellent," Margaret beams. "Just in time, too. We need to get Connor down to the convention hall to the main stage. As you can see, every seat is filled." Margaret glances out the wall of windows in the hallway. They reveal the interior of the convention hall below.

The huge room is at least the size of two football fields, if not larger. It's packed with booths and people from end to end. Countless colorful banners on standees and banners hanging from the rafters combine with an ocean of thousands upon thousands of circulating people to create a vivid confetti of visual overload. Although the windows mute the sound, the white noise of people is a low level hum of excitement seeping through the glass.

At the near end of the hall, there is a large pink stage. Hundreds of people are already seated in front of it, obviously waiting for Connor to unveil himself.

Margaret smiles at Connor, "They're all waiting for *you*, Connor. I don't know if you realize how excited the fans are to finally meet you." Her eyes are glued to Connor's handsome features. "I don't think anyone was expecting you to be so... *gorgeous*." Her face glows with obvious desire.

Connor chuckles casually, "Thanks."

I cringe. I want to say, *You can't judge a romance novel by it's cover, Margaret.*

One of the young women in a red STAFF polo shirt wears a headset. She mumbles something to whoever is on the other end of the mic. To Margaret, she says, "Five minutes until show time."

Margaret smiles. "Why don't we take you downstairs, Connor. Electra, would you like to watch from backstage so you can get an inside look? Or would you like to watch from the audience?"

"Oh, I was just—" I stop myself. I can't tell Margaret that I was just leaving.

She waits for me to finish my sentence.

If I walk out of here, I'll be acting like a spoiled child. I can only imagine how Vince will chew me a new asshole when I tell him I can't hack it. I would hardly blame him. It's not like I'm in an actual warzone risking my life while getting shot at. This is a *romance* convention, for god's sake. But we're talking about Connor Hughes. I really don't want to be in his presence for one more second.

Indecision grips me. If I bail, I can count on Vince to stop giving me any new assignments. If that happens, I won't be able to pay rent this month. If I get evicted, I'll have to start couch surfing. When I wear out my welcome with the few friends I have, I'll have to move back in with my parents until I can build up some savings.

My parents.

Ugh.

They would love to have me come home. I can imagine what they'd say if I told them about my current Connor dilemma. *If it doesn't make you happy, don't do it, Electra. Life is too short to waste it working for a bunch of corporate criminals. Why buy into their reality when you can create your own?*

My parents' casual attitude is *exactly* why I have to tough this out. I don't want to go back to living with them. Ever since I graduated from high school and they bought that failing walnut farm on the outskirts of Oxnard, there's no way I'd ever move back in with them. Some people might enjoy living in an orchard in the middle of nowhere, but I don't. I like civilization. Nothing like hot running water and a toilet that isn't an outhouse. Every time I visit their farm, the seclusion drives me bonkers. So does the outhouse. It *really* stinks. I don't know how they stand it. To this day, the thought of it gives me shivers.

I groan inwardly. Time to suck it up.

But I don't have to like it.

In fact, I hate it.

But I'm a professional and an adult.

Time to be a big girl and pay the bills.

Chapter 5

ELECTRA

While I sit waiting in the crowd near the front of the stage, I check my phone.

Damn. Several texts over the last hour from Austin Thayer, the photographer from *Trending Magazine*.

11:57am: *In the lobby.*

12:34pm: *Where are you?*

12:47pm: *Going to convention hall. Meet u there.*

1:43pm: *Show's about to start. Are u here?*

I realize now that like always, I turned off my ringer before starting Connor's interview.

I fire off a text to Austin: ***I'm in the front row.***

I send it and twist around in my seat, looking for him. Everybody behind me watches me. I ignore them. After scanning the crowd, I see Austin standing at the back of the seating area. I wave vigorously.

He trots up the aisle between the rows of seats, hunching down to be less conspicuous until he squats beside me. "Hey, Electra."

"I'm so sorry, Austin. I totally spaced. I had my phone off during my interview. I was—"

He grins, "No worries. I kept myself busy taking a bunch of shots of the attendees and the authors. There's a lot of famous writers here, from what the fans are telling me. But I don't recognize them."

I grin, "What, don't you read romance novels?"

He grins sarcastically, "Do you?"

"No," I whisper guiltily.

I've always liked Austin. We've worked on assignments like this before. He's very cute in that clean-shaven surfer-next-door sort of way, but he definitely fills out his tight O'Neill surf T-shirt nicely. He has one of those long swimmer's bodies with just the right amount of muscle to be manly, and wavy sun-bleached blond hair from actually surfing. His tan legs flex noticeably beneath his khaki shorts when he shifts positions. His forearm muscles dance when he fiddles with his camera. He holds it up to show me the view screen on the back. The photo shows a middle-aged brunette woman surrounded by two dozen grinning women of all ages. "Check it out."

"Who's that?" I ask.

"E.L. James. She wrote Fifty Shades of Grey."

"*She's* here? I've heard of her."

"I guess Rom Com Con is a pretty big deal."

"Wait, I thought you don't read romance. How do you know who she is?"

"Because there's a giant sign behind her that says her name?"

"Oh, right," I giggle, leaning against his shoulder for a second.

When we met two years ago, Austin had a girlfriend, otherwise we might've ended up dating. As far as I know, they're still together. Ever since I found out, I've kept our conversations purely platonic.

"Do you want to sit?" I offer.

"No, thanks. As soon as this thing starts, I'll be moving around to get good photos."

"Got it."

The stage in front of us is currently empty. Women in red STAFF shirts have stuck their heads out now and again, but the only thing to look at is the huge projection screen hanging from the back of the stage. A slideshow of book cover images has been playing on it since I sat down. I don't recognize any of the covers except *Stepbrother Obsessed*, which Romeo showed me this morning. But I do recognize Connor's body in all of them.

As nice as the photos are, they don't do justice to what it feels like to be standing inches away from the real thing.

Or to be kissing the real thing.

Heat flushes through my body as I remember our kiss.

I have *never* been kissed like that.

It was like Connor was *fucking* me with his tongue. Even now, the sense memory makes me shiver.

"You okay?" Austin mutters.

"Yeah, I'm fine." I knot my hands in my lap and shift on the cushioned chair. I'm suddenly very aware of my feminine folds. I wish I'd had time to go to the restroom before the show because I realize I'm still quite wet.

I submerge into memories of Connor's hard body and his hard cock pressing up against me through my skirt. My desire to feel him inside me sweeps through my entire body in a hot wave. What I wouldn't do right now to rewind back to that moment. Too bad Romeo showed up when he did. Who knows what might have happened if he hadn't.

"Who's ready to meet Connor!!" The voice blares from the PA speakers hanging above the stage.

The crowd of fans erupts in high pitched squeals of approval. I resist the urge to plug my ears. I never realized a room full of grown women could be so incredibly loud. If it was a bunch of twelve year olds at a Katy Perry concert, I would understand. But these women range in age from sixteen to sixty.

The announcer on stage stands to the side of the stage with a mic in hand. I have no idea who she is, but she's wearing slacks and a blazer over a red Rom Com Con polo shirt. She says, *"You all know him from the countless covers he's done in the past five years."* She looks up at the projection screen to watch more Connor Covers flash by. *"What do you think ladies? Is Connor hot or what?!"*

The crowd cheers approval.

"I bet you're all dying to see Connor in the flesh!!"

More cheers.

"Do you ladies think the rumors are true? Is THE Connor heinous? Or is he handsome?"

An immediate roar of disagreement from the crowd.

"No!!"

"He's gorgeous!!"

"Handsome!!"

Some of these women are getting red in the face from shouting so loud. I can't believe how invested they are in what amounts to no more than a fantasy. It boggles my mind.

"I won't keep you ladies waiting any longer. You've waited five years for this moment! Without further ado, here he is! The REAL Connor Hughes!!"

Thumping dance music pumps through the PA speakers. The stage lights flicker and flash all over the place. Smoke billows out from both sides of the stage. The projection screen fades to a blue glow, revealing a fifteen foot tall muscled silhouette behind it.

The crowd shouts with bold desire.

The screen raises and a spotlight trains on Connor, who is a mere six-foot-whatever, but the screen lights up with larger-than-life video of him. He saunters through smoke to the middle of the stage. He's wearing the baseball cap, aviator glasses, T-shirt, jeans, and boots. He starts to writhe in time to the dance beat pumping from the PA.

The women go wild.

Austin crouches and duck-walks up to the foot of the low stage and starts shooting photos.

Connor is quite the dancer. After a few moves, he grabs the brim of his ball cap and frisbees it into the audience. A group of women suddenly jump up to catch it. They fight for it desperately. They all want a piece of *The* Connor Hughes.

Random women scream from the crowd:

"I want your baby!"

"No, let *me* be your baby mama, Connor!"

"Come home with me, Connor!"

"I'm getting a divorce!"

I can hardly blame them.

Based on how well he's dancing, Connor either has training as a male stripper or he's a natural dancer. I'm not sure which. He gyrates his hips hypnotically. He really can move.

As he waves his body up and down, he grabs the collar of his T-shirt and slowly tears it open, revealing his incredible chest and abs. The big projection screen shows a gigantic image of his writhing muscles.

A surge of desire spasms in my core. I was pressed up against that mythical body only a few minutes ago.

I squeeze my knees together and gasp audibly. If it wasn't for the chaos of all the screaming women, I'd be embarrassed. But nobody can hear me in this noise. I'm cocooned in my own world of high definition arousal. What would it be like to have Connor's hard writhing body between my legs? To have that thick cock of his filling me up, pounding me to orgasm? Oh god, I'm going to come in my panties right here just thinking about it. My entire body shivers as pleasure blooms in my stomach. At this rate, I'm going to soak right through my fitted skirt. I need to get a grip.

Connor wads his tattered T-shirt into a ball and throws it to the other side of the crowd. Another wave of women rise up to fight for it.

This is insanity.

Connor starts taking off his sunglasses. He does it with the same languorous slowness I imagine he'd use when removing my panties. The crowd gasps with electric anticipation. Oh gawd, I'm melting into my seat. I swear I'm about to come from all the excitement.

Nothing prepares me for what happens when Connor *finally* removes his sunglasses. The women go absolutely crazy. The sound of the desperate screams is deafening. It's worse than Biebermania or Beatlemania or whatever kind of mania you can imagine. Some of the women surrounding me are literally hysterical. Others are merely in awe of Connor Hughes.

He throws his sunglasses into the crowd and continues to dance, making his way toward the front of center stage. He continues to twist and swivel his hips with seductive finesse.

All of the energy pouring off the women surrounding me combined with Connor's dancing is having a strange effect on me. Not twenty minutes ago, this man who is melting the minds of all these women, wanted *me*.

Not *them*.

Me.

Little Electra Warmoth.

Does it make me shallow that I care what everyone else thinks of Connor, that *them* wanting *him* makes *me* want him that much more?

I don't know.

But I do know that Connor is looking right at me.

Me.

He has that same stupid cocky grin I know so well and he's pointing it straight at me while all these women *wish* he was looking at them. Some of them are literally begging for his attention.

"Connor! Over here!"

"Please, Connor!" another woman screams desperately, on the verge of sobbing.

"Connor!!!!"

But he's only looking at me.

Connor is doing all of this for me…

CONNOR

Between the PA and the women, it's louder than a Metallica concert in here. But I don't notice any of it. I'm 100% focused on Electra.

She's all I'm thinking about.

I'm dancing for her.

Lord knows I've tried every other fuckin trick in the book to get her to lower her defenses. I've never tried so damn hard to get a woman to fuck me. Usually they're the ones doing all the work to get on my cock. But when all else fails, do a striptease in front of a thousand other drooling women. If this doesn't show her the light, nothing will.

Based on the way her luscious lips are opened in a pouty O, I think it might be working. Fuckin finally. My dick stirs in my pants. Those fuckin *lips*…

Something flies at me from the crowd.

I catch it easily.

A black thong. I have no idea who threw it. I wish it was Electra, but we all know it wasn't hers. Remembering I'm here to do a job, I stretch the underwear over my head and wear it like a choker.

The women go wild.

I keep dancing.

There's two more minutes left in the song. I'm already sweaty. All the stage lights are hot as fuck. A bunch of photographers at the foot of the stage are snapping away. I think it's safe to say I'm going to get a lot of press out of this. My face is going to be all over the internet in less than an hour.

All these fuckin women are screaming their heads off. It's fuckin ridic—

—*screamscream*—

A flash of pain spikes through my brain.

I gotta focus on dancing. I don't want to lose my shit right in the middle of

—*scream-scream-scream-scream*—

I grit my teeth, trying to focus on my moves.

—*why did you*—

The stage tilts, nearly knocking me down.

The crowd gasps.

I recover by falling backward and rolling into a handstand. Then I do two slow handstand pushups like it's nothing. It takes all my strength, but I do it smooth. On the bottom of the second one, I let my legs scissor out into splits. I hold the handstand for several seconds, my arms shaking slightly. I push up slowly, point my legs back up at the ceiling, then kick out of the hand stand, landing on my feet.

The crowd goes crazy.

Right then, the song ends on a crescendo.

I hadn't planned on ending the song this way, but whatever works.

Confetti bombs go off and I take a bow. A rainbow rain of confetti flutters down all around me as the lights strobe like lightning. The smoke machines fog the stage and I exit stage left.

If that doesn't get me into Electra's pants, I don't know what will.

<<<<<<<<>>>>>>>>

ELECTRA

The stage lights go dark.

"*The one and only Connor Hughes, ladies!!*" The announcer says over the PA. "*He will be signing autographs and anything else you want him to sign over in Autograph Alley in thirty minutes.*"

"I wasn't expecting that," I mutter to Austin

"Yeah," he says absently, kneeling beside me and wheeling through the photos he just shot.

"How'd they turn out?"

He holds up the camera so I can see the screen.

"Nice action shots, Austin. You really have an eye. The angles are incredible."

"Thanks," he grins.

"Should we head over to Autograph Alley?"

"I need to get to a wifi hotspot and upload these photos to Vince ASAP. There's wifi in the hotel. Wanna come with? You can finish up your article. I know Vince is waiting for it."

Oh shit.

Is he kidding?

After the trouble I've had with Connor? I barely have anything. What am I gonna do? I'll just have to fake my way through my article. I don't have any other choice.

"Come on," Austin says.

We worm our way through the glue of all the giddy fans. It's going to take forever to get back to the hotel at this rate.

"This way," I say. "It's faster."

Austin follows me out the back of the building and we stride toward the hotel, past the tennis courts, the pool, into the spa, and finally the lobby, which is no longer packed with people. There are Rom Com Con attendees milling about, but nothing like earlier. Everyone's inside the convention hall.

Austin and I find two stools at the hotel bar. He pulls a MacBook Air out of his bag and starts transferring files from his camera to the laptop. I pull out my Microsoft Surface and unfold the keyboard. We both order sandwiches from the bartender and get to work.

Austin pages through his photos and starts editing his selects in Photoshop.

Me?

You know that feeling when you're *starting* your term paper minutes before class on the day that it's due, the one you put off for weeks and weeks? This is that times a thousand. But I'm not in danger of getting an F. I'm in danger of pissing off my best client and not getting paid. This is a disaster.

Am I surprised that anything involving Connor Hughes is anything less?

Nope.

The first thing I do is open a web browser to *TMZ* and check their latest headlines. Nothing on Connor yet. Why would there be? He's not famous. Yet. But after what I saw on the convention hall stage? Forget it. If I'd known about the dance routine, I would've told Vince we needed a camera crew. No time to worry about it now.

I open writing software and bang out ideas, throwing down catchy headlines and anything else I can think of. This article is going to be nothing but bullshit.

Austin sits back from his computer and takes a bite from his sandwich.

"Are you finished?" I ask, distressed.

"Yup. Uploading now."

"Crap."

I hunch my shoulders and go to work. If I don't email something to Vince in the next ten minutes, I'm going to hear from him.

Ten minutes later, Austin is finishing his sandwich. I haven't touched mine. But I do have 500 catchy words and a punchy headline that I send off to Vince's email.

MYSTERIOUS MODEL CONNOR HUGHES HAS GOT THE GROOVES

I may have rushed through it, but I think it's pretty good considering how little time I had. I refresh the *TMZ* page one last time, scanning for anything Connor related. Nothing.

I breathe a sigh of relief.

Finally, I pick up my sandwich and take a bite.

My phone rings five minutes later while I'm chewing on a fresh bite of turkey and cheese.

It's Vince Pitts.

I hold the phone up to my ear, prepared for the worst. "Yeah?"

"This is shit, Warmoth!" Vince shouts on the other end of the line "You call this a story? It's useless fluff! I could shred it and fill my cat box with it and my cat still wouldn't piss on it!"

I didn't think it was *that* bad. Sounding sarcastic, I say, "You have a cat?" I can't believe Vince Pitts has a cat.

"No! You're missing the point! Where is my story? That's the point! Your article is a few boring facts and too much filler. I need meat! Something readers can sink their teeth into! Nobody likes to take a bite out of shit, Warmoth."

At that thought, I set my sandwich down and wipe my fingers on my napkin. Although Vince's string of gross metaphors are vintage Vince, they're also appropriate. I know the article was rushed. Sure, it's not terrible, but it's far from my best work, and it's definitely not a revealing exposé. It's just color.

Austin gives me a sympathetic smile. He knows how annoying Vince can be.

I take a deep breath. "Vince, I've been under a bit of a time crunch. I didn't have much to work with."

"Whose fault is that, Warmoth? Who decided to *walk out of the interview* before it started? You lost almost two hours because of that stunt!"

"I'll fix it, Vince. Is that what you want to hear? I'll get you something good."

"You better, because as it stands, your story isn't worth printing. *TMZ* already posted a piece on their website."

"No they didn't! I just checked."

"Check again."

I refresh the *TMZ* webpage. Shit. They did.

"And they have video, Warmoth! Where's my video?!"

"Nobody told me it was going to be a Broadway show! I figured it would be a basic photo op! Not a dance routine!"

"Maybe if you hadn't've run away from the interview, Connor might have told you himself."

"I—"

"That video has been on *TMZ* for ten minutes. Can you guess how much traffic it's getting?"

"More than *Trending Magazine*," I sigh.

"I'll tell you how much—" he stops himself, surprised. "That's right. More than *Trending*. The only advantage we have right now is this exclusive exposé interview. I need something juicy, Warmoth. Something that will sell magazines. So go find this Connor schmuck—" To my surprise, I bristle when Vince calls Connor a schmuck. "—and get some dirt on him. I don't care what it is. Draw him out. Use your feminine wiles—"

"Sexist, Vince," I warn.

"Effective, Warmoth. Do what it takes. You don't have to sleep with the guy. Just get inside his head. I need an angle."

"Fine. I'll make it happen."

"That's the Warmoth I remember."

"But I'll need a few extra hours."

"At this rate, it won't matter when we publish to the web. The only way people are gonna read *your* article is if you get me a feature that knocks everybody's socks off."

"All right, Vince. I'm on it."

"You better be."

"I am. So kick your shoes off now because your socks are going next."

"Cute, Warmoth. Cute. Get to it. And don't call me until you have something I can print."

Chapter 6

CONNOR

"Please tell me you did the reveal," Gloria says over my phone.

"Yeah. Went off without a hitch." I'm taking a break from signing nonstop autographs by leaning my head under the autograph table and plugging my free ear so I can hear. It's fuckin loud in the convention hall.

"Thank goodness," she sighs. "I was worried I'd have another fire to put out."

"Nope."

"And the interview?"

"Did that too."

"How did it go?"

"Great." Do I tell her I was *this* close to fuckin Electra Warmoth on the meeting room table? Probably not.

"That's my Connor." Her voice is all smiles again. "Would you like to celebrate later?. Just the two of us?"

"I don't know how long I'm gonna be here, G. I'm still signing autographs and the line is out the door. I don't know when I'm gonna finish."

"Have you signed any breasts yet?" There's an edge of envy in her voice.

"Hundreds. Tits all over the place." I say it sarcastically so she'll wonder if I'm fuckin with her or telling the truth. The truth is yes, I've signed plenty. One woman said she wanted her tattoo artist to ink my signature into her skin.

"You must enjoy being the finest fox in the henhouse."

"You know you're the only hen in my henhouse, Gloria." It's bullshit. But it's what she wants to hear. Gloria was never interested in the truth.

"That's right," she purrs. "Let's keep it that way." She sighs thoughtfully. "But I know you have a part to play. Sign all the breasts you want. It's good for business. Just don't sleep with any of your fans. That would be bad for business." It's a warning.

"Sure. No fuckin the fans. Got it."

"Then we're on the same page." Gloria likes to pretend I'm on a short leash.

"Always, G."

"Don't have too much fun without me. You're there all weekend, right?" She's trying to trip me up.

"Right. All weekend."

"Good. I'll check in with you tomorrow."

"Great. Laters." I end the call.

One of these days, I'm going to kick Gloria Powers to the curb.

ELECTRA

"I can't get over how many hot men there are at the show," Romeo swoons.

Austin and I bumped into Romeo when we returned to the convention floor to cruise the crowded aisles. The second I find Connor, I'm going to drag a good interview out of him with dental pliers if I have to. Austin is snapping candids as we make our way toward Autograph Alley. It's taking us forever to get there because of all the people squeezed inside the hall. I bet the show has exceeded maximum capacity by at least a thousand attendees.

"Earth to Electra," Romeo says.

"Sorry. You were saying something about men? This place is all women."

"I mean the other cover models," Romeo says. "They're everywhere."

I hadn't noticed. Why? Because I'm thinking about my article and I'm thinking about Connor and what we did in that meeting room two hours ago.

But now that I look around, I realize Romeo is right. The hot muscled men stand head and shoulders above the women, either at the author booths or circulating in the aisles. The women surround them to flirt and pose for pictures. Some of the models are shirtless, showcasing their incredible physiques. Others, equally gorgeous, wear period costumes: ancient Egyptian princes, Greek gladiators, loin-clothed barbarians, pirates, and everything in between. A few guys sport charcoal gray suits, who I assume are supposed to be Christian Grey from the 50 Shades books.

"Wow," I marvel. "You're right, Romeo. There really are a lot of beautiful men here."

"I know," he beams. "I feel like a kid in a man candy store! Too bad all of these hulking hunks are straight."

"How do you know?"

"I asked."

"All of them?"

"It didn't take long. I work quickly. Tho I still haven't asked your friend the photographer." Romeo nods toward Austin who is busy taking photos and doesn't hear us. "He sure is cute. But he's obviously *far* more interested in you than me."

I wrinkle my nose, "I think he has a girlfriend."

"Perhaps. But he keeps checking out your fabulous ass."

"Really?"

"*Yes*, your ass is fabulous, and *yes*, really. But I imagine you've been too busy thinking about that illicit kiss you shared with Connor up in the meeting room to notice."

I grimace. "Is it that obvious?"

"You *know* you'd love to have Connor vajizzle your clizzle, girlfriend."

I break into laughter. "You sure have a way with words, Romeo."

"I attribute it to my fondness for the bard."

"Shakespeare?"

"Yes! Are you a fan of the bard as well?"

I chuckle, "Um, not so much. But I read enough Shakespeare in high school that I'm pretty sure he never used the phrase *vajizzle my clizzle*."

"Then you must not be familiar with *The Comedy of Errors*."

"I don't know that one. But I doubt they say *vajizzle my clizzle* in it."

"Then I suggest you read it."

I frown. "Really?"

He breaks into a mischievous smile. "Kidding."

We wander past more booths.

Romeo stops in his tracks. "What pray-tell is *this*?!" He drags me over to a booth filled with extremely lifelike male mannequins. The sign on the banner at the back of the booth reads *The Real Dude*.

"It's a realistic sex doll!" Romeo practically squeals.

"The *Real* Dude?" I wince. "That is *so* gross. I can't imagine any woman buying a realistic sex doll."

"Who said it was for women?" Romeo titters as he steps up to the nearest doll, which is dressed in a charcoal gray suit. "Hey look, it's Christian *Gay*!"

I can't help but laugh.

As I examine the dolls, I notice they all have a blank look on their faces. "Don't you think they're kind of creepy?"

"Not at all," Romeo muses.

I lean closer. "They don't look very real to me."

Romeo grabs the crotch. "Seems real enough to me! I can even feel *veins*," he moans.

"What are you—" That's when I notice the life-size doll has mammoth wood, or should I say plastic or latex or whatever it is, under its slacks and Romeo is *stroking* it. "Romeo!"

People walking by gawk and giggle.

Romeo jiggles the fake dick of the suited doll so vigorously the whole doll starts to sway back and forth on its stand.

"Please *release* the merchandise, sir!" the nerdy guy running the booth says sharply, glaring at Romeo.

"But I'm trying to give him a hand release right now!" Romeo gibbers.

The booth guy grabs at Romeo, who finally lets go.

"Okay, okay," Romeo pouts. "But you know the doll was enjoying it."

"*Iiii* wasn't," booth guy says seriously. "Please leave, sir. And don't come back."

Romeo sulks over to me and mutters, "Prude."

"Let's go, Romeo." I pull on his arm.

"I got photos of all of that," Austin chuckles while scrolling through them on the back of his camera.

My eyes bulge in horror. The idea of someone having photos of *me* or anyone else I know doing something so incredibly embarrassing is horrifying. They could easily be used as blackmail material.

Romeo is obviously not concerned. He leans against Austin's arm. "Let me see! Oooh! You got my good side in that one. Oh! That one's a keeper! I look very dashing, don't you think?"

"Totally," Austin grins.

"Can you email them to me?"

"Sure," Austin laughs. "You want prints?"

"Can you make me a life size one? It'll be the next best thing to having the actual doll!"

"Let's go, you two," I giggle, pulling them along.

After another twenty minutes of shouldering through the dense crowd, we make it to Autograph Alley. The line of women waiting for Connor is *really* long. It snakes up and back so many times, I can't tell where it ends. I don't know how I'm going to manage interviewing him like this.

I move up to the security ropes around Connor's table to get a better view. Connor is not shirtless like I expected. He's wearing a red Rom Com Con STAFF T-shirt someone must've given him. It stretches nicely over his bulging chest and shoulders.

Maybe I can interview him while he's signing autographs? I watch for a while. I'm surprised by how polite and gracious Connor is with everyone. He has a friendly smile for every single woman. He certainly wasn't that nice to me. Even more annoying is the fact that all the women are practically groping Connor every chance they get, thrusting their boobs in his face and god knows what else. Why do they have to be so shameless?

Not that I care.

Connor, on the other hand, looks like a pig in shit. He's having the time of his life basking in the adulation.

That's when I realize the whole Connor kiss earlier was just a joke. Truth Or Dare nonsense. It wasn't real. There's a reason why I always called him The Con Man. Nothing about Connor is real. Having sex with him would've been a *huge* mistake. I would've been one more fuck for him. He'd forget all about me by morning, like he has done with every other girl he's had sex with. Because he knows a hundred other women will be along a minute later.

I was stupid to think he was dancing for *me* when he was on that stage. He was dancing for himself.

Like he said, this is just his job.

And I'm here to do mine.

That's it and nothing more.

I wish I could leave.

I *should* leave.

Too bad I have rent to pay.

CONNOR

"Oh my god! This is so exciting! I finally get to meet you, Connor!"

The woman saying it stands across from me at the table where I've been sitting and signing autographs non-stop for an hour.

You would think having all these women worship me would go straight to my head. Both of them. All it does is make me feel ten times worse about being here and doing this. I don't deserve this. People who do good things deserve this level of praise. Not me. I should be in jail or six feet under.

I sigh to myself between fans.

Moments like this make me feel like the only thing I've figured out about my life is how to cover up the pain. Nobody wants to know about your pain. When people ask you how's it going, they usually don't want to hear you say "Shitty."

From the outside, I look like I have my shit together. On the inside, everything has gone to shit. I'm a mess that can't be fixed. You don't come back from what I've been through. You never get over it. The guilt eats away at your guts until you're nothing but a shell of regret. When people say at the end of your life you regret the things you didn't do, they don't know what they're talking about. It's because they never did anything really stupid, something so stupid you wish every single night you *hadn't* done it. That's how my life played out.

—*SCREAM-SCREAM-SCREAM*—

My entire body goes cold as the memory bites into me. I push it away, but I still feel icy tendrils snaking through my guts.

I'll regret that shit until the day I die.

Until then, I'll keep acting like I'm not as miserable as I feel.

"Seriously, Connor, you are such an incredible dancer!" the woman squeaks.

"Thanks." I force out a grin.

"Were you ever, you know, an exotic dancer or something?" She looks ready to faint, she's so excited.

I do my best to tune into her excitement so I don't sound like a corpse. "No, but thanks anyway." I peel a color headshot off the stack on the table next to me. 'What's your name?"

"Kimberly. But you can call me Kim." Her upper lip is quivering. It's like she's losing her mind talking to me.

"Kim it is," I scribble her name on the bottom of the photo and sign it *XOXO Connor Hughes*.

"Oh my god, thank you."

"Any time." I give her my best yearbook picture smile.

She blows on the signature, drying it. "Would you believe I have every one of your books?"

They're not *my* books. I'm just paid to be on the covers, but I'm not gonna bother to correct her. "Every one? I've done hundreds."

She nods confidently, "214 to be exact."

"Wow." I forgot how busy I've been for the past five years. "Is that right?"

"Yup," she grins proudly. "I have a few with me, if you want to sign them?"

Paula, the woman in the red Rom Com Con STAFF shirt standing beside Kim, says to her, "The limit is two books per person."

"Okay," Kim says, shaking nervously. She reaches frantically into her bulging book bag and pulls out two. One is *Stepbrother Obsessed*, one of my favorites. I was particularly pumped that day. The other is the latest. She lays both on the table.

I scribble my name inside both and hand them back to Kim.

"Next!" Paula calls out, waving the next person in line forward to the table.

"Oh!" Kim gasps. "I wanted to get a photo with Connor!"

"I'm sorry," Paula says, "but you'll have to get back in line."

"It's okay," I say, standing up.

Kim already has her smart phone out.

I lean over the table and put my arm around Kim. She snaps a selfie of the two of us. "How was that?" I ask.

"Perfect," Kim grins. "Thank you so much, Connor!" She lunges at me, wrapping her arms around my neck, and gives me a huge smooch on the cheek. "You don't know how much this means to me!"

"I think I do," I smile genuinely. "Thanks for coming out."

"Next!" Paula hollers, practically pushing Kim away from the signing table.

That's when I notice Electra and that Romeo dude standing off to the side. And some tall tan surfer looking photographer whispering in Electra's ear. What's that shit about? I watch them from the corner of my eye as I sign another autograph.

Surfer Dude says something that makes Electra laugh. A happy laugh. I've never seen that look on her face and it pisses me the fuck off she never smiled that way for me.

Who the fuck is this guy?

Electra laughs again and she looks happy. I've never seen her happy. I didn't think she could do happy.

Surfer Dude glances at me for a second then touches Lex's elbow. What the fuck is he thinking? That's my fuckin elbow!

Lex glances at me briefly.

I'm not looking right at her, but I can tell she's looking at me from the corner of my eye.

She giggles again as Surfer Dude says whatever.

Are they talkin shit about me? What the fuck! Now I'm pissed. I want to jump over the table and butt in to their conversation until I find out what the fuck they're saying. If I have to, I'll punch Surfer Dude in the teeth. But I'm stuck signing autographs.

Man, I hate being tied down.

"Hey, Lex!" I holler. "Come here a sec!" Man, I sound like a goon.

"What?" she calls out.

It's really noisy in here, and she's trapped behind the nylon crowd control belts. "I said, come here a second!" I'm feeling stupider by the second.

"I'm sorry, what?"

Do I have to fuckin yell? This is ridiculous. I'm not gonna yell.

Surfer Dude mumbles in her ear and she's grinning again.

Meanwhile, I have more autographs to sign. I barely pay attention to what I'm signing because most of my focus is fixated on the conversation between Lex and Surfer Dude.

"What an asshole," I imagine the dude saying to her.

"I know, right?" Lex probably says. *" I can't believe he thought I'd actually have sex with him."* Or something like that.

"Let's go back to my place and fuck."

"Okay. Your cock isn't as big as Connor's," she says, *"but it's the motion of the ocean, right?"*

"Yeah. I know all about ocean motion from all the surfing I do."

"Totally. I want to ride your wave as soon as we get back to your place."

They turn away and fade into the crowd.

"Fuck!" I grunt in frustration.

I never planned on snapping the Sharpie in my hand in half, but I just did. It makes a huge fuckin mess when it spills all over the white table cloth and the headshot I was about to sign.

The girl waiting for me to sign it for her gasps. "Are you okay?"

I hold up my ink soaked hand, "Yeah. You got a napkin or something?"

CONNOR

Two hours later, I'm finally finished with autographs. I have to sign more tomorrow, which is fine. I don't want anyone who wants shit signed going away empty-handed. But I'm happy for the break.

I cruise through the packed convention hall looking for Electra. I wish I hadn't thrown my hat and shades into the crowd during the stage show. People keep staring at me and whispering my name. I don't stop unless they chase me down, which happens a few times.

Being famous is fuckin strange.

Too late to do anything about it now. Hopefully, things'll die down when I'm not in the middle of a fuckin romance convention. In the mean time, I really need to find Electra. I need to... Fuck, I don't know what.

Yeah I do.

I need to talk to her. I don't like how things fell apart when Romeo walked in on me and her when we were about to fuck. And that Surfer Douche needs to back the fuck off.

I stop dead in my tracks.

What the fuck is my problem?

I'm *chasing* some chick.

I don't chase women.

Ever.

Get a grip on yourself, you pussy.

I don't need Electra. I'm surrounded by 45,000 women who would all be happy to jump on my dick. Or, I can walk up to Sunset Boulevard a couple miles from here where some of the hottest women on the planet will *also* try and jump on my dick. It's just the way it is.

But for some fuckin strange reason, I don't give a fuck about any of them. All I want is to talk to Electra.

"It's him!" some random woman gasps. She waves to three friends behind her. "It's Connor, you guys!"

Shit.

"Can we take a picture with you? Our book group will *flip* if we get a picture with you."

"Yeah, sure," I mutter.

The next thing I know, I've got my arms around the three friends, ready to say cheese for the camera.

"Wait!" one says. "You have to be in the picture too, Joanne!"

I smile politely while Joanne gets a random person walking by to shoot the group picture for her.

Shit twice.

Now the random woman who took the pic for Joanne wants to take a picture with me too, so I do that one. Ten minutes later, I'm still taking pictures with other women who walked up while all this was going on.

The whole time, all I can think about is Electra. Where the fuck is she? "Sorry ladies," I sigh. "I really need to go."

"Ooooh," they all whine like I'm breaking their fuckin hearts.

I feel like an ass, but I need to go. "Call of nature," I lie as politely as possible. I grin to myself. It's actually true. Just not the bathroom kind of call of nature. More like the Call Of The Wild. Where the fuck is Electra? That Surfer Douche could be in her pants by now.

I charge into the crowd, heading for the nearest exit.

Once I'm outside, I realize I have no idea where Electra is. She could be in fuckin Mexico for all I know. Who would know how to find her?

Gloria.

She's my only option. I call her office and her assistant Madeleine puts me on hold. After ten minutes of waiting, Gloria finally fuckin answers.

"Connor," she purrs. "Did you miss me?"

"You know I'm always fuckin hard for you, G."

"Mmm. I like the sound of that. What can I do for you?"

"I need the number for your guy at *Trending Magazine*."

"Why?"

"I just need it."

"I would be more than happy to give it to you if you'll tell me why."

I was hoping she would just give me the number. I sigh, "I need to get a hold of the reporter who did my interview."

"I thought you said you finished it already."

"Sort of. I had to cut it short for the reveal thing. I don't think they have much to work with." I avoid using the words *she* or *her* because I know Gloria will start asking questions.

"And why is that, Connor?"

"Fuck, I don't know. We didn't get into much depth. I think more time with—" I almost said *her* "—the *reporter* might be good."

"What aren't you telling me, Connor?"

I run my hand through my hair. "I'm telling you I didn't finish the interview. If you want me to have a great article, I need to get a hold of that reporter."

"What's the hurry, Connor? You can finish the interview tomorrow." She's suspicious.

"They need it for their deadline. Something about getting it to the printers." I'm making this up.

"Is that right?"

"Yup."

"Why don't I believe you, Connor?"

"I don't give a shit if you believe me or not, G. But if you want me to finish the fuckin interview so I can look good, which means more cash down the line for both of us, get me that number."

Money is Gloria's one weakness.

She doesn't say anything for a long time. "Fine, fine, Connor," she sighs. "You're lucky I have a dinner thing tonight with my friends over at Warner Brothers, otherwise I'd sit in on the rest of your interview with you. I'll have Madeleine get the number for you." She puts me on hold.

I wait.

And I wait.

Turns out Madeleine doesn't have Electra's number. She has to call *Trending Magazine* to get it from them. It takes forever. While I wait, I wander over to the tennis courts behind the convention hall and watch people smack balls around. The waiting drives me nuts. I haven't smoked in years, but all of a sudden I *really* need a cigarette. Right as I'm about to head into the hotel to find a pack, Madeleine texts me Electra's phone number.

I thank her by text and fire off a message to Electra: *Saw you at the booth. I was busy signing. Back at the hotel. Do you want to finish the interview?*

I stare at my phone and wait for a response. When I don't get one, I start thinking about those cigarettes again. My hands shake and I realize I'm cracking up. I fist my hands at my sides and force myself to stare at the tennis game on the court in front of me.

Back. Forth. Back. Forth.

I'm not going to get—Back—a fuckin—Forth—cigarette.

Back. Forth.

The bouncing yellow ball manages to hypnotize me. I zone out on it for who knows how long. I jump when my smart phone pings with a text from Electra.

Do you have time? Or are you too busy with your fans?

I can't tell if she's being sarcastic or not.

My first thought is to text back something ballsy. But I don't want to piss her off. For all I know, she'll refuse to meet up with me. I don't know why it's so fuckin important I see her again today, but it is. *I got time right now.*

My skin crawls while I wait what seems like thirty minutes for a response, but in reality is only thirty seconds.

Electra: *Where do you want to meet?*

Me: *Unless you want fans asking me for autographs the whole time, we should meet in my room.*

Her: *If I do that, we need ground rules.*

Me: *What?*

Her: *No Truth Or Dare. I ask questions. You answer them. NO questions from YOU. Agreed?*

Me: *Sure.*

Her: *I'll be there in ten minutes. Let's get this over with.*

Me: *Cool.*

Her: *If you're naked I'm kicking you in the balls. You've been warned.*

I grin to myself and haul ass up to my room.

Chapter 7

ELECTRA

"Did you bring a ruler?" Connor asks, fully clothed.

I half expected him to be naked again. I'm a tad disappointed he's not. No I'm not. I need to finish this godforsaken interview. "What do I need a ruler for?"

"To hit me across the knuckles if I misbehave."

"Huh?"

"You were such a ball-buster in your texts I thought maybe you wanted to play out some hard ass school teacher fantasy. Make me clean the chalkboards and erasers and shit. I didn't realize you were kinky like that, Warmoth."

"You wish. I don't have time for games, Connor. We're doing this interview. Then I'm leaving. Got it?"

"Whatever you say, *Miss* Warmoth."

"Don't call me Miss." I stride into the room. "You sit there." I point at the chair by the window.

"Yes, ma'am."

I frown at him. "Don't call me ma'am."

"Yes, Miss Warmoth." He drops into the chair.

"Quit it, Connor!"

He chuckles and hangs his muscled arms on the arm rests. "Anything you say, Miss Warmoth."

I groan and sit down in one of the other chairs, facing him. "Let's get one thing straight," I growl. "I'm not your *teacher*, I'm not your *mother* or whatever other sick fantasies you have in mind. I'm here for the interview and then I'm leaving."

"Mother? I hadn't thought of that one." He fakes a shiver. "That kind of turns me on."

I grimace. "That is disgusting, Connor."

He nods knowingly. "I get it. You want me to be your daddy."

Angry, I stand up from my chair and flash my eyes at him. "Bye, Connor." I march toward the door.

"You're not going anywhere." It's half command, half a statement of fact.

"I'm not? Watch me." I grab the door handle. Then I hesitate.

"You push the handle down to make it work," he chuckles sarcastically.

I spin around and stare him down. "Fuck you, Connor! I've had it with you!" I shake my fists and take a step forward. "I've had it with your filthy mouth!" I take another step toward him—"I've had it with your childish behavior!"—and another step—"And your rude comments!"—and another—"And the insulting way you've *always* treated me!"—and a final step until we stand toe to toe.

He smirks at me with that dirty fucking grin of his.

I shout in his face, "And I'm sick and tired of your god damn cooler-than-thou attitude!!"

"Yeah, well I'm over your sexier-than-thou attitude."

"My what?!" Did he just call me sexy?

"Face it, Warmoth. You want me."

"No I don't!"

"You've *always* wanted me. Admit it."

"I do not! I never have! Do you want to know why? Because I *HATE* you, Connor Hughes! I've hated you since the day we met! I hated you all four years of high school! And I've *never* stopped hating you!" I shout so loud I'm red in the face.

He chuckles. "You want me."

"Fuck you!" I whip my hand up to slap him across the cheek—

Except he grabs my wrist blinding fast and twists me around, pinning my arm behind my back, and forcing my chest down against the table top. His hips press right up against my ass.

I can't move. "Let go of me, Connor!"

"Not like this, I won't."

I claw behind me with my free hand and grab for him. All I get is a handful of hard muscle on his side. I barely have any nails, but I dig my fingers in as hard as I can. "Let go!"

"You tried to hit me, War Mouth! I'm not letting go until you calm the fuck down." He's amused by this. He's also totally overpowering me.

"Get off of me!" I growl and squeeze harder with my fingers.

"Ow!" he chuckles. "You have strong hands!" He leans his weight onto my back.

"You're damn right! Now let go of me before I tear your skin off!"

He grabs my free arm by the tricep and squeezes back. "Let go, Warmoth."

"No!"

"Fine." He forces my free arm onto the table top with ease.

Now I can't move either arm. I growl and push back against him with my ass, trying to throw him off balance, but he's made of bricks. I can't budge him.

"What are you doing, Warmoth? Are you trying to grind on me?"

I squirm beneath him. "I'm trying to—get—you—off—"

He laughs. "You're trying to *get me off?*"

"Of! Me! Move it, Connor! *Get off of me!*"

"I'm not going anywhere. You're dangerous."

"You bet I am! Now move!" I bang my butt into his hips. What can I say? It's the only body part I have left to work with. That's when I notice my knitted skirt has climbed half way up my ass. My cheeks are pressing against his jeans.

"What. *The* fuck, woman. Are you wearing a thong? I never pictured a tight ass like you wearing a thong. How the fuck do you get it up that tight ass of yours?"

"Same way as anybody else." I strain against him, arching my back. This inadvertently positions my center of passion directly against his denim covered crotch. I bang at him again. This is humiliating. Or something else entirely.

"What the fuck are you doing?" he laughs. "Are you trying to fuck me, Warmoth?"

"No! Let me go, Connor. I'm serious."

"Promise me you won't hit me and I'll let you go."

"I'm not promising you anything!"

"Then I'm not letting go."

That's when something inside me flips.

I can't decide if I feel exhilarated or humiliated. Maybe both at the same time. I'm caught on a high wire between giving up and letting go. No matter which way I lean, there is no net to save me. One way or the other, I'm going to fall into the unknown. When in doubt, look at the facts at hand: An ultra hot man who I've known for years is pressing up against me. I have intense feelings for this man. They may be feelings of hate, but they are very real. Somehow, it drives me wild. I'm ashamed. Embarrassed. Literally *bare*-assed. And insanely turned on. I whisper, "Fuck me, Connor."

"Is that an order, *Miss* War Mouth?"

I hiss. "Shut the fuck up and fuck me, Connor *Screws*. You know you want to."

"I thought you'd never ask."

"I didn't. It's an order."

"You're not in a position to give any orders, Warmoth."

"Stop being such a pussy and fuck me, big man. Or can't you get it up for a real woman?" I almost laugh. I can't believe I said that. I've *never* said anything like that. I have zero experience with dirty talk of any kind. My vanilla bedroom experience involved only grunting and moaning.

"I can get it up, Warmoth."

Something jingles behind me. Sounds like his belt buckle.

"I've been waiting to do this forever," he grunts.

My drenched thong is pulled away from my folds. Something hard and stiff parts my slick channel, the backs of my legs spasming and my thighs quivering as it slides up and down, up and down. "Is that your finger?"

"Yup."

"Where the fuck is your cock? What are you doing?"

"Inspecting the fuckin merchandise."

"I'm *not* your fucking *merchan*—" My words are cut off when his finger wetly circles my clit. Pleasure pours into me and I moan long and low.

"You like this, don't you," he mutters in my ear, his chest hard against my back. My breasts are pressed against the table top. The cups chafe against my nipples, which are swollen and tight.

"Mmmm," I moan. His finger fills me again, probing deeper. This is the first time a man has touched me downstairs in *years*. I never realized a fucking finger could send me to the moon. When he releases my other arm, I throw both hands on the table top in front of me. "Take me, Connor. Put your cock inside me." I push my hips back against him.

His other hand grabs me by the hip while he caresses my clit. Every muscle in my pelvis starts to squeeze as a powerful orgasm begins to build. Breathless, I gasp, "I'm going to come, Connor. I'm going to—"

"No you're not."

Suddenly his finger is gone and he pulls away.

The tinkling sound of his buckling belt.

"What are you doing, Connor?" I look behind me.

"Leaving you hot and bothered. Let's do this interview."

"What? No! Finish what you started, you piece of shit!" I glance over at the pristine king size bed, which was obviously made up by the maids since this morning.

He laughs. "What happened to the all important interview? I thought this was your *job*." He's mocking me. Standing there fully dressed while I'm bent over a table with my ass in the air and my skirt around my waist and he's mocking me.

I twist around and yank my skirt down. "Screw you, Connor! I'm leaving!" I grab my purse off the floor and glare at him.

"You don't know what you want, do you?"

"I—" Deflate. He's right. I don't. "I hate you, Connor," I pout.

"Me too. Weird, isn't it?"

"You hate yourself?" I quip.

"Yup. And you."

I frown. "I don't hate myself."

"You sure?"

"I don't know. Stop asking so many questions."

"*Me* asking so many questions? Are you hearing yourself, Ms. Interviewer?"

I stare up at him, unable to stop myself from smiling. "You know what's funny?" I ask it with mild amusement.

"What's that?"

"My job is to get people like you to admit things they would never tell a soul, then it gets printed in a magazine and on the internet so the whole world can read about it. Then I get paid. And what do they get? I mean, really?"

"Is this a serious question?"

"Yeah."

He shrugs. "I don't fuckin know. Validation? Publicity? Notoriety?"

I snort. "I don't know either." Today has been confusing from beginning to end, to say the least. I flash a smirky smile at him.

"Did you want me to finish raping you?" He arches a thoughtful eyebrow.

"No means no, Connor," I quip.

He laughs. "I don't know about you, Warmoth, but I could use a fuckin drink."

"Me too." I walk toward him and slap him across the mouth.

He chuckles, completely unaffected. "What the fuck was that, Warmoth?"

"That's what you get for not finishing what you started, Connor *Screws*." I strut proudly past him toward the door. "Let's go. I need that drink." I open the door. "Are you coming?"

"Later." He glares at me with wild eyes. "When you finish what we started."

"Maybe after we have that drink. *Maybe*." I wink at him and walk out of his hotel room.

"Have fun," he hollers out the door. "I'll be here when you get back."

"I thought we were getting a drink?"

He shrugs.

"Can you be *any* more frustrating?"

"Yes."

I roll my eyes and—

CONNOR

I slam her up against the inside of my hotel room door. She claws at my shirt and our tongues fight for dominance as we kiss with mad passion. I force her skirt over her hips and pull her into me by the front of her thong. She pushes my shirt up and smears her hands across my chest. I rip her blouse open, sending the buttons flying off in every direction.

I expect her to say something about the blouse, but she doesn't. I roll her bra up without bothering to unhook it. I squeeze one gorgeous tit and bite the other by the nipple.

She moans and sinks against the door.

I grunt and lift her back up by the thong.

She whimpers as I force my tongue back into her mouth. My finger slips inside her wet pussy.

I'm hard as a fuckin rock.

"Fuck me, Connor," she whispers. "Please."

Hearing her beg makes me twice as hard.

I pick her up by the ass and she wraps her legs around my waist. I walk to the bed and throw her on the comforter.

She pushes up on her elbows.

I dive between her legs and bite her thong, pulling on it like it's dinner.

"What are you doing?" she gasps.

I snarl and let the thong snap against her. She yelps. I yank them all the way off and throw them in the trash. Two points. I glare at her.

Her eyes flash.

"I'm going to eat your wet fuckin pussy until you lose your fuckin mind."

"Connor, I—" She sounds worried.

She should be. My mouth is all over her heat a second later. She tastes so fuckin sweet I can't get enough.

Her hands grab my hair in knots.

My tongue laps her tangy wetness. I'm so fuckin thirsty for her pussy I swallow every last drop.

She moans loud.

"Come all over my face," I grunt.

She comes hard.

Her hips buck against my mouth as I suck her clit and drink her down. Fuck she tastes so fuckin good.

She gasps like she just finished a four minute mile. Every time she says a word, her chest fills and her stomach flattens. "Connor— That— Was— So— Fucking— Good—"

ELECTRA

"I want you inside me right now," I gasp, completely out of breath. I can't believe how hard I just came. I've never had a man *ravish* me like that. I want more.

"Fuck," he hisses.

"What?" I'm worried.

"I'm out of condoms."

"What? *Noooo*," I groan and drop my head against the comforter and stare at the ceiling.

"Yes."

"You're kidding," I laugh.

"Nope."

"I'm not on the pill. And you're not pulling out. My friend in college got pregnant that way. And you probably have more diseases than the CDC."

"I'm clean. I use condoms with everybody. I'm not stupid."

"I didn't say you were."

This is seriously ruining the mood. "Want a blow job?" I say it sarcastically and with no enthusiasm whatsoever.

He snorts. "Not from a corpse."

"I'm not a corpse."

"You sound like one. Let's go get that fuckin drink." He sounds angry.

I kind of don't care. I sigh. "Sure." I sit up on the bed. "Can I have my panties?"

"No."

"What? Give me my panties."

He shakes his head. "They're mine. You got an orgasm, I get your panties."

"You're a pervert," I laugh.

"Says you," he grins. "Let's go."

"I'm not going anywhere without my panties."

"Yes you are. Get up. Let's go."

I stand up. "You're crazy, right? My blouse has no buttons!"

"Tie it."

"No, Connor! This is an expensive blouse! I'm not going to tie it in knots."

"It's already ruined. What difference does it make? We'll go up to the Strip. Nobody will care."

"I'm not going to the Sunset Strip looking like this! I need to change into a different outfit!" My brows knit. "Oh shit! My clothes!"

"What?"

"My laundry," I groan, slouching over with my elbows between my knees. "I had to pull everything out when it was still wet this morning. So I could come back and interview your sorry ass," I smirk at him. "My wet laundry has been sitting in my trunk all day. I really need to go home and go to Lucy's so I can rewash everything and dry it."

"Why don't you do it here?"

"At the hotel?"

"They have laundry service. I can charge it to my room."

"That's sweet, Connor. But I can't ask you to do that."

"So let's go to Lucy's. We can watch the spin cycle together like we're the fuckin Brady Bunch."

"No," I chuckle. "I'm not going to make you sit in a laundry mat with me until midnight while my clothes dry. I can do it myself."

"You shouldn't be hanging out at an all night laundry mat by yourself, Lex. This is L.A. Not the valley."

"Why do you keep calling me Lex?"

He shrugs. "I don't know. It feels right."

My heart starts to flutter for no good reason. "Stop staring at me."

He doesn't. His blue eyes penetrate mine.

Liquid energy slides down my spine and pools between my legs where there's already a tempest of pent up desire. God damn it, I wish he had a condom.

"Let's get your clothes out of your car. Come on," he commands, nodding toward the door. "I won't take no for an answer."

I knot my blouse below my boobs and grab my purse. At least he didn't tear my bra off. Then I'd have to go topless. That gives me an idea. I pull my blouse off.

"What are you doing?" he chuckles.

"Whatever I want." I unsnap my bra and throw it at his face. "You can have this too, asshole." I retie my blouse. "Let's go."

He folds my bra up and shoves it in his back pocket. "I can totally see your nipples through your blouse."

I glance down. He's right. They're not just poking against the thin rayon, they're visible through the light colored fabric. "Good. Then maybe I can find some other idiot smart enough to keep condoms handy so *he* can screw me. Let's go." I walk toward the door.

He's staring at me.

"What?" I'm suddenly embarrassed, but I try to hide it.

"Do you *ever* let your hair down?"

"I thought I just did." Going braless and pantyless is definitely what I'd call letting my hair down.

"No," he chuckles. "I mean *actually* let your hair down?"

I reach up and touch my bun, which I can tell is coming apart. "Shit. How does it look?" I step into the bathroom and flick the lights on.

Connor steps up behind me. In the mirror, he looms over me.

"Get out of here! I'm fixing my hair."

He chuckles. "You're crazy. I just had my face in your pussy and you're worried about me seeing you fix your hair?"

"I don't need to make sense to you. Out."

"I'm not going anywhere."

"Fine." I unknot my bun and let my hair fall. I run my fingers through it, shaking it out.

"Damn, Lex. You have incredible hair. I didn't realize it was so damn long."

"Thanks," I smirk, trying to figure out what to do with it.

"You know, I don't think I ever saw you wear it loose in high school. You always had it in a pony tail."

"I did?"

"Yup. Oh, wait. Except on grad night."

The room freezes.

We stare at each other in the bathroom mirror.

I frown. "Don't talk about grad night."

He heaves a sigh and lowers his eyes. "I'll let you fix your hair." He walks out of the bathroom.

What was that about? Was that regret I saw on his face? It should be. He was a total asshole that night. I shake my head. I don't want to think about it.

I play with my auburn hair, considering options. My lipstick is gone and my eyeliner is a shadow of its former self. Fuck it. I don't even care. I storm out of the bathroom, "Let's go before I change my mind about that drink. This day has been a complete disaster." I stare at him, challenging him to disagree.

"I'm enjoying it," he chuckles.

"You would," I scoff, but find that I sort of agree with him.

To avoid bumping into any convention-goers who might still be wandering the hotel hallways, we take the stairs to the underground garage where my car is parked. Surprise, my clothes are still damp and soapy. To my further surprise, Connor insists on carrying my laundry basket for me.

"Can I have my panties back?" I ask as we walk back toward the stairs. It was one thing to go commando up in his hotel room. Now that we're out in public, I'm very aware of how little I'm wearing.

"No."

"Fine," I grumble. That's when I realize my nipples are hard not because of the warm summer evening weather, but because wearing no underwear in a vaguely public place (there's no one in the parking structure) while in the presence of Connor Hughes is turning me on. I guess I have an exhibitionist streak I didn't know about. I smile to myself.

Two minutes later, we're standing in the marble-floored lobby of the hotel. The main bar off the lobby is crowded, but no one notices us as we approach the concierge desk.

A cute young woman smiles at us from behind the desk. "How can I help you two?" She has a blonde chignon and wears the resort's standard burgundy blazer and gray slacks. Her gold name tag reads *Finch Barksdale*.

"Hey," Connor smiles at her. "I'm a guest here. You guys have a laundry service, right?"

"Of course," Finch says.

"You think you can run a load or two for us?" Connor holds up the basket.

"It would be my pleasure. What room are you two staying in?"

I say, "We're not staying—"

"714," Connor cuts in.

"Excellent," Finch says, reaching over the counter to take the basket from Connor.

His phone chimes in his pocket. "Hold on. I gotta take this call." He walks back toward the stairwell, already muttering to whoever is on the line.

"Your boyfriend is *hot*," Finch says in a low voice.

"He's not my boyfriend," I say nervously.

"He's not?" She seems doubtful. She also notices my outfit for the first time, but doesn't say anything.

I guess Connor was right about no one noticing. "We, uh, knew each other in high school."

Finch frowns, "You better get on that, girlfriend. You don't want a guy like that getting away."

"He—we—" I sigh. "It's complicated."

She nods compassionately, her face serious. "Guys that hot always are. My friend River dated this guy named Drakken who was that hot, and he was drama drama drama." She rolls her eyes.

"In other words, I should end things before the drama gets any worse? Wait. I didn't mean *end* things, because there is no thing. He and I are nothing."

"Are you sure?" she asks coyly.

I glance at Connor's back. "I am *sure* sure."

Her face brightens. "In that case, since you don't want him, can I have him? I haven't had a man in *forever*. Maybe he could break my dry spell?" She looks at me hopefully.

I'm suddenly tense. Every muscle in my body locks up like bridge cables. This isn't my normal state of tension. It's a hundred times worse.

"I'm sorry," Finch says. "I didn't mean to step on your toes."

"Oh, it's okay. I really don't mind. There's really nothing going on between us."

"Are you sure? Because I could've sworn you were ready to claw my eyes out a second ago."

"What? No! I'm not, I mean, you can—" I stop myself when I realize how ridiculous my denials must sound.

"Maybe you guys need to mend some fences and move past whatever is holding you back. That guy obviously likes you."

Memories of grad night gnaw at me. I shake my head. "I think *hate* is a more appropriate word."

"Hate? He's doing your laundry for you. That's not hate, girlfriend. That's love."

I scowl.

I hate that she's right.

Chapter 8

CONNOR

"How was your dinner with the Warner Brothers people?" I ask Gloria, trying to sound friendly.

"Draining. Don't ask. Why didn't you answer my call earlier?" she whines.

"What call?"

"I called you an hour ago."

"You did?"

"Yes I did. Why didn't you answer?"

"I didn't hear the phone ring,"

A group of guys in business suits coming out of one of the hotel elevators erupts in laughter as they pass by.

Gloria asks, "Where are you?"

"At the hotel. What do you want?" My right hand is still covered in black ink from that damn Sharpie I broke signing autographs earlier. That shit never comes off. I stuff my hand in my jeans.

"I'm lonely," she pouts. "Come over, Connor."

Jesus fuckin Christ. She always does this. "So watch a movie."

"Come *over*." She sounds fourteen.

"I'm busy."

"Too busy for your agent? With what?" Now she sounds thirty- or forty-whatever she is. She keeps her age a trade secret.

"Doing what you told me. I'm schmoozing the fans."

"At the hotel? The convention closed at six or something, didn't it?"

"Yeah." I glance over at the crowded hotel bar and see the sea of pink Rom Com Con t-shirts. "But a group of fans kidnapped me," I lie. "They're staying here at the hotel and they've been buying me drinks all night."

"Oh, I get it. You're too busy with a bunch of desperate horny housewives to have time for me?"

"Whose desperate and horny now?" I try to sound as flirtatious and fun as possible. I don't want to deal with her shit right now.

"I'm always desperate and horny for you, Connor. Come over. I'll suck that thick cock of yours and let you come in my face."

"You always let me come in your face," I chuckle. "You'll have to offer more than that if you want me over."

Gloria is always horny as hell. You'd think it was her biological clock, but she wants kids about as much as she wants an STD. She's too busy living the Hollywood lifestyle to make time for anyone other than herself.

"Anything you want, Connor," she says seductively.

"You gonna let me fuck you in the ass?" In reality, I don't give a shit about ass fuckin one way or the other, no pun intended. I've back-doored plenty of hotties. It's been a thing with women my age for years. But Gloria missed that ship and she fuckin *hates* the idea. I'm just saying it to turn her off so she'll back down.

"You know I don't like anal, Connor. Your cock is too big..." she giggles.

"If you let me fuck your ass, I'll be right over."

"Con-*nor*," she whines.

"Come on, G. You know how bad I wanna fuck your ass."

"No, Connor!" Suddenly she sounds like she's reprimanding a kid.

That shit pisses me off. I'm not her fuckin plaything. "I gotta go, G."

She explodes with jealous rage. "Fine! Have fun with your fans, Connor! I'm sure all of them would *love* to let you fuck them in the ass! Just remember who your agent is. *Connor*." She says my name like I'm a piece of shit.

I don't know what she's bitching about. When it comes to ass pains, she's given me more than her fair share.

"I can hear you smirking, Connor."

I'm not smirking. I'm rolling my eyes. Gloria's jealousy is older than dinosaurs and I'm over it.

"You're not hot shit, Connor. You're just a book cover model. I have plenty of *talent* that earns ten times what you do."

By *talent* she means the other hot young guys she reps.

Now I'm pissed. "So go fuck one of them, Gloria. Or did all of them get sick of your shit already?"

"Fuck you, Connor," she hisses before hanging up.

Fuck her.

I shove my phone in my pocket and stare at my ink black hand. I clench it into a fist. I don't know why I'm still using Gloria as an agent anyway. Fuckin controlling bitch.

Anger flares up and my skin starts to itch.

I don't need to put up with her bullshit.

I don't need to be a fuckin male model.

And I don't need the fuckin money.

—*scream-scream-scream-scream*—

My whole world spins as the memories hit me like a shotgun blast. I stumble and find the nearest wall to lean against so I don't fall over.

"Dude, are you okay?" a bellhop asks as he pushes an empty bellman's cart past me. "You look like you're about to pass out."

"I'm good. Thanks, man." Only now I'm bent over with my hands on my knees like I got sucker-punched in the gut.

—*it will get worse over time without surgery*—

"You sure? You don't look too good."

"I'm okay. Really. Thanks."

"Maybe you should sit down for a minute. Do you need some water or something?"

"Thanks, man" I wince, my voice strained. "I'll be fine. Gettin over a bad cold," I lie. "I was sick for two weeks."

He nods, "Some bad viruses going around. Take it easy." He wheels his cart across the lobby.

I finally manage to stand up straight. I wipe my forehead and it's covered in clammy sweat. I gotta get my shit together before Electra sees me like this.

ELECTRA

"Who was that on the phone?" I ask. Why do I feel like I'm prying?

"Nobody," Connor sighs, his eyes dancing around evasively.

"One of your girlfriends?"

He shakes his head, "It was my agent. She can be a ballbuster. I'm supposed to answer the phone whenever she calls in case it's some big deal bullshit."

"Oh. I know what you mean. My editor at *Trending* is the same way. He's a pain in my ass most of the time."

"Right?" Connor agrees, smiling. "Can't live with 'em, can't kill 'em."

"Something like that," I giggle.

"Ready for that drink?"

"About that. I'm kind of tired. Can I take a raincheck?"

"You only live once, Warmoth."

"Can't it wait until tomorrow? My feet are pretty sore from walking around all day in these pumps. I'll feel a lot better after a good night's rest."

"I'm not taking no for an answer." He grins.

His grin is difficult to resist. I sigh, considering. "Can we just have a drink at the main bar here in the hotel?"

"That's a bad idea."

"Why?"

The entire bar area is filled with women in pink Rom Com Con attendee T-shirts.

"*It's him!*" Some random women squeals.

And like that, dozens of faces turn to gawk at Connor and I. They all stare, wide-eyed and hopeful.

"*It's Connor Hughes!!*" The women start filtering out of the bar, creeping toward us uncertainly.

"That's why," he grimaces, "Let's get out of here." He drags me to the stairs and we exit through the parking garage on foot.

My feet are killing me by the time we get to the bottom of the resort's long driveway. "How far is it to Sunset?"

"Do you want me to call an Uber car?"

"I can make it." I may have blisters by the time we get there, but I'll suck it up.

"Fuck that. I'll call one."

"How chivalrous of you." I mean it.

Five minutes later, a guy driving a Nissan sedan picks us up and drives us to the Sunset Strip. Keenly aware of my lack of panties, I keep my knees squeezed together the entire time. When we arrive, I ask Connor, "Do you need any money?"

"I got it on my credit card. Don't worry about it."

"Thanks."

He climbs out and offers his left hand.

"Such a gentleman," I smile, taking his hand. I suddenly worry he'll see up my skirt. Then I realize maybe I *want* him to look. I slide my ass across the seat, feeling the contours of the cushions rubbing against my swollen desire. When my pumps touch the sidewalk, I let my legs open. With my skirt on, they don't open very wide, but I feel like a slut letting it all hang out like this. It's not like there's a bunch of photo spot lights shining on me, but the soft glow of neon from all the lights on Sunset is more than enough for Connor to catch a glimpse.

He smirks and stares between my legs. "Do you want me to push you back in that car and roll your skirt up so I can fuck you on the back seat?"

If it wasn't for the fact that the driver totally smells like Corn Nuts and is watching all this, I would instantly say yes. I nod toward the driver, "We can't..."

"Fine. I'll push you up against the nearest wall and fuck you like the secret slut that you are."

"I'm not a slut," I protest.

"But you wanna be. Every woman does whether they admit it to themselves or not."

"You're *such* a manwhore, Connor."

He helps me climb out of the car. "And proud of it. Let's get inside a club or I really am gonna fuck you."

I linger for just a second, considering his threat. Why does all this sound so damn yummy?

On the sidewalk, I purposefully hang back for a few seconds so I can steal a glance at Connor's ass while he walks. It looks incredible in his tight black jeans. I picture it thrusting in and out of me. Oh, *gawd*...

He stops up ahead and turns. "Are you coming?"

"*Uhhhh*... yeah! Coming!" Why does his butt have to be so *perfect*?

At a stop light, we wait before crossing the nearly gridlocked Sunset Boulevard. The Strip is party central pretty much around the clock. When the light changes, a random guy in a blazer crosses toward us. An unlit cigarette dangles from his lips as he searches his pockets. He nods at Connor, "Yo, man. You gotta light?"

"Sorry, bro," Connor says, "I quit."

The guy chuckles, "You and me both. I've already quit thirteen times."

"Fourteenth's the charm," Connor grins as we pass the man.

"You quit?" I marvel. "You *always* had a cigarette in your mouth. It was your trademark."

Connor smirks, "When I started getting winded after running for two minutes, I decided it was time to ditch the cancer sticks. Smoking and cross training aren't a good fit."

"Makes sense. It's better for your health anyway."

"What do you care?"

"I don't *really* care," I grin sarcastically. "I just don't like the idea of people getting cancer when they could avoid it. My concern is more of a general one. It applies to everybody. Even big jerks like you," I giggle.

"The only thing big about me is my—"

"Don't say it!"

"I was going to say that the only thing big about me is my heart." He bats his eyelashes comically.

I break into laughter. "Ha! That is *so* not true."

"What do you know, War Mouth? You don't know what I've been up to for the past seven years." He sounds amused, not angry. "Maybe I rescue puppies and kittens and volunteer at an old folks home."

"Do you?"

He shrugs.

"The only thing you volunteer is your services for sluts."

"Harsh, Warmoth. Way too harsh."

"It's true."

"If it is, that makes you a slut too."

"Let's go." I pull him along by the wrist toward the closest club. "How's this?"

He looks up at the marquee. "The Cobra Lounge? They usually have bands."

"They have drinks too, don't they?"

"Let's check it out."

The line of hipsters is a mile long. "We'll never get in. My hair's a mess and my outfit is trashed. Maybe we can find a quiet bar?"

He grins. "We don't need to wait. Look at us. You're a fuckin fox."

I blush.

He smirks, "You're almost as good lookin as me."

I scowl. "Cocky as ever, aren't you?"

"Yup." He grabs my hand and pulls me past the crowd of bored people in line. Nearly all the women stop whatever they are saying as we pass and drool at Connor.

I have to admit, it is *slightly* thrilling seeing the glaring jealousy on the faces of all these beautiful women.

When we get to the bouncers, I expect them to tell us to wait in line with the rest of the peasants. The taller bouncer with a shaved head stares at my chest. I fold my arms across my knotted blouse. Without my bra or a sweater or panties, I'm all nipples. What am I doing? Feeling suddenly bold, I unfold my arms. Let him look.

The tall bouncer checks our ID's while the other bouncer, who looks like a burly old ex-Marine, grins at me, his eyes traveling all over my body.

"Gettin a good look?" Connor grunts. He's jealous, which amuses me.

"You want in the club, dawg?" the tall bouncer challenges him, handing back our ID's.

"They can look all they want." I grin. Leaning forward with my hands on my thighs, I arch my back like a pinup girl so both bouncers can look down my top. I don't know why I'm acting like this. I'm never this big a flirt. I blame Connor. He stole my underwear and got me all worked up without doing anything about it, so he'll have to deal with it.

Both bouncers stare at my boobs for a while, smiling approval.

Connor's eyes flash with hot murder.

"Is something bothering you?" I tease.

Connor forces a strained smile, "No, nothing's wrong." He mumbles in my ear with obvious amusement, "But I'm the guy with your panties and bra in my pocket."

"So?"

He shrugs confidently, "If you think either of them has a cock half as big as mine, or can drive you half as fuckin wild as I already have, be my guest. Go home with one of them. Shit, take them both home. But you and I both know they won't measure up and you'll go home lonely and disappointed."

He's calling my bluff and he knows it. I glance at the two burly bouncers. They're both manly enough, but neither is nearly as gorgeous as Connor. "You're a cocky sonuvabitch."

He presses up against my ass and I feel his throbbing cock. "Say the word and I'll fuck you right here."

I grind my ass into his jeans.

"Save it for the dance floor," the older bouncer chuckles, waving us past.

Inside, the DJ spins a summery electro house mix I don't recognize. Imagine the standard *BOOM-cizz BOOM-cizz BOOM-cizz*. The crowd on the dance floor bounces to the jagged rhythm.

"*Let's get some drinks,*" Connor hollers over the loud music.

"*Okay,*" I holler back.

—*BOOM-cizz BOOM-cizz BOOM-cizz*—

He reaches out for my hand with his right.

Does he want to hold it? Then I notice his palm looks weird. "*Why is your hand black?*" I shout.

He shows me the palm. "*This?*"

"*It looks terrible.*"

He leans toward my ear, "*Some fungus I picked up. Highly contagious.*" He reaches up to touch my face.

Horrified, I jump back and nearly trip over two random dancers. "*Connor! Don't!*"

He breaks into an easy smile. "*Relax. It's permanent ink. I broke a pen signing autographs. It won't come off.*"

I wince, *"Are you sure?"*

"Gimme your hand."

I recoil. *"No!"*

"Gimme."

I relent. *"Here."*

He strokes the back of my hand with his warm palm.

My skin tingles and my heart flutters and sizzles travel up my arm and down my spine.

"See? It doesn't come off."

I look down at my hand as he continues to rub it. None of the ink comes off.

"See?"

"Yuh — yeah."

He keeps rubbing my hand, circling his thumb around my palm.

It does amazing things to me that I can't explain.

— BOOM-BOOM-BOOM cizz-cizz-cizz —

As the thumping music and Connor's erotic hand massage starts to carry me away, I am suddenly reminded of my lack of panties and bra. Am I going to drip on the floor? At this rate, it's bound to happen. Damn, I'm turned on.

He releases me. *"Let's get some drinks."*

I hold my hand to my chest and rub it thoughtfully. I can't respond to Connor because that was somehow the most romantic thing he's ever done. Well, after doing my laundry, or should I say having it done for me. Either way, I feel the echo of his thumb still circling, like he's still doing it. But he's not. What the hell did he just do?

— cizz-BOOM cizz-BOOM cizz-BOOM —

He drags me to the neon blue bar and works his magic on one of the cute female bartenders. Despite the crowd, she takes his order right away. A minute later, she hands him two shots and two mixed drinks. He offers me a shot.

"What's this?" I ask.

"Drink it," he orders.

"How do I know it doesn't have roofies in it?"

"Quit kidding yourself," he smirks, *"You already wanna fuck me. Pound that shit and let's dance."* He swallows his shot then gulps down the mixed drink in three seconds.

I sip the shot. It tastes like Tequila. The mixed drink looks like a Cosmo.

"This isn't a fuckin taste test! Pound that shit!"

"Okay, okay, Frat Boy!" I swallow the shot easily but it burns my throat. My eyes bulge and I make a flame-thrower face. Connor laughs.

Then I tip my head back and drink the Cosmo as fast as I can. I nearly choke, but manage to get it all down without spilling it all over myself.

He grabs my hand and pulls me onto the packed dance floor.

—BOOM-cizz BOOM-cizz BOOM-cizz—

Connor is instantly into the dancing. He breaks out the slithery pelvic gyrations he showed earlier during the convention reveal. Somehow, he manages to include me in his dancing. He snakes around me in fluid movements. I try not to look dorky. I've never been a good dancer. Connor is a master.

I'm intimately aware of the fact that my skirt keeps riding up. It's not meant for dancing. I keep yanking it down by the hem. Luckily, it doesn't take long for the shot and Cosmo to take effect on my empty stomach.

A few minutes later I'm bouncing to the beat with my hands over my head.

Connor worships me, sliding his body all over mine.

Everybody is watching us. Or should I say, watching Connor. I feel like a statue. So I shake my ass. Connor is instantly behind me. I circle my butt against his jeans as best I can.

—BOOM-BOOM-BOOM cizz-cizz-cizz—

He leans into my ear, "*Everybody is watching you, Lex. All the guys in here want this ass.*" He punctuates his words by grinding his crotch against my cheeks. "*They all want to fuck you, Lex. But they can't. I won't let them because this is mine.*" As the alcohol takes effect, the sexual energy pouring off everyone in the club feeds into my desire. A hard hand roams up my stomach. I'm only vaguely aware it's Connor's hand. In the moment, I almost don't care whose hand it is. He squeezes my breast through my knotted blouse. My nipples ache with desire, throbbing to the dance beat.

—BOOM-cizz BOOM-cizz BOOM-cizz—

I close my eyes and tip my head back, leaning it against Connor's muscled shoulder. Heat blooms against the top of my head.

Connor's face is buried in my hair. "*You smell fuckin incredible, Lex.*"

I'm pretty tall, but Connor is way taller than I am. Having a big hot guy wrap himself around you like this is heaven. I grin to myself, my eyes closed, shaking my ass as he massages my other breast, boldly twisting the nipple. I sit my ass onto his hips, leaning onto his hardness for support. The front of my skirt suddenly tightens against my thighs and lifts. A hot hand cups my folds.

"*You're soaking wet for me, aren't you?*"

I nod my head against his shoulder.

"*You want me to fuck you right here, don't you?*"

I moan a reply.

He chuckles lustily against my ear.

His fingers start to circle against my wetness. It feels incredible. Vaguely aware that people might be able to see up my skirt, I open my eyes a slit. The people surrounding us swim in a deep ocean of blue light. I'm so turned on, everybody seems to be moving in slow motion. I'm completely enveloped by Connor, floating in his hard heat and sexual energy. Slowly I become aware that people *are* staring. The men. The women. Everybody. They're captivated by what Connor and I are doing. I feel like a porn star. When he starts to massage my clit, I realize I don't fucking care *who's* watching. I melt all over his hand.

—*BOOM-cizz*—

His finger slides inside me.

—*BOOM-cizz*—

I moan loud, *"Fuck me, Connor…"*

—*BOOM-cizz*—

Nobody can hear me over the loud music.

Nobody except Connor. He growls into my ear and he pushes his finger deeper. I sink into his hand, wanting more. Some part of his hand is rubbing my clit just right. It sings with ecstasy. The first spasm of orgasm starts to build and my muscles clench around his deep finger.

And then his hand is gone.

Damn him! He did it again! I shout, *"Connor —"*

His tongue fills my mouth. We're chest to chest. He squeezes my ass hard. I straddle his thigh, pushing my skirt up, grinding my core against his denim covered leg. If it wasn't for Connor's hands on my ass keeping my skirt from riding any higher, it would be around my waist.

Our tongues go to war as we kiss on the dance floor.

This is easily the dirtiest thing I've ever done.

But god damn it, I'm going to come if it kills me. Because *not* coming *will* kill me. I've never been so turned on in my entire life. I continue to grind against Connor's muscled leg. I have no doubt I'm leaving a wet streak on his jeans. I don't care. The muscles inside me clench in a slow rhythm. Each time they squeeze it feels exquisitely good. But it's like I *can't* come unless there's a cock inside me. I try to pretend his tongue in my mouth is his cock invading my tunnel, but it doesn't work.

This is beyond frustrating.

Still kissing, I grab his belt buckle and start to undo it.

He pushes my arms behind my back and pins them there. He stares at me with his deep blue eyes. *"You're not gonna come until I say you can come."*

"I need to come, Connor!"

He smirks and withdraws his thigh from between my leg, moving it with the music so I can't straddle it anymore. *"You're not ready yet."*

"God damn it, Connor! You fuck me right now or I'm going to kill you!!"

He laughs, his lush mouth pulling over his perfect teeth. He's the most incredibly handsome man I've ever seen, bar none. And he's just as infuriating as he's always been. I smack the bottom of my fist against the granite of his chest.

He shakes his head, ignoring it.

"I hate you, Connor Hughes!"

"I hate you too, Lex," he grins, still dancing.

ELECTRA

"I need a break, Connor! My feet are killing me!"

"Let's grab a seat at a table!"

He takes me by the hand and leads me off the dance floor. The little round bar tables hugging the walls are all filled with people. We finally find one that is stacked with at least thirty dirty glasses and a litter of wadded up napkins.

"How's this?" Connor asks.

—*BOOM-cizz BOOM-cizz BOOM-cizz*—

"Dirty?" I yell.

"I'll clean it."

"Let's just find another one."

"There aren't any others. Hang tight. I'll find a waitress or something. You gonna be okay here by yourself?"

"I'm a big girl. I'll be fine."

"You're not that big," he grins.

I ball my fists and hold them up like a boxer, *"Don't mess with me! I'll mess you up!"*

He laughs, *"I'm shakin in my boots. I'll be right back."*

—*cizz-BOOM cizz-BOOM cizz-BOOM*—

I glance around the club and watch the people. A bunch of green glow sticks wave in the air above the crowd, wielded by the wasted dancers. Strobe lights flash in time with the music as the bass beat pulses. I can feel it humming beneath me on the barstool.

—BOOM-BOOM-BOOM cizz-cizz-cizz—

I shift uncomfortably, feeling the ache of my drenched sex. Damn it, if Connor doesn't have sex with me tonight, I'm going to explo—

Somebody bumps into my back.

I twist around on the stool. *"Hey! Watch it!"*

The table next to ours is surrounded by five big guys in cheesy blazers and collared shirts. They ignore me.

Assholes.

I look around for Connor, but I don't see him.

It doesn't take long for the bums in the blazers to bump me again.

"I said, watch it!"

They can't hear me.

—BOOM-cizz BOOM-cizz BOOM-cizz—

I tug the blazer of the nearest idiot.

He turns around. His face can best be described as toad-like.

"Please be more careful! You keep bumping into me!"

He smirks, obviously drunk. *"Suck my dick, bitch."*

My eyes headlight. *"Fuck you!"*

"Any time, baby. Any time." He stares down my top.

"You're disgusting!" I turn around and fold my arms across my chest.

WHAM!

I'm thrown against the table, rocking it forward. I grab the edge of it so I don't fall on my ass. When the table and I rock back to standing, several half-empty drink glasses keep going and spill into my lap. *"God damn it! You ASSHOLE!!"* I instinctively catch one of the glasses, but two more fall to the floor and shatter. The sound is buried beneath the music.

—Cizz! Cizz! Cizz! Cizz!—

I stand and yank on the sleeve of Toad Face.

He turns and glares at me sleepily.

"Look what you did! You spilled drinks all over me!" My wrinkled blouse and my bare stomach are covered in sticky alcohol.

He scowls and turns away.

I grab his arm through his blazer and tug on it.

He shoves me and I stumble back. Nothing is behind me. I can't regain my balance. I'm going to crash into the floor and get trampled by dancers. I wheel my arms, trying to catch myself. It's too late. I fall right into—

Connor's arms. *"You okay?!"*

"That guy pushed me!!"

"What?!"

I charge forward, circle around to the front of Toad Face and slap him on the cheek. "*Jerk!*"

CRACK!!

I reel, holding my hand to *my* cheek as I sink to my knees. My glasses hang cockeyed from my nose. Starlight twinkles in my vision as I sit down on the dirty dance floor. My cheek seems to have disappeared. I can't actually feel it. But I do know one thing:

Toad Face. Just. Punched. Me.

With a fist.

—*BOOM-cizz BOOM-cizz BOOM-cizz*—

My mouth O's. I gasp.

Chaos ensues.

Connor slams Toad Face by the forehead against the bar table and he pours to the floor. The other four guys in blazers turn on Connor. He punches the next one in the throat and the guy crumples into the guy behind him, grabbing for his neck as he knocks over a barstool that clatters against the sticky floor.

—*cizz-BOOM cizz-BOOM cizz-BOOM*—

Connor punches the third guy in the stomach and the guy folds over into a heap.

The remaining two guys stare wide eyed at Connor.

Everything happened so fast, I don't know what to do.

Connor sweeps me into his arms and carries me away.

I wrap my arms around his neck and watch the two guys still standing at their table gape open-mouthed at us. They're too scared to follow.

As Connor worms through the crowd, he spins me so I'm over his shoulder like a sack of rice. He pushes through the people jamming up near the front doors. We finally burst past the bouncers who let us in earlier.

The burly ex-Marine bouncer catches my eye as we pass. He looks as surprised as I feel. Connor is running so fast, I don't want this guy to think I'm getting kidnapped. I wave at him and holler, "We had a great time! He's taking me home. See you next week!" I laugh.

The bouncer grins and shakes his head, "Make sure you guys use protection!"

I've got all the protection I need carrying me over his shoulder down the sidewalk.

Chapter 9

ELECTRA

"It doesn't look that bad," Connor says, inspecting my cheek in the lights of his hotel bathroom.

I sit on the sink. "My cheek feels like it's the size of a grapefruit."

He grins, "It looks like a tomato."

"What?" I twist around to see myself in the big wall mirror. Turning my neck makes my whole head throb. "Ow, shit. This *hurts*."

"Let me get some ice. I'll be right back."

Fifteen minutes later, he still hasn't returned.

I'm getting worried. *That* doesn't make any sense. There's no good reason why *I* of all people should worry about Connor Hughes. Then again, he just came to my rescue. Maybe I need to re-evaluate my position on him.

The hotel door finally opens. "They keep the ice machines hidden behind a secret door in this place. It took me forever to find it." He sets the bucket of ice cubes on the counter and wraps a bunch in a washcloth. He holds it carefully to my cheek.

I wince. "That stings."

"Sorry."

"I'm fine."

"Why did that guy knock you down?"

"He knocked me into our table. A bunch of drinks spilled all over me."

"That's why you smell like barroom floor."

I frown at him, which hurts. "Anyway, I slapped him."

Connor laughs. "You slapped him? Shit, Warmoth. You should change your name to Warhead." He ruffles my hair.

"Stop," I giggle.

"What am I gonna do with you, Lex?"

"Take me to bed."

His eyes search mine. "Do you mean *put* you to bed or *take you* in bed?"

I snicker and hang my head. My loose long hair curtains my face. "The latter."

"How about later. I don't know about you, but I'm starving. I haven't eaten anything since breakfast."

"Do you want to order room—" My phone rings in my purse on the counter beside me. "Fuck. Hold on." I look at the number. "It's my editor. I have to take this call."

"Go for it."

I answer. "Yes, Vince?"

"Where's my story, Warmoth!"

I press my fingertips against my forehead and sigh, "I'm working on it."

"I don't want to hear excuses, Warmoth!" His voice is loud in the quiet bathroom. I hold the phone away from my ear. "You've had all damn day! What is taking so long?! Do I have to come over there and hold your hand?"

"No, Vince." I hang my head again, feeling like an incompetent child.

"Get this shit done, Warmoth! No article, no paycheck. It's that simple."

"Please, Vince. I'm working on it. I swear. But it's… complicated. You have to believe me." I can't believe how *desperate* I sound. For the first time in my career, I'm blowing my assignment. And it pains me. I've dropped the ball all day long and I feel ashamed of my own incompetence. "I just need until morning. I promise."

"Did you at least finish the interview? Tell me you finished the interview and you just have to polish the article."

"No, I—"

"Jesus, Warmoth!"

Connor takes the phone from my hands. "Relax, buddy. You'll get your interview."

"Who's this?" Vince barks.

"I'm the interview. She'll get it done. And she'll have your article for you tomorrow afternoon." He gives me a look.

I nod and mouth the words, *"Thank you."* I reach for the phone so I can talk to Vince.

Connor ends the call. "That guy is a dick."

"You hung up on him!"

"He deserved it. Let's order food and finish your interview."

I can't argue with that.

ELECTRA

"Remember that time Elliot McKinney got caught sneaking into the girl's locker room?" Connor sits shirtless across from me at the round room service table that was wheeled in here an hour ago. A white table cloth is draped over the table. It's covered with everything on the menu. Connor insisted.

I laugh. "Oh yeah! I was there! Mrs. Navarro caught him and chased him across the quad during brunch and Elliot kept shouting 'I am Seymour Bungholio! I am Seymour Bungholio!' over and over! That was hilarious!!" I'm wearing a hotel bathrobe and my wet hair is up in a towel. I needed to shower off all the booze that Toad Face spilled on me.

"Elliot McKinney was crazy," Connor chuckles, spreading butter onto a dark seven grain bun.

"Were you friends with him?" I take a bite of my wild greens salad.

"Sort of. I knew all the guys on the football team."

I scowl. "I hated those guys. Whenever you were around them you were twice the ass you usually were."

He looks at me for a long time before lowering his eyes. "Sorry."

"Wait, what? Was that an apology?" I chuckle. "I can't believe Connor Hughes is apologizing to *me*. Where's my phone! I have to call Vince Pitts and tell him to stop the presses! Someone get CNN on the line! This is breaking news!!"

He snorts. "Whatever."

"Oh, gosh, Connor. Do you feel bad? Did I hurt your widdle feewings? Grow up, Connor. The world is a harsh place. Anyway, I'm over it. What you did to me in high school is ancient history." I stab a crab cake with my fork.

The truth is, I'm not over it. I don't want to talk about it. What Connor did to me for four straight years is far too big for a simple sorry. And while punching out a few guys I could've handled myself was nice, it doesn't make up for much. He could apologize for *years* but I doubt it would make any difference now. Connor *changed* me. Permanently. I see that now. A big piece of who I am is a result of how Connor always treated me. There's no denying it and no taking it back.

I just want to forget about it.

Changing the subject, I ask, "When are we going to finish your interview? You told Vince I'd be finished by morning."

"No, you said morning. I said tomorrow afternoon to buy you some time so you don't have to rush."

I sigh, "I'd rather just get it over with." Then I yawn. My cheek throbs when I do. Before we started eating, I took some aspirin I had in my purse and it helped a little. "Fuck it. I don't want to do your stupid interview right now. I want to go home." I stand up. My feet ache the second I do. I walk into the bathroom and grab my skirt off the counter. It's still sticky from all the drinks that got spilled on it and needs to be dry cleaned. I step into it, my robe still on. "Can we meet in the morning?" I holler. "Maybe talk over breakfast?"

"You're not going home." Connor leans against the door frame.

"Shut up, Connor. I don't want to play any more games tonight, okay?"

"Sleep here tonight. You'll be safer with me."

Why does that make me feel special? I don't know, but it does. But... no. "Thanks, Connor. I'll be fine. Those guys aren't going to follow me to my apartment or anything."

"You never know."

"Trust me. I've met way more dangerous people than those douches. I'll be fine." I pull my blouse off the shower curtain rod. It's still damp from hand-washing it. Whatever. "Can I have some privacy?"

"No." He puts one hand in his pocket, making his chest and shoulder flex impressively.

"Are you flexing your abs for me?"

"Maybe," he grins.

It's impossible not to be affected by his charming smile and the incredible body attached to it. Muscles and tattoos are an irresistible combination. I grin, "Do you think your model body is going to change my mind or make me forget about my black eye?"

"I have a black hand." He holds up his ink stained palm.

I snort. "What's that have to do with anything?"

He shrugs. "I don't know."

I roll my eyes and shrug the robe off. Now I'm topless. Nothing he hasn't already seen. "Can I have my bra?" I hold out my hand expectantly.

He smiles, eyeing my boobs. "No. I told you. It's mine."

"Why do you want my bra?"

"It's a memento. It'll remind me of today."

"Why do you need a reminder? I want to forget it."

His eyes flash and he looks away. "Something tells me I'm not going to see you again."

"That's stupid. We have an interview to finish, remember?"

He does this non-committal shoulder shrug and head shake. He almost looks... sad.

I don't believe it. It's just part of his charming act. Injured Heartthrob Needs Shoulder To Cry On. It may work on unsuspecting girls, but I'm not a kid anymore. I know better. I know the real Connor Hughes. The one who lived to hurt me and insult me. All that talk about high school brought back an army of painful memories that I feel brimming beneath the surface of my thoughts. Everything that has transpired over the course of this epic day has left me completely drained and confused. I need space. I sigh, "I'll see you tomorrow, Connor. Give me my bra. And panties."

He grins and shakes his head. "Nope." He locks eyes with me.

I am not amused. A wave of exhaustion whips through me, stealing the last of my good humor. I am *really* tired. "Whatever." I break eye contact with him and jam my arms into the sleeves of my blouse and yank the tails into a tight knot around my ribs. I shoulder past him and grab my pumps from by the door. The second I slip them on, my feet sparkle with pain. I ignore it. I swipe my purse off the chest of drawers. "Thanks for dinner. I need to go." I reach for the doorknob.

"What, no kiss?"

I smirk and walk up to him. He leans down and I peck his cheek.

"Is that it?"

"Yes, that's it."

He smiles hopefully. "You're tired. I'll drive you home."

I sigh. "Is your car here?" I don't know why I asked.

"My motorcycle is in the garage."

"I can't carry my laundry on your motorcycle."

"Leave it here. Come get it tomorrow."

"No. I'm going home. Tonight."

He lifts an eyebrow. "You drove a car, right?"

I'm ready to fall asleep standing up. I sigh again, "Yeah, why?"

"I'll drive you," he grins.

"How will you get home?"

"I'll call Uber."

I consider it. I really am tired, maybe too tired to drive. But no. "No, Connor. I just want to be alone right now. I should go." My freshly cleaned laundry is neatly folded and stacked inside my basket by the door. There's even a folded card resting on top of the clothes with gold embossed B.H.R. initials in elegant script. I pick up the basket. "Good night, Connor."

He opens the door and flashes a grin. "After you. I'll walk you down."

"You don't need to do that. I'll be fine."

"I'll carry your basket for you."

"I've got it." I step into the hallway. "Quit trying so hard."

He follows, closing the door behind him. He wears only his jeans. He stuffs his hands into his pockets bashfully and wiggles the toes of his bare feet, swaying back and forth. He looks like a boy.

A boy I will always hate. "Goodnight, Connor." I turn and walk away. I don't look back. If I do, I might do something stupid.

"Wait!"

I turn around. "What?"

"Just a sec." He dashes into the room.

I rest the laundry basket against my hip. "What now?" I can't tell if I'm exasperated or excited.

He jogs back out of the room and stops inches from me. "You forgot your glasses." He holds them out. "You left them on the sink when we came back from the club."

I reach for them and our fingers touch.

I stare at his hand and my eyeglasses.

Somehow, those glasses tie everything together. They bring me right back to that moment in the meeting room upstairs at the convention hall. Truth OR Dare. That first passionate kiss. Watching him dance at the convention reveal. Punching those guys out at the club without a care for his own safety.

I'm going to do something stupid.

Chapter 10

ELECTRA

We crash onto the bed in his room, him on top of me, our mouths locked together in mortal combat. He rips my blouse open and his hard hands attack my breasts, squeezing, twisting, pinching.

It hurts but it also drives me wild with wicked pleasure.

His teeth sink into my lower lip and he tugs until my lip pops out of his mouth. He glares at me like a wild animal. "Fuck, Lex. I've been thinking about fuckin you since the second I saw you this morning."

I suddenly remember the girl who marched out of his room, the one he'd obviously had sex with before I arrived on *this* bed. My heart squeezes in my chest. This is the stupidest thing I've ever done. I want to run out of here.

His hand sneaks up my skirt to my naked cleft. "You are soaking fuckin wet, Lex. You're dying to fuck me, aren't you?" He massages my folds, finding my clit, circling it.

Heat. New arousal explodes between my legs. "Make me forget all the shit that happened today," I moan.

'I'm going to make you forget your own name, Lex." A stiff finger slides inside me.

My head drops to the mattress and I moan.

Connor's blue eyes blaze into mine. "You've wanted my dick since you saw it."

I shouldn't be doing this. Because I *hate* those blue eyes. I've *always* hated them. I moan throatily, my voice husky. "No." *Yes.*

"You were thinking about this when I was on stage and all those girls were screaming my name."

"No I wasn't." *Yes I was.*

"You were thinking how you wanted to scream my name while I was deep inside your wet fuckin pussy, weren't you?" His finger forces deeper, filling me. His thumb relentlessly massages my clit.

Fireworks go off inside my core and shoot up to my chest. It's getting hard to argue, but I still have some fight left in me. At a loss for words, I simply snarl.

He grins, "You're a fuckin animal, Lex. I always knew it. A wildcat."

"That's right," I hiss. "So you better shut your filthy mouth and do something or I'm going to claw your dick off and throw it to the wolves." My eyes pop open. I can't believe I just said that.

Connor's face twists into a strange smirk. Then his expression turns dangerous, but he's still grinning.

Are all the feminists wrong? Do women *want* a man to force themselves on them, to prove their fitness, their strength, their determination? Do we want to fight a man in the bedroom to find out if he is resilient enough to care for us and our offspring? I don't know, but right now, I know one thing: this is my moment and I can do whatever the hell I want.

Connor can only have me if he can *take* me.

That thought, combined with the magic his hand is working between my thighs sends me over the edge. A powerful orgasm tears through me, stopping my breath. My back arches and lifts off the bed and my hips thrash.

"Come all over my hand, Lex. Come all over it. Fuck yeah."

My breath comes in sharp gasps as the intense pleasure slowly fades in my veins and I relax onto the mattress. His weight presses down on my chest. Our noses are tip to tip. Rough hands peel my skirt up over my ass.

He leaps off the bed and stands over me. "God damn, Lex. You have the most beautiful pussy I've ever seen. I can't stop staring at it." He shakes his head. "Fuckin incredible." He kicks his jeans off, revealing his straining length. "You want this, don't you?" He grabs himself by the base and strokes slowly. He can't get any harder. The head is purpled with blood. Pre cum swells from the tip. "You want to know what it's like to have a real man fuck you with a real dick, don't you?"

My eyes are locked on his cock and the glistening pearl of pre cum. We don't have any condoms. He is going to get me pregnant. I don't care. The haze of arousal swirling in my brain blots out all rational thoughts. I want this man to fuck me. To plant his seed inside me. To impregnate me so that I can carry his young. "Fuck me," I moan. "Fuck me now."

He bends over and pulls a condom from the front pocket of his jeans. He tears the package open and sheathes his sword.

A sense of vague relief whispers in the farthest corner of my mind, as if someone other than me is thinking about condoms and birth control. From the neck down, all I'm thinking about is cock and cum.

He flips me over onto my stomach and yanks my hips to the edge of the bed.

"Fuck me hard. If you're man enough." I push up with my hands and thrust my ass in his face.

He chuckles. "You think you can handle it?"

I smirk, "You're all talk, Connor. You don't even know how to use that big cock of your—"

The tip of it sinks into my wet folds and I drop my head to the mattress, my hair piling over my face.

"Be careful what you wish for," he growls as he slides himself in.

"Oh, god…" I shiver as every inch fills me to the hilt.

He pauses, deep. His cock pulses inside me. I tighten down. "Yeah," he grunts. "Like that." He slowly withdraws and I keep squeezing. "Milk it." He pushes in again.

His slow thrusting steals my sanity.

My pleasure mounts with every stroke.

He leans over my back and collects my hair like reins, pulling my head up.

"I'm gonna ride you like an animal," he grunts.

"Fuck me with that race horse cock of yours, Connor." I'm barely aware of how absolutely dirty that sounded.

"Mmnnmm…" he moans as he picks up speed.

I surge backward with each thrust, timing my movement with his. My body waves into his, bringing intense pleasure with it. I'm so turned on I bite my own shoulder. Sex has never been *this* good.

"Fuck, Lex. I can't get enough of your pussy. It's so fucking… *fuuuck…*" He trails off, his deep voice straining with ragged pleasure bordering on pain. He is unraveling, losing his mind as his hard muscled body overtakes mine.

He is in complete control of me.

And his cock is suddenly gone.

"No!" I'm terrified and furious at the same time.

He flips me over and drives his heavy cock home.

He thrusts into me savagely with his thickness, his heavy balls slapping against my ass.

Electricity arcs through me from every point of contact with his body.

The stirrings of a violent orgasm begin to build.

My body thrills with sensation as he plunges harder and deeper. My legs clamp around his narrow waist. My hands claw at his muscled back.

My mind reels knowing that Connor Hughes is fucking me. The boy I hated through four years of high school finally got his way. The boy who I swore would never lay a finger on me, let alone fuck me, is bringing my body to an earth shattering climax I never believed I was capable of having.

My heart doesn't know what to do.

The overwhelming pleasure of his sex deep inside mine mingles with the pain of knowing I'm sleeping with the enemy as I come undone.

His strong fingers dig into my ass as he tilts my pelvis just right and the head of his cock grazes back and forth across my G-spot with expert perfection.

I can't stop him.

I wouldn't if I could.

It feels too damn good…

I want to moan, but I won't. I'm suddenly afraid I'll scream his name if I let it all out. I can't let myself do that. It would somehow be my final betrayal of myself. He can fuck me, but he can't keep me.

I won't scream his name.

I won't.

It's the only shred of dignity I have left.

But it feels too good…

Needing to let *something* out, I begin to whimper.

"Come on my cock, Lex." He pulls my hips into his over and over, his body weighing down on mine.

"*Yes…*" I moan, my face buried in his muscled shoulder.

"Squeeze me as hard as you can."

"*Yes…*"

"Fuckin come, Lex. Come now!"

"Yes!"

"*Come right the fuck now!!*" He growls.

"Yuh—!!" The first wave of my orgasm hits me, stopping my voice in my throat.

"*Fuck yeah!*" He roars, his voice all gravel and passion. He explodes inside me.

At the same moment, a powerful orgasm tears through me. I squeal as the muscles of my core clench around his pulsing manhood as his final desire surges into me. I can't stop myself. I scream. "Connor!!!"

He heaves on top of me, pulling me into him as hard as he can, his entire body quivering for a long time.

As the electric tempest dies down, I turn my face to the side and gasp for breath. I clamp my eyes shut and cover them with my arm.

What have I done?

I'm not sure, but the guilt and shame I'm feeling is positively delicious.

I.

Fucked.

Connor.

HUGE.

I laugh like a loon.

No matter how big of a mistake this was, I want more. Now. "Do you have any more condoms?"

ELECTRA

The lights of Santa Monica twinkle in the distance. Somewhere beyond them lies the dark Pacific Ocean. The two people in the pool seven floors below the balcony are making out. They think no one is watching them.

I am.

I'm also getting fucked from behind by Connor and I'm completely turned on once again. I didn't think it was possible, but Connor is a master cocksman. I mean, I heard the rumors for years. But they really were true.

The couple in the pool are wearing bathing suits.

I'm not wearing anything. I'm completely naked except for my pumps. Connor insisted I put them on for balcony sex. Who was I to say no? Something about wearing them makes me feel extra slutty. I like it. Add to that the fact my feet are killing me from walking in my pumps all day long and I can't help but imagine what strippers go through after a long shift strutting their stuff on strip club runways.

I smile to myself.

I'm just a working slut and I love it.

Maybe I should look into becoming a hooker?

What am I thinking? I almost laugh but then I moan when another swell of pleasure pushes through me. I squeeze the steel railing in both hands and lean into Connor's languid thrusts. I never realized how much I like standing doggy style. I had always thought it was impersonal so I avoided it. Nope. It's somehow twice as intimate. I can't explain why. Maybe because I've never done it before. I don't know.

Connor grunts, "I am *hooked* on fuckin you, Lex. You fit me like a fuckin glove. *Fuuuuck...*" He reaches beneath me and fingers my clit as he slides in and out.

Jolts of ecstasy stab into me. "Oh, god, Connor. I'm going to come again. I'm going to come..." I start to whimper and I pull myself forward, my chest against the cold steel railing as Connor's hot steel fires into me.

The couple in the pool below suddenly turns up and stares. Damn it. I wish I had my glasses on so I could see better. But I can tell that they're looking at me, their faces white blobs in the blue glow of the pool lights.

Unashamed, I stare right back at them and come on Connor.

CONNOR

"I hope you have more condoms," Electra pants, lying beside me on the sheets.

"You ready to go again?" I'm lying beside her, propped up on my elbow, my hand resting casually on her wet pussy.

"I am." She frowns. "Unless you're out of condoms?"

"You think I'd just get two? I got ten more."

"Ten? You're *waaaay* too cocky for your own good, Connor. And speaking of condoms, when the hell did you find some? I don't remember you stopping to buy any."

"I got them when I went looking for ice."

"You're such a liar, Connor! *Couldn't find the ice machine*? Ha!" She's throwing my words back at me. "Wait, were you thinking about screwing me while you were tending to my wounds?"

"At the time, I was thinking about the fact you were sitting on the bathroom countertop with no panties on that sweet pussy of yours while I cleaned your face. I couldn't let you out of here without fuckin you, could I?"

She giggles and yawns. "You're a sex fiend, Connor Screws."

"Look who's talkin, Warpussy."

"That's terrible," she cackles and drops her head on the pillow, her eyes half shut. She smiles at me for awhile. Her eyes close all the way.

She's so damn hot it hurts.

In the back of my mind is the idea that she's going to throw her clothes on and leave once we're done with the fuckin. That's one reason I went along with the sex. I would've been happy if she'd just slept here. I didn't want her to go. But make no mistake. The other reason I went along with the sex is Electra Fuckin Warmoth. Are you kidding? This has been the best sex of my life, bar none. That's saying a lot considering all the chicks I've banged.

But when you know, you know.

Why? I have no idea.

Electra gets this little frown line in her forehead. She's asleep.

I pull up the sheet so it covers her shoulder.

The little line goes away.

I smile to myself.

The good news for me is that I came so hard tonight, I'm sleepy as fuck. Usually after the fuckin, I kick them out like I booted Babe this morning, or I bail. I always get jittery after fuckin at night. Whether it's my place or theirs, it doesn't matter. I can't sleep after sex. I never figured out why. With Electra, it's different.

I'm relaxed as a fuckin cat.

If you scratched behind my ears I'd fuckin purr.

I'm grinning to myself as my eyes start to close.

The only thing I can think about is seeing Electra Warmoth in my bed when I wake up in the morning.

CONNOR

My phone buzzes on the table next to the bed, ripping me awake. I swipe it off the wood so it stops making so much noise. It vibrates in my hand less loud.

The first thing I do is make sure Electra is all right.

She sleeps quietly beside me, her back to me.

Good.

I check the number on my phone. Fuckin Gloria. It's also four fuckin thirty in the morning.

I jump out of bed and take the phone into the bathroom, closing the door quietly behind me. "Why are you calling so late?" I whisper, sitting on the toilet.

"Why are you whispering?"

"Because I was sleeping. What do you want that's so important it can't wait until fuckin morning?"

"I forgot to ask you earlier." She sounds pleasant. "How did your interview go with Electra Warmoth?"

Fuck. I don't say anything for a long time.

Gloria laughs. "I got her name from Madeleine. Funny how you played the pronoun game when we talked this afternoon."

"The what?"

"You kept saying *they* and calling her *the reporter*. So I asked Madeleine for *their* name. Surprise, *they* was a *SHE*. I looked her up on Facebook. She's very attractive." It's not like Gloria to stalk me this bad.

"So?"

"Are you with her right now?"

I look around the empty bathroom. "No."

"So why are you still whispering? Who's going to hear you in an empty hotel room?"

"The fuckin neighbors. I'm here alone so you can fuckin relax." I say it in a regular voice. It echoes against the tiles and tub. Fuck.

"You're in the bathroom, aren't you?"

"I'm takin a piss, Gloria."

"I don't hear any pissing."

"I'm sitting on the toilet because I didn't wanna turn the light on. Or make a mess for the maid." I stop myself before the lying gets too obvious. Less is always better.

"So thoughtful of you, Connor." She doesn't say anything for several seconds. Maybe she believes me. "She's in your bed, isn't she?"

Fuck. I lean my elbows on my knees and run my hand through my hair. "What do you care? I thought we had an agreement. Don't ask, don't tell."

"Maybe it's time we change our agreement, Connor."

"Fuck that shit."

"Fuck. That. Shit, Connor?"

"You heard me."

"Someone is getting too big for their britches. I think all that adulation you got today at the convention is going to your head, young man."

If she only knew. I'm so pissed right now I want to punch a hole in the wall. Or her face. I shoot to my feet. "What the fuck do you want, Gloria?"

Her voice goes cold. "Who do you think you are, *Connor Hughes*?

The next Channing Tatum?"

"I don't think I'm anybody."

She chuckles. "That's right. You aren't. You can't even act. You're just a body model. I can name twenty other nameless hard bodied men doing the fitness circuit in this town who think their abs are their ticket to stardom. But guess what? They'll fade away just like you will."

I snort a laugh.

"You think that's funny? You think you're *special*? You think you're going to be the next big thing? The only reason you're anything, Connor *Nobody*, is because I made you something. *I* did. Without me, you're a minimum wage waiter someplace still hoping for a Sears Catalog underwear shoot."

"Fuck you, Gloria."

"That's right," she says, satisfied with herself.

"What?"

"Fuck *me*. Make *me* happy. Ditch that little bitch you're playing with and come by my place," she purrs. "I'll show you what a real woman can do. Then we'll see what we can do about your career."

I drop my phone in the toilet.

Fuckin cunt.

Chapter 11

CONNOR

"What is the length of the hypotenuse, Connor Hughes?" the faceless teacher demands. She is topless and has super fake balloon tits that look ready to pop.

"I don't know." I always sucked at math.

The students behind me in class all laugh like dogs. They have evil Halloween mask faces like melting zombies.

"What is the length of the hypotenuse, Connor!!!" The teacher screams and is now also wearing a melting mask. Her tits melt like plastic. It's not gross because it's like a melting wax statue or some shit. But it freaks me the fuck out.

"Fuck, bitch! I don't fuckin know!" I'm naked and afraid. I'm always naked.

"You're a dumbass, Connor!" Electra laughs across the room. She doesn't have a mask on her face.

"You're a brace-faced bitch, War Mouth!" I hate her.

She cries like a baby robot. No tears come out.

We never had Geometry class together.

Teacher points at me with a ruler. *"Go to the Librarian's Office, Connor Hughes! Go where all the fuckups go!"*

I walk naked through crowded high school hallways. Everyone stares at my dick.

The library is on fire.

I don't want to be burned alive...

Devils push me inside.

The sexy librarian stands up behind her flaming desk. She has glasses and a tight skirt and a hair bun. But it's not adult Electra. It's Gloria Powers. Her eyes are flames. She unbuttons her blouse and squeezes her own tits. Her forked tongue licks one nipple like a snake. She pulls up her skirt and her pubic *hair is fire. I want to fuck her until my dick burns off.*

She laughs evil. *"You're in trouble now, Connor Hughes. I have to spank you. Bend over my desk."*

I do.

She has a yardstick. It's on fire. She spanks me again and again.

I like it.

My dick is hard.

It jerks every time she spanks me.

She grabs my dick and strokes it. She licks my ear and whispers, "You like it. You like it when I make you come."

She sticks her burning yardstick up my—

—scream-scream-scream-scream—

"Fuck!" I gasp, sitting up in bed.

My heart machine guns in my chest. I feel like I'm having a heart attack. I can't be having a heart attack. I'm twenty fuckin five years old.

—it will get worse over time without surgery—

I rip the sheet off my legs and stand up.

The bed is empty.

Where is Electra?

Panic.

Not on the balcony.

Not in the bathroom.

Naked, I rip the hotel door open.

No sign of her in the hallway.

Emptiness.

…This is all your fault…

I start to shake.

I fall to my knees and crawl inside the room and hide behind the door.

CONNOR

Later that morning, I sit in Autograph Alley at the same table I was at yesterday, signing autographs. The crowds are worse today. After I scribble my name on another headshot and pose for another selfie with a random fan, some metro looking guy walks up in a suit.

"I'm Xavier Soto with Torrent Films." He holds out his hand.

Never heard of him. I shake his hand anyway. "Connor Hughes.

What's up?"

"My business partners saw your video on *TMZ* yesterday."

"And?" I lean to the side, looking past this Xavier dude at the mile long line of pink-shirted fans waiting for face time with me. This guy gets the same two minutes they do.

He smiles. "We liked what we saw."

I'm only half listening, but something about him makes me say, "I don't do porn."

He chuckles, "We're not a porn company. We make feature films." People throw bullshit around this town all the time, but you never know if you're talking to someone genuine.

"Yeah? You got a deal with any studios?"

"First look at Lions Gate."

Lions Gate isn't a major player like Warners or Paramount or Sony, but they make real movies that make it into theaters. "Nice. Whadda you need me for?"

"We're packaging a feature based on a Nora Roberts novel. One of her older novels that has been languishing in development hell for ten years. We think now is the time for it, and you might just be the man to play the male lead."

"No shit." I've never done a cover for a Nora Roberts book, but I know exactly who she is.

"Would you be interested in doing a screen test for us?"

I've been in Hollywood long enough to know that everybody and their brother is working on a movie. For all I know, this guy doesn't have shit and he's lying about the Nora Roberts thing. "Who's funding the movie?"

"We've secured half from private investors based on our script and leading lady. Once we've signed a male lead, we'll get the other half."

"Really?" He sounds like he might be for real.

"Yes, really," he grins. "If you test well against our leading lady, who knows. You might get the part." Nobody ever promises anything in Hollywood if they don't have to. "So, what do you think?"

"Sounds great." I don't bother to mention I've never acted before.

"Who's your agent?"

I'm about to say Powers Talent Agency, but I stop myself. Do I want Gloria knowing about this deal? Or do I want to start cutting ties with her now, before she gets a piece of a big payday? "Uhh..."

"You do have an agent, don't you?"

"Not right now."

"Never mind that. We can work out details later. But I want to get you in for a screen test with our leading lady as soon as possible.

What's your schedule look like next week?"

At the moment, all I can think about is finding Electra. Until I do, I don't want to think about anything else. But this guy seems legit. If I want to get rid of Gloria, this would be a great way to do it. "Free and clear. Tell me where you want me and when. I'll be there."

He pulls out a business card. It looks expensive. "That's my direct line. Call my assistant and she will give you details."

I stand up and shake his hand. "Thanks, man."

"Have fun at the show." He turns to glance at the fans. "You have a lot of admirers and I believe more will be waiting for you when you walk the red carpet."

I grin, "Shit, Xavier, you don't have to suck my dick. I'll be there."

"Please do." He nods knowingly and smiles like he either thinks he owns me or is better than me.

Same old shit.

"Next!" Paula hollers, waving the next fan forward.

With a smile on my face, I sign, selfie, and hug yet another woman in the line.

Today is one surprise after the next.

ELECTRA

Last night was a huge mistake.

So huge, that the only thing I can think to do is call my mom. I *never* call her when I have problems. I solve them myself.

But for whatever reason, I can't work through this one on my own. It's so bad I ditched the convention and came home. Screw Vince Pitts and that stupid interview.

Today, I can't deal.

I open the last bottle of iced coffee I had in my fridge and walk outside where it's marginally cooler than my oven of an apartment. It doesn't have A/C and I can't afford a wall unit. I sit down on my cement doorstep and stare at my phone before dialing. Am I really calling my parents to whine? I guess I am.

Their house phone doesn't have voicemail. It rings and rings. Mom finally picks up after fourteen times.

"Hello?"

"Hey, Mom."

"Elle! I knew you would call today!"

"No you didn't."

"I did too."

"Then why didn't you answer 'Hello, daughter'?"

She laughs like sunflowers. "Of course I knew it was you. Don't be such a know-it-all, Elle. I could *feel* you wanting to call me all afternoon."

I roll my eyes. Same old hippie druid nonsense. "No you didn't. I decided just now to call you."

"Well, I didn't know the exact *time*. But I knew. Ask Gerry. I told him over lunch." My mom and dad *always* call each other by their first names. It's a hippie thing.

"Sure, Mom."

She ignores my bitchy attitude.

I can't help it. My parents have rubbed me the wrong way since I was little. They mean well, but I think the stork delivered me to the wrong house when I was born.

"Phew!" She breathes heavily into the phone. "Sorry it took me so long to answer. I was moving sacks of bird seed from the truck to the barn." Water runs in the background. "I need a drink. Just a sec. Ahh. Much better. So, tell me. What's wrong?"

"Nothing's wrong. How's the farm?"

"I know you didn't call to talk about walnuts, honey. Tell me what's bothering you."

I sigh. "Remember Connor Hughes? From high school?"

"Yes. What about him?"

One of the tenants in my building walks by on the pathway that leads to the street. I have no privacy here when it's hot.

I lower my voice to a whisper. "I slept with him last night."

"You did what?"

"I—"

Right then the tenant turns on his heel and walks back toward me. I don't even know the guy's name. I just recognize him and his bald head and the Hawaiian shirts he always wears during summer.

When he's gone, I hiss, "I *slept* with him."

"How did *that* happen?"

"I was supposed to interview him yesterday."

"So how in the world did you end up sleeping with him?"

"It's complicated," I sigh.

"Sounds like it. I thought you hated him. Wasn't he the boy who always made fun of you and called you names? I thought he made you miserable?"

"He still does."

She laughs a friendly laugh. "Then why on earth did you sleep with him, Elle?"

"I've been asking myself that same question all day."

Sex has always been an open topic with my parents. Not that there has been much to talk about on my end. But they wanted me to feel comfortable bringing it up if I needed to. They were always saying things like, *"Do you have any boyfriends? Are you sleeping with anybody? Don't forget protection. If you get pregnant, come to us. We want you to make your own choices for yourself, but we want you to be informed. We will love you no matter what you do. You're our sunshine, Elle. The light of our life."* I nearly get Adult Onset Diabetes thinking about how sweet they've always been. Sometimes, it was just too much. Too good to be true. I'm a born pessimist. Like I said. The stork dropped me at the wrong house.

"I thought you hadn't seen Connor since..." Mom trails off. "Since grad night, wasn't it? Wasn't that the last time you saw him?"

"Don't remind me."

"Oh, that's right. I remember you came home—"

"Please, Mom."

"I'm sorry, honey. I know how much he hurt you."

"He didn't hurt me, Mom!"

"Denial doesn't change what happened. You have to face it some day."

"Mom!"

She sighs. "I know it's hard, honey. Maybe you should come home for a few days. Spend some time with Gerry and I here on the farm."

"No, Mom. That's not gonna help."

"Then what do you need, Elle? Tell me. I will do anything I can to help."

Unconsciously, I start reading the ingredients label on my iced coffee, which I've nearly finished drinking. SHAKE WELL. BEST SERVED COLD. REFRIGERATE AFTER OPENING. FOR MORE INFORMATION, CALL 1-800...

"Elle? Are you all right?"

"I'm fine, Mom. It's just that... It's just that—" I'm not gonna say it. I nearly throw my empty bottle against the cement pathway, but stop myself. My neighbors walk here.

"What, Elle?"

"It's just that..." I switch directions with a huffy sigh. "He's been texting me all day, Mom. He wants to see me."

"I'm confused. Do you *not* want to talk to him?"

"I don't have any choice."

"You *always* have a choice, honey."

"No. I have to finish his stupid interview."

"So talk to him," she says calmly.

"You don't get it!"

"I think I do, Elle." That stupid sunflower smile of hers shines through the phone.

I don't register her words. I just barrel forward. "I think maybe I like him, Mom!"

"That's great, Elle."

"But he's an arrogant asshole! An annoying jerk! An inconsiderate womanizer! I *can't* like him. It would be the height of stupidity to like him. I'd be better off liking a tornado or an earthquake!"

"Oh, honey. These things don't always make sense."

"What's wrong with me, Mom?"

"Nothing is wrong with you, Elle. But I think you need to talk to him."

How did I *know* she was going to say that?

I didn't even need to call her.

Damn her.

<<<<<<<<>>>>>>>

CONNOR

During my afternoon break, I sneak behind the wall at the back of the booth and chug a bottle of water. I also check my new phone to see if Lex has texted me back yet. She hasn't.

After I got my shit together this morning, I hopped on my bike and headed to the nearest phone store to get a new one before the show started. Fuckin Gloria. If it wasn't for her, I wouldn't have dropped mine in the toilet last night. Good thing I memorized Lex's digits so I could text her the second I got the new one.

The area behind the booth is the closest thing to privacy I'm gonna get. The only thing between me and all the fans on the show floor is a bunch of curtains. There isn't even a roof to keep the noise out. Listening to 45,000 jabbering people all damn day gets pretty damn loud.

I kept hoping I'd hear Electra's voice. I never did. I also kept hoping she'd poke her head in the booth and surprise me. Didn't happen. At this point, I'm losing hope. She's giving me the brush off. I knew she would. I saw it in her eyes last night.

The curtain suddenly ruffles and I nearly shit myself with excitement.

Electra.

Romeo leans his head in. "There he is! The star of the show!"

Fuck. Wrong head. I smirk at him. "Something like that."

Romeo pulls the curtain closed behind him. "Where's your co-star?"

"Who? Electra?"

"Yes!"

"Shit, man. I was hopin you'd seen her."

He shakes his head. "Not today."

"Fuck."

He gives me a look. "Are you pining for her?"

"What?"

"Pining? Yearning? Longing?"

I laugh. "Dude, speak fuckin English."

"If you weren't so dashing, that would be rude. I simply meant, do you miss her so much it hurts?"

"No," I scoff.

"Liar! I see it in your eyes."

Something about this Romeo guy makes me feel like he won't judge me. Everything comes pouring out. "I texted her a hundred times today. She never responded. We're supposed to finish our interview today. I don't know what the fuck happened. First I was like, fuck that bitch—" Romeo smiles. "—then I was like, I wish she'd fuckin text me back. Like, if she doesn't, I'm gonna lose my shit and run out of the convention hall and search all of L.A. until I find her."

Romeo gives me a weird look, "Just so you could finish your interview? Yesterday you didn't seem all that interested in answering questions."

"Fuck, I don't know."

Romeo nods like he knows shit. "Let me guess. Did you two... *seal* the *deal* last night?"

"What, like fuck her?"

"What other deal is there to seal?"

I grin. "Yeah. I fucked her. Best sex I've ever had."

Romeo nods again. "I imagine she felt the same way."

"That's not your asshole talkin, is it?"

"Elle Oh Elle, Connor Hughes."

"Well, is it?

"If you're suggesting that I imagine sex with you would be incredible, you are correct, sir." He winks at me and puts his monocle in his eye. "But no, I believe Ms. Warmoth has had a thing for you since… well, since long before I watched you two interact yesterday morn. Venom like that doesn't come from lack of passion."

"Huh?"

"She likes you. I daresay she feels even more strongly than that."

"I don't know about that, man. Haven't you had a hate fuck?"

He smiles like a girl. "I don't kiss and tell. But let me ask you this. How many women whom you've hate fucked do you text the next day?"

"Shit, bro. I don't text *any* women I fuck the next day."

"As I suspected. You don't hate her, my friend. You are feeling what is commonly called love."

I burst into laughter. "Bull fuckin shit."

"Methinks the gentleman doth protest too much."

I snort. "The what?"

CONNOR

What a fuckin day.

I must've signed ten thousand headshots. My hand started to cramp at the end. But that Sharpie ink on my palm never gave out. It's still there since yesterday.

It takes me an hour to leave the convention hall because more fans want selfies and shit. I say yes to everybody because I hate being a dick. These women are so damn nice, I wouldn't think of it. They're total strangers and they're all treating me like a fuckin saint.

What they don't know won't hurt them.

I finally get to the parking garage and hop on my bike. Before I put my helmet on, I text Lex.

Do you want to finish the interview tonight? I'll buy you dinner.

Her boss is expecting it.

I'm sure she'll say yes.

It's already five o'clock.

I wait a few minutes for her to reply, but she doesn't so I cruise home through traffic. At my place, I sit on the edge of my couch staring at my phone on the coffee table for over an hour.

Nothing.

At quarter to seven, the phone rings and I can't breathe. I jump off the couch and grab the phone.

Fuckin Gloria.

I sigh hard.

Do I answer?

Shit.

I grunt, "What?"

"I thought you'd be busy with your girlfriend."

"She's not my girlfriend." It hurts to say it.

"So you just fucked her for a night?"

"Yeah. So what."

"Are you going to see her again?"

"I doubt it." It *kills* me to say it.

The smile in her voice is loud and clear. "Come over, Connor. It's the weekend and I'm horny."

I don't fuckin care.

"Come over, Connor," she purrs. "You know you want to. I know how you like to come on my tits." Her voice is sultry. My dick should be hard as a rock. It's soft as a sock. "Come on over and you can come on Mama's tits."

Mama? I look around for the nearest toilet to drop my phone in. But I'm in my living room and the phone store is gonna close soon. "Not tonight, Gloria. I've got a fuckin headache." I almost laugh at myself.

"Don't be a bitch, Connor. Who do you know who will suck your dick for a solid hour? Do you think I do all that yoga and Pilates just to stay healthy? No way, mister. I do it for you."

"I'm serious, G. The convention was exhausting. I need to chill tonight."

"Unacceptable. I'll buy take out and be right over."

"I might not be here."

"I thought you said you wanted to chill?"

"Chill, as in, do fuckin nothing."

"Do me, Connor. I'll make it worth your while."

"I gotta go, G." I hang up on her.

An hour later, she's standing on my doorstep looking extremely fuckin hot for however old she is. She holds a bottle of wine and takeout something. "I brought Thai. I like to eat light before a marathon fuck session. And wine. Here." She jams the bottle in my hand and barges inside.

She's lucky Lex didn't text me back otherwise I'd throw her out.

She sets the dinner bag on my dinner table and gets plates and forks from the kitchen like she owns the place. She's been here so many times she knows where everything is. "Don't you think the dining room set I picked out for you is *so* much nicer than that ratty old thrift store table and chairs *you* had? It gives this place that modern touch."

It also gives it *her* touch. I don't know why I let her redecorate. She doesn't live here.

She opens one cupboard after the other. "Are you out of napkins?"

Fuck if I know. I stare at her.

"Fine. We'll use paper towels." She smiles at me as she unpacks the food. She looks pretty damn good in her skin tight yoga outfit that looks like she bought it this morning before her workout. She probably did. "Well? Are you going to pull out my chair for me?"

I roll my eyes and walk over to the table so she can sit down like a fuckin lady.

"Sit down." She points at the chair next to her.

"Jesus Christ, Mom. Do you take away my allowance if I don't do what you say?"

She grins. She has nice fuckin lips. Probably gets injections, but she spends so much you can't tell for sure. "Oh, you want to roleplay tonight? I can be your momma, Connor. Now sit down and eat your dinner like a good little boy or I'll send you to your room."

—You're in trouble now, Connor Hughes. I have to spank you. Bend over my desk—

I almost puke in Gloria's face thinking about that nightmare from this morning.

"What's wrong, Connor?" Gloria is smiling like a true friend. "Are you okay?" She stands up and rubs my elbow. "What's wrong? Tell me."

If she didn't sound like she actually cared, I'd shout at her to get her fuckin hands off me. But she's being nice. I sit down so she'll let go of my arm. "It's nothin. Gimme some of those noodles."

We eat while she talks on and on about the latest insider Hollywood gossip. She throws A-list names around like she's talking about her personal friends. She almost is. She's been in business in this town a long time.

I try to tune her out.

I eat.

My phone is one of those new Samsung Edge ones where your messages only light up the strip on the side. It's hanging half out my pocket so I can see it but Gloria can't. It's been sitting that way all through dinner.

The message strip lights up.

Lex.

Let's meet later this week. I got an extension on your interview.

I hide my smile the rest of the night until Gloria leaves.

Chapter 12

CONNOR

Morning sun warms my face as I peel my helmet off. Still straddling my parked motorcycle, I listen to the voicemail from my parents on my phone before I buzz inside the building to finish my interview with Electra.

"Mount Rushmore was incredible, son. You need to go whenever you have the chance."

"It was *so* small!" Mom laughs.

"It just seems that way, Kell. If we had been closer, it would've been gigantic. The sign said the heads are sixty feet high! That's six stories! Who do you know who has a head that big?"

"You do!" she laughs. "We could put your head up there next to Washington or Lincoln and it would be the *same* size."

Dad chuckles. "I walked into that one. Anyway, son, just wanted to give you an update. We're on the road headed for the Great Lakes. We should hit Chicago by nightfall. I hear they have the best summer weather anywhere in the country."

"It's the windy city, Connor!" Mom hollers. "Everyone there is a blowhard like your Dad!"

"Enough of that, woman!"

They both laugh and cheer, "Bye, Connor!"

I climb off my bike and trot up the stairs to the building. The guy behind the desk inside tells me to take the elevator to the fourteenth floor.

Just as the doors are closing, some blonde haired hottie with icy eyes comes running up, her heels clicking on the marble. "Wait!"

I jam my arm in the doors and she steps inside. "Where you going?"

She looks at the panel. "Oh. Same as you."

The doors close.

We're all alone.

She's totally checking me out but pretending not to. This shit happens to me all the time. Great ass. Fake tits. L.A. all the way.

The doors ding when we arrive on 14.

"After you." You gotta be polite.

"Thanks." She steps off the elevator and lingers.

The glass doors of *Trending Magazine* are straight ahead, but the hallway T's in both directions.

We both step forward at the same time.

"Sorry," she giggles.

"My bad."

"Are you here to see someone at *Trending*?"

"Yeah. You too?"

"Audrey Fisher. I'm a senior contributor for *Trending*." You can tell she's proud of herself. She jams out her hand to shake. She's got a strong grip. "Who are you here to see?"

"Electra Warmoth."

Her eyes widen. "Oh. *You're* the interview." She's still holding my hand.

I pull mine away. "What's that supposed to mean?"

She starts walking toward the doors, implying I should follow. She reminds me of Gloria. A hot bitch who's way too full of herself. She makes my dick curl up like a hermit crab. But, since I'm going the same way she is, what the fuck.

We walk.

She lowers her voice, "The rumor around the office is that Electra missed her deadline because she was having trouble getting your interview. That she couldn't handle you." She eye fucks me. "I don't know what the problem was. Did you scare her off?" What a bitch.

"No." I open the glass *Trending* door for her. Again, you gotta be polite. But I feel like bashing her head between the two doors. "After you."

"Thank you. Such a gentleman." She grabs me by the wrist and stops me by the doors. "If you don't feel like… *Electra* is giving you a good *interview*," she means sex, "let me know. There's a certain *art* to it, if you know what I mean."

"Sure." *There's a certain bitch to you, if you know what I mean.*

"Here's my card. Call me any time." She makes sure to brush her tit against my elbow. "I'm always available."

"Uh huh."

ELECTRA

"Tell me today is the day, Warmoth," Vince Pitts says, sitting behind his desk with his feet up. He stretches his retro suspenders out with his hands and lets them pop against his white-collared pinstripe shirt.

"I promise. I will finish the interview in the conference room before lunch and have it on your desk by five."

"Famous last words, Warmoth."

"Vince. Have some faith."

"You know I'm an agnostic. I don't believe in shit until it's handed to me on a platter."

"I will have a platter of shit for you at five." Vince respects people who can volley back his profanity.

"You can't polish turds, Warmoth. Make it a platter of gold. Award winning, Pulitzer-worthy gold."

"It's just an exposé, Vince."

"Shoot for the moon, Warmoth. You never know what you're going to hit. Maybe he secretly saves babies in the Sudan."

"I'll ask."

"Please do. This Connor character is getting a lot of buzz on social media since that convention last week. He might be the new it guy this summer. If you get me a good story, I'll put it on the cover."

He keeps waving the cover carrot in front of me, but with what Connor has given me so far, I think Vince might be barking up the wrong tree.

Vince's assistant buzzes through on his intercom, "I have Hal Barrett on line two."

"Got it. I'll take it right now." He punches the blinking button on his phone and waves me out of the room.

Hal Barrett is the publisher of *Trending Magazine*, so I make myself scarce.

I don't know what I was thinking inviting Connor to the *Trending* offices to finish his interview. I told myself it would be neutral ground so he won't try anything stupid and I won't cut and run if he gets out of hand. I need to finish this interview. Now I'm thinking this was a horrible idea.

No reason in particular.

Just Connor Hughes.

Trouble always finds him.

At least the glass conference room here is a controlled environment with minimal distractions. And with the wraparound glass walls, he's not going to try anything. Everyone would see us. I'll be safe and I can finish my interview.

If you guessed that I haven't figured out how I feel about Connor, you would be right. It doesn't matter if the sex was impossibly good. It doesn't matter that I've been thinking about the feel of his cock inside me ever since he pulled it out of me. What matters is getting this interview finished.

End. Of. Story.

Now if I can only find Connor.

He was supposed to be here thirty minutes ago.

Am I surprised he's late?

Not at all.

We're talking about Connor Hughes.

I make it out to the lobby and the first thing I see is Connor chatting up Audrey Fisher.

What was I thinking?

Like him? I *loathe* him.

CONNOR

Electra barks at me and this Audrey chick, "Are you two *done*?"

Fuck, Lex is hotter today than at the convention. I don't know how she does it. Do I have a thing for sexy librarians that I didn't know about until now? The dick stirring in my pants says yes, as long as they're not demon Gloria.

"Oh, hi, Electra," Audrey smiles at her. It's fake. They hate each other.

"Trying to steal my story?" Electra snarls at her.

I want to laugh. Cat fight.

"Steal it?" Audrey snorts. "You already dropped the ball, Electra. I was just picking it up for you."

"I can pick up my balls myself."

Audrey tries not to laugh.

Me, on the other hand, I try not to think about my balls because seeing Electra fight for me like this gives me a case of raging blue steel in my jeans. She can pick up my balls any time she wants.

Electra pistols across the polished cement floor on her pumps and grabs me by the arm. "Let me take you to the conference room, Connor. So we can start our *interview*."

This is nice. I've had chicks fight over me before, but this is my favorite. Because it's never been High Tension fighting over me. I never thought I'd see the day. I'm tempted to drag my feet and see if I can get these two to go at it. Something tells me Electra would rip this Audrey chick's shit apart.

I smile to myself.

Some other time.

Electra drags me into the glass conference room and closes the door. It's behind the reception desk out front. We're in a fish tank. I can see into everyone's offices and they can see in here. Most people are busy at their computers or on the phone or whatever, but a few glance at us.

The only sound in the conference room is the A/C blowing through the vent hanging from the exposed ceiling. The rafters are concrete and steel.

I sit down in one of the leather chairs surrounding the glass table and kick my boots up.

"Get your feet down," she snarls as she pulls up a chair across from me.

"How's your shiner?" I can see purple and yellow beneath the concealer on her cheek.

She raises her hand to touch it but stops herself. "Better. Thanks for asking. Your hand still black?" She remembered.

Grinning, I hold up my palm. "I rubbed all the ink off stroking myself thinking about you."

She frowns, "That's disgusting, Connor."

"That's true, Lex."

"Does that mean your—" She stops herself, shaking her head. "I don't want to know."

"What?" I chuckle.

"No, Connor!" She busies herself with her notepad.

"Aren't you gonna offer me water or coffee or some shit?"

She places her palms on the table and scowls. "I'm not your servant, Connor."

"Don't be like that. I mean, wouldn't you offer water or coffee to your interview if it was someone other than me?"

She sighs like a bull winding up to charge the guy with the red cape. "Fffffine." She flips her head and bolts to her feet. "What do you want to drink?"

"What do you have?"

"I don't know, Connor!"

"Let's go find out." I stand up and follow her past a bunch of offices and cubicles to the kitchen.

She opens the fridge. "You can have anything on the bottom shelf."

"Ice water looks good. You want one?" I hold out a bottle for her.

"No. I mean, sure. Thanks."

"Can we start the interview now?"

"Lead the way."

We walk a different route back, passing down a hallway.

"What's in here?" I ask, opening a frosted glass door.

"The copier room."

"Let's check it out."

I roll my eyes. "It has a copy machine. And paper. What do you need to see?"

I grab her wrist and pull her inside, closing the door behind us. It doesn't have a lock. Oh well. I push her up against the door, which rattles.

"Stop it, Connor!" she hisses.

"Do you *always* wear tight skirts, War Mouth?"

Her arms hang at her sides. "I don't know. What do you want?" She stares up at me.

I lean my arms against the glass, trapping her. "You."

She looks away. "I don't want you."

"You did at the convention."

"That was different. This is my workplace."

"If I were to lift up your skirt..." I reach down and grab the bottom and jerk it up an inch.

She shivers, her eyes half closed. "Connor..."

I jerk the skirt another inch. "And stick my hand between your legs..." I reach up and feel the heat trapped down there. "What might I find?"

"Someone might walk in..." she moans.

I find her hot thong. I peel it aside. Touching her pussy is heaven. I have died and gone. I stroke her slick slit. "You are wet, Warmoth. Any idea why?" I tease my middle finger back and forth, working my way through her lips until I find the tip of her clit. I circle it slowly.

"Mmmmmm..."

"Tell me to stop." I plunge my finger inside her wet hole.

"MMMMMMmmmmmm..." Her eyes are completely closed.

I lick her lips. The sweet fuckin lips I've dreamed about kissing since I was fourteen. They part and my tongue slides right in. We slow fuck each other's mouths.

"MMMmmmmmm…" She rests her palms against my chest.

I slide my finger out and massage her clit while squeezing her breast through her blouse and fuckin her with my tongue.

"MMMMmmmmmm…" Her thighs start to quiver.

"Yeah, babe. Let it out." I maintain a slow but forceful motion on her sweet spot.

"MMMMMMMMmmm…" She's gonna lose it. She breaks the kiss and tips her head against the glass. She starts to pant. "Uh. Uh. Uh. Uh."

My dick is so hard it's gonna punch a hole in my pants. I almost pop when she starts to come, bearing down on my whole hand with her pussy. I hook my finger and feather her G-spot.

"NNNNNnnnnnn…" Her pussy clamps down and she lets it all go, coming hard.

After a minute, her muscles start to relax. She falls forward and catches herself by bracing her palms on my chest. Her head hangs, her forehead against my skin. "Fuck me," she whispers like she's about to pass out. "I need you to fuck me right now."

I grab her by the ass and pick her up. I spin us both around, looking for the nearest thing to sit her on. I drop her down on the first thing I see and tear her panties in half at the crotch with both hands. The fabric stretches, pops, snaps.

She gasps.

I yank my belt off. I can't get my dick out fast enough. I rip a condom package open with my teeth and whip it on a split second before I fist my dick by the hilt and plant it in her wet pussy. The second the head touches her entrance, I go crazy. "Fuck, Lex. God damn it. Fuck. *Fuck*. Fuck!!!" I grunt. I want to spill my guts and say more while I'm inside her, but I'm afraid to say what I'm thinking. I don't want to scare her off. The truth is, I never thought I would be inside her again. I'm fuckin *grateful* to be fuckin her. After she snuck out of my hotel room, I thought that was it. I was going nuts wishing I was inside her again. No matter how many times I rubbed one out thinking about *this* moment, it wasn't the real thing. This is fuckin paradise. I've never known one chick where I *couldn't* get enough. This is a whole new mind fuck for me. I'm hooked on her pussy.

I fuck her slowly.

I don't want to make too much noise. With no lock on the door, someone could walk in any second and I wanna finish what I started.

So does she.

She wraps her legs around my waist and her arms around my neck. "It's so good, Connor. I can feel you hitting my clit every time you—

ooooh, god… " She clenches her pussy around my cock in time with my thrusts. "Fuck me, Connor. Like that. Yes, yes, yes."

I hook my hands under her ass and claw at her cheeks while I plow into her. "Fuck yeah." It's so damn good my head is spinning. I barely know what's happening except my dick is in her pussy and I need to pound her as hard as I can until she comes so bad she ends up as hooked on me as I am on her.

She leans back on her hands and throws her head back, moaning low in her throat.

Something beeps.

A fan whirs.

A flash of light.

She tips her chin down and peels her lips over her teeth. "Fuck me harder, Connor," she hisses. "Fuck me as *hard* as you can…" She's a beast.

And I'm the man with the plan who can tame that hungry pussy of hers.

ELECTRA

I never knew sex could be this good. The kind of sex where you lose your mind and all you can think about is how damn *good* it feels.

I've had three orgasms since Connor entered me.

Three.

Four, if you count the one he gave me with his hand while we were leaning against the door.

This is addiction, people. Because I can't think. I'm only aware of the sweet ache between my legs that can only be filled by Connor's cock. No matter how many times I come, I need to come again.

But, like all things. The key is moderation. Four orgasms is enough. For now. "Are you ready?"

"Fuck, I'm dying, Lex." He grits his teeth, his sweaty face inches from mine.

"Come inside me, Connor. Fill me up with your cum."

He rocks into me savagely and I savor his explosive orgasm.

Make that five. His passion fires mine and I come one last time.

Five orgasms.

I lean against him, spent.

He breathes heavily, the last spasms of his orgasm fading inside me. My clit is still singing. This is the best feeling ever. Me. Him. Our bodies locked together in the afterglow of incredible sex. I never want it to end.

But we're at my work. Someone could walk into the copier room any second. I'm surprised someone hasn't already.

"We should…" I whisper.

"Yeah."

When he reluctantly withdraws from me, I rest my hands on the glass of the copy machine I'm sitting on.

Oh, shit.

Copy machine?

I look around the room.

There is a literal snow drift of photo copies on the floor beside the copier. "Connor?" My voice shakes as I slide off the machine and push my skirt down.

"Yeah?" He tosses his condom in the trash on the far side of the copier before I can stop him. Casually, he zips up his jeans.

"Is that photocopies of your cock inside my vagina?"

"What?" He turns to look. "Oh. Would you look at that. I believe that it is." His smug grin stretches from ear to ear. He squats down to pick one up. He holds it in both hands like a work of art and turns it from side to side. "I'm telling you, Lex, you have the most beautiful pussy I've ever seen. My cock isn't bad either," he chuckles. "Can I keep this one?"

"No!" I grab for it but he whips it away and holds it over his head where I can't reach it.

"Fine. But don't show it around."

Connor folds it up and slides it in his front pocket, grinning at me.

I grin back. It gives me a secret thrill that he has a picture of our privates *fucking*. I've never taken a selfie of my privates, but this is the next best thing. No, better. Because Connor's cock is inside me. Being a slut is a lot more delicious than I realized.

But I don't have time to savor the thought. How many copies did we make? I look down at the control panel on the copier and see the numbers. Reality comes crashing back. "Five hundred! We switched on the auto copy function!"

"Well, fuck," Connor chuckles, looking at the pile of papers. "If you bind them together you could make a flip book and watch it like a movie."

"This isn't funny! We have to clean this up!"

A shadow appears behind the frosted glass of the copier room door.

I slam my hands against it. "You can't come in here!"

"Who's in there? Is that you, Warmoth?" It's Vince Pitts.

Shitts!

"There's been a major meltdown!" I yelp.

"What's going on, Warmoth?"

"There's toner everywhere! It's a disaster area! I, uh, dropped the toner cartridge and it broke and it's like a coal mine explosion in here! Unless you want to ruin your clothes and get black lung, DO! NOT! COME! IN!" I glare at Connor and point frantically at the pile of paper.

He starts scooping all the copies up in a rush.

"Should I tell Elizabeth to call the copy repair guy?"

"No! It's too big a job for him! Call a chimney sweep!"

Connor smirks at me, holding a big wad of copies, and mouths the words, "*Chimney sweep*?"

I flip him off then holler at Vince, "You might need to call the fire department!" I wince, regretting I said it.

"The *fire* department? Is something burning in there, Warmoth?"

"No! Forget the fire department! I've got it covered! Just don't come in!"

He rattles the doorknob. "Open up, Warmoth!"

"No, Vince! I'm serious!" I lean all my weight against the door and squeeze the knob as hard as I can.

Connor has all the paper in a jagged pile at his feet. He scrunches it together into a mound and crumples it up into a blooming wad of corners and curls.

The momentary distraction is enough that I relax my hand on the door knob. The knob turns and the other knob walks into the room. Vince's eyes ping-pong between me and Connor. "What the hell is going on in here, Warmoth?"

Embarrassment explodes in my chest. Based on the heat of my skin, I imagine I am lobster red from head to toe. I got caught having sex at the office!! By my boss!! And there are 500 pieces of evidence as proof. Who knew paper could be such a problem? I thought the ability to endlessly duplicate files on computers was an issue. But this is worse. I can't just press DELETE and make these copies go away. I need a huge paper shredder or a flamethrower to get rid of them. I have neither.

Connor wads the big stack of papers tighter against his chest. It's huge and crumples loudly. A single sheet of paper slips free and seesaws to the floor, landing at Vince's feet.

I gasp.

Vince bends down to pick it up. "What is this?"

I rip the paper from his hand so quick, he's still holding a torn corner. "Nothing!"

"Copier malfunction," Connor says, as if that explains everything.

"Uh huh," Vince nods suspiciously, looking at the shard of paper in his hand. He turns his head this way and that, but he can't make sense of the partial image.

I snap it from his fingers and wad it up with the rest of the copies in my hand. "All fixed now!" I twist around, looking for any other stray copies. That's when I noticed the gargantuan *smear* on the copier glass. I bang the lid down on it. "Just give us a few minutes to tidy this up!" I grin insanely.

He holds up a sheet of paper. "I need to make a copy."

"NO!" I shout in his face. Not with my bodily fluids on the copier glass he isn't!

"I'm sorry, what?" He totally heard me.

"I need to put more toner in!"

His brows furrow. "I thought you said you spilled toner everywhere?"

"I did! I already cleaned it up!"

"Something smells fishy in here, Warmoth."

I drill him with a hateful glare. He better not be talking about me.

Connor steps up to Vince.

Vince glances down at the wadded paper in Connor's hands. It's far larger than the neat ream it started as. It's bigger than a basketball. You can see black and white images of our privates peeking out from the crinkled mess.

Vince gazes at the wad.

Please let them be too blurry to recognize.

"You guys aren't wasting paper, are you?" Vince asks.

"It wasn't a waste," Connor smirks and winks at me.

I repress a smile.

Connor takes another step toward Vince, imposing his presence without doing anything overt.

Vince glances up at him then away. "I'll come back later. Let me know when you have the machine up and running."

"Will do," I nod frantically.

Vince closes the door behind him.

"Holy shit," I hiss. "That was close."

"What do we do with these?" Connor asks, holding up the wad of copies. "Put them in the trash?"

"No! You have to take them out of here!" I bend over and grab his condom out of the trash. "And take this with you!" Why are used condoms so gross, even when they're yours? I don't know. Maybe it's the same thing as how you don't want your own spit back in your mouth once it's left. And, sweaty latex *stinks*.

Connor takes the condom and stuffs it in the back pocket of his jeans. Why is that so gross? He doesn't seem to care. He reaches for the doorknob.

"You can't walk around with the copies out in the open! Put them under your shirt or something! I need to clean the copier glass. I'll meet you in the conference room in a few minutes."

"I'll wait here." His shirt is stretched over the jagged ball of paper.

I laugh.

"What?" he asks.

"You're paper pregnant."

He looks down at his belly. "So I am."

"What am I going to do with you, Connor Hughes?"

He grins, "I have a few ideas."

"Go!" I grin.

"Do you want me to come get you if my, uh, sawdust breaks?"

"What?"

"You know, when my sawdust breaks. When I'm ready to deliver my paper baby?" He pats his belly.

"No!" I laugh.

"Or is it pulp? What do they make paper out of?"

"I don't know! Now get out of here!" I wave him out the door, still giggling.

CONNOR

Electra comes walking into the conference room a few minutes after cleaning herself up in the ladies' room.

My feet are kicked up on the glass table. The huge ball of copies is centered on the table where I left it.

"Nice center piece," she chuckles. "Maybe you should put it under the table so no one can see it."

"I like it right where it is."

She shakes her head and grins. "Can we finish your interview now?"

"Are you still wearing your torn panties like a garter belt?"

"No," she frowns.

"So you're not wearing any panties? Your pussy is completely exposed inside your skirt?

"Stop it, Connor." She sits down across from me.

I lean my head under the table.

"What are you doing?"

"Trying to look up your skirt so I can see your pussy. Duh."

She clamps her knees together. "Stop it, Connor!"

"What if I don't?"

She's enjoying this. "Then you may as well throw me on the conference table and screw me right here so everybody can watch."

"That's not a bad idea," I chuckle. My dick starts to harden in my jeans. "I can't get enough of your pussy, Lex. It's worse than heroin."

"Be that as it may," she smiles at me over her glasses, "we need to finish your interview. We can talk about table sex *after*. Are we clear?"

"Ooh," I fake a shiver. "Are you telling me what to do, Miss Warmoth?"

"Yes. Now shut your mouth for ten seconds so I can ask you my next question."

"Yes, ma'am."

There's a knock on the conference room door. "What?!" She barks.

I love how bitchy she gets without the slightest hesitation. A big smile melts into her face, so I twist around in my seat to see who it is. It's Surfer Douche, the photographer who was all over Electra at Rom Com Con. He holds a canvas camera bag in one hand.

What the fuck is he doing here?

"Hold on a second," Lex sighs, standing up and walking to the door.

Surfer Douche opens the door before she gets to it and leans inside. "Can I talk to you for a second?"

"Sure," she says. "Let's talk outside."

They're out the door before I can stop them.

Who the fuck gave him permission to open the door? Or talk to Lex? The *fuck* he think he is?

They walk into the main lobby. I can't hear them through all the glass. He's standing really fuckin close to her and smiling like an idiot. I need to rearrange that guy's fuckin face.

Electra giggles at something he says and touches his bicep with her fingers.

What the fuck? We *just* had sex and she's flirting with this fuckin guy? Fuck me! I shoot to my feet and bang the glass conference room door open and barge into the lobby.

"Totally," Surfer Douche chuckles.

It takes everything I have not to wrap the strap of his fuckin camera bag around his neck and hang him with it. "I hate to bug you guys, but I'm in a hurry."

Lex smirks at me, "Just a second, Connor. I'll be right there."

I look at my wrist like I'm wearing a watch, but I'm not. I feel stupid but follow through, still staring at my wrist like there's a watch there. "I've gotta be outta here in fifteen minutes, so make it snappy." Once again, I feel like a goon because of this stupid fuckin Surfer Douche.

"*Snappy*?" the Douche chuckles and mumbles to Electra. "Who *is* this Barney?"

Barney is surf lingo for straights who can't surf, or anybody who doesn't live on a surfboard. Does he think I can't hear him? "Shut the fuck up, Spicoli," I growl. I've seen *Fast Times at Ridgemont High.*

"Calm down, Connor," Lex grumbles. "I'll be in there in a second."

Surfer Douche smiles like he owns Lex or some shit. "You can go. *Bra.*"

I can kick his ass. No question. But am I going to do it in front of Electra and the receptionist? And the guy walking by me in the hallway sipping his coffee and staring at me? Fuck. I'm not that big a tool. If Douche took a swing at me, it would be over in two seconds. But he's just standing there with that fuckin douche smile on his douche face.

Fuck it.

I'll have to jump him in a back alley later.

I let the door close and sit back down at the table. I stare at the big ball of copies. I seriously consider peeling one off and slapping it up against the glass so Surfer Douche can see my dick up inside Lex's pussy. Then I imagine him not knowing what it is, or should I say *who* it is, and me having to explain. I'd have to point at myself then Lex and say, "Me. Her. Fuckin. Right down the hall in the copier room."

How would that play with Lex's office buddies?

Scrap that idea.

I need to think of something quick or I really am gonna go kick his ass.

"Geez, Connor," Lex says, walking into the conference room. "Can't you wait five seconds? You're worse than a toddler." She sits down across from me.

Surfer Douche walks past the conference room and into the offices. My eyes track him until he's gone. Then I glare at her. "Is there something going on with you and that guy?"

She looks stunned. She blinks several times and folds her hands on her notepad. Her face tightens. "What do you care? You had sex with another woman the *same* day we did."

"It's not the same." It's not the same because I forgot all about that woman the second Electra walked back into my life like a gift from god.

"It's not? Could've fooled me, Connor!"

"Hold on. Are you saying you had *sex* with Surfer Douche?"

"His name is *Austin*, Connor."

"I don't give a fuck *what* his name is. Did you have sex with him or not?!"

"That's none of your business!!"

"Tell, me, Lex. Did you sleep with him?"

"Would you calm down! People are staring."

Red haze stains my vision as I glance around at the surrounding offices and cubicles. Sure enough, people are watching. "So the fuck what?"

"So *what*? This is my workplace, Connor. Is it not enough that you are once again trying to ruin my interview, but now you have to try and ruin my entire *career*?"

"Is that all you care about? This interview and your fuckin *career*?"

"At the moment, yes. So either we drop this and finish the interview, or you need to go."

I grind my jaw like I'm chewing nails.

"*Well* Connor?"

I hiss, "Did you sleep with Austin or not?"

"It's none of your business, Connor!! It's not like we're dating! We're not boyfriend and girlfriend so back the hell off!"

My face goes grim. "That's right. We're not. And we never will be."

"What?"

"You heard me."

She folds her arms across her chest. "So you just wanted to fuck me, is that it?"

"I guess so."

"Screw you, Connor! It's just like I said to you on grad night seven years ago! I'm just another notch to you! One more girl you want to fuck and forget! You disgust me, Connor Hughes! You are a piece of shit!"

I smirk. "So what?"

"Get out of here!" she screams, jumping to her feet.

<<<<<<<<>>>>>>>>

ELECTRA

I'm on the verge of tears. But I will never show them to my arch nemesis. "Go, Connor!" I spear my finger toward the door. "Leave! Go home, or wherever your next notch is waiting for you! You probably have ten girlfriends for all I know! Get out of my sight!"

Without saying a word, he yanks the glass door of the conference room open and skulks out the front doors in the lobby.

I nearly fall over after he's gone. My entire body is shaking. I pull out the nearest chair from the conference table and drop into it.

The basketball sized wad of copies sits on the middle of the conference room table, mocking me.

Ugh.

The shame of knowing I slept with Connor Hughes after vowing I would *never* allow such a horrible shallow womanizer like him to lay one finger on me literally breaks my heart in two.

How could I have been so stupid?

I sit motionless for almost an hour. I literally can't stand up or even move. I'm surprised I can still breathe.

The truth is, I have feelings for Connor and it scares the shit out of me. Who am I kidding? It *embarrasses* me.

I've only loved one person. Dylan Montgomery. And that ended up in disaster. It took two years before I even thought about men again. And another year after that before I went out on a single date. Dylan nearly broke me.

I don't want to go through that again.

I thought I'd learned my lesson. But here I am doing it again. Letting an asshole into my heart. To make matters worse, Connor isn't some random guy I met in college. Connor is the man who harassed me for four years. He's the man who ruined grad night for me in a big bad way. He's a horrible person. Considering our history, it seems stupid to consider *anything* with Connor.

I can't date him.

I hate him.

With good reason.

It doesn't matter how much I crave him. Lust isn't love. Yes, he's hot. But millions of men are hot, and none of them devoted themselves to making me miserable.

I let things go way too far with Connor.

I need to walk away now before I get any more confused. Heck, I should thank *him* for doing the walking away just now. He made himself perfectly clear when he left.

"Warmoth!"

I nearly have a heart attack. I didn't know anyone had come up behind me. I slowly turn around, half dead to the world.

Vince leans his head in the conference room, smiling. For once. "I forgot to tell you the good news."

All I can do is stare at him.

He steps into the conference room. "Hal Barrett wants this story on the next cover."

I still can't respond.

Vince is a happy camper and rambles on. "Hal thinks we need to attract a larger female demographic. He watched that dance video of Connor at Rom Com Con on *TMZ* and asked when he could expect to see *the* Connor Hughes on the cover of our next issue."

The Connor Hughes. Hearing that makes me want to vomit.

"Speaking of, where is he? Did you finish the interview already?" He checks his watch. "It's nearly noon, so I'm assuming yes?" Vince is boyishly jubilant. He rarely gets like this.

Great. What do I tell him? That after Connor and I had sex on the copier, Connor informed me that I was just another random fuck for him, so I threw him out of the office before finishing the interview I promised Vince I'd have done by lunch? I'm sure Vince would *love* to hear that.

Vince looks suspicious. "Where is he, Warmoth?"

I'm suddenly furious. "I don't know, Vince! And I don't care!" I smile like I'm crazy.

"Ex-*cuse* me?" Vince's happy time is clearly over.

I sigh like a woman ten times my age. "It's complicated, Vince."

Furious, Vince slaps his forehead. "What is it with you and this god damn interview, Warmoth? How many times can you screw it up?! I swear, you're going to give me a heart attack before I eat my lunch today!!"

"I'm sorry, Vince." He doesn't deserve this. This is all my fault. I never should've slept with Connor. I *knew* better. But I did it anyway. Now *I'm* the one ruining my own career. I need to suck this up and make it happen. I need to behave like a professional. It doesn't matter if Connor is an asshole. I have a story to finish. I will get it done if it kills me. In fact, *not* finishing it would somehow mean that Connor won. I'm not going to let him have another victory at my expense. I am better than him. "Vince, I'll take care of it."

"Take *care* of it? It sure looked like you were taking care of *something* in the copier room earlier when you should've been interviewing him!" His eyes flick toward the copy paper ball of shame on the table top.

"It wasn't my fault, Vince! He—" I stop myself. I can't blame Connor for this. I'm as guilty as he is for letting things go too far in the copier room.

"He *what*? What, Warmoth?"

I hang my head.

Vince jams his hands on his hips. "Are you sleeping with him, Warmoth?"

Shocked, I gasp. "No!"

He narrows his eyes. "You could've fooled me." He nods knowingly, picking up steam. "That's it, isn't it?"

"What?"

"Yeah, that's *exactly* what it is."

"What, Vince?" I'm suddenly afraid Vince is going to start listing all the dirty things Connor and I did on that copier. He's going to call everyone in the office into the conference room and read off my list of transgressions like a prosecutor at a murder trial while playing back security camera video of the entire dirty deed.

Vince shakes his head with intensely parental disappointment. "You let me down, Warmoth. You lost your objectivity."

"I'm not *sleeping* with him, Vince!"

Vince snorts. "That's quite the denial, Warmoth."

"I—" stop myself before I make this worse.

"It doesn't matter if you are or not. The outcome is the same. You're a part of this story. You're no longer in a position to handle it like a professional."

"It's an *exposé*, Vince! Not Watergate! I can handle this, Vince. I swear!"

He crosses his arms and strokes his chin with one hand, thinking. He nods.

A good sign.

He shakes his head. "You've had your shot, Warmoth. I'm pulling you off this story. Audrey will take over from here. You're done."

"What?! You can't do that!"

"Yes I can."

A voice booms behind Vince:

"No you can't." It's Connor, his voice hard.

While turning around, Vince says "Who are you to tell me what I —" He stops when he sees Connor.

"Do you want my interview finished today or not?"

Vince glares between me and Connor. "I don't know what exactly is going on between you two, but I have a general idea. I need you to understand something, young man. A number of people's *jobs* are at stake. Mine included. In case you haven't noticed, the internet is quickly replacing printed publications like *Trending Magazine*. I've given Warmoth plenty of chances to get this right. For whatever reason, she can't hack it. I'm replacing her with Audrey Fisher. *She* will get this job done, I promise you."

The idea of Audrey Fisher all alone interviewing Connor turns my stomach.

Connor stares at Vince. "You're not putting anybody on this story except Electra Warmoth. This is *her* story."

"Look here—"

"No, buddy. You look here. If you don't let Electra finish the interview, I'll take it to *GQ*."

For a full minute, Vince looks ready to chew through a chain link fence. "Get me a goddamn story on my desk by five, or you can take your interview to *GQ* and shove it up their collective ass." He storms toward the door of the conference room and drills me with his gaze. "I want it on my desk by five o'clock. No excuses!" He glares at both of us. "And get rid of that goddamn paper ball. I don't want it in my conference room. It looks terrible."

Chapter 13

ELECTRA

"Why are we here, Lex?" Connor asks.

We stand on the sunlit grass field behind North Valley High School. School is out for the summer. Except for the old guy throwing a ball for his dog with one of those whippy ball launchers, we're the only people here. This was the location of our grad night seven years ago.

I sigh, "This is where everything ended for you and me. I think it might be a good place to begin."

"I don't."

"The last seven years of your life are a complete mystery to me, Connor. I don't know where you went or what you did after high school."

"You don't want to know," he chuckles morbidly.

"If I'm going to get an interview out of you worthy of the cover of *Trending Magazine*, I *need* to know."

He smirks to himself and stares at the grass, digging into it with the toe of his motorcycle boot.

Being here brings back a host of bad memories for me. Grad night did not turn out like I hoped. I was determined to enjoy myself that night. I wore my hair down for the first time ever and the new off-the-shoulder white dress I bought. Mom wanted to sew one herself, but I wanted a *new* dress. Not a homemade one. Something trendy and fresh. Fat lot of good that did. A mix of emotions tries to strangle me. It's not just grad night I'm thinking about. It's four years of Connor and everybody else at North Valley treating me like I was garbage. I often wonder if I would've been invisible and left alone if it wasn't for Connor. But he made sure the spotlight shone on me every single day. He made me a target for *everybody* else. I'm suddenly ready to run away from this field and never come back. The only thing stopping me is my need to understand why Connor was so mean to me. "Why were you such an ass to me on grad night? I've never forgotten what you did, Connor."

He looks away. "I don't want to talk about grad night."

"I do. I need to get past it. Past what you did to me."

"You and me both."

"What's that supposed to mean?"

"Nothing."

"What, Connor?"

"What do you want me to say, Lex?"

"I want to know why you did it."

He looks at me with haunted eyes for a long time.

Am I missing something?

"If I could take back what I did on grad night, I would. Every fuckin day, I wish I had a do over for grad night."

The tone of his voice is so sad, so strained, it seems out of character for the Connor Hughes that I know. "I'm confused, Connor. What you did to me was a jerk thing to do, but it's not like you ruined my life or anything." I giggle nervously because I'm not entirely sure I believe my own words, but it seems like the right thing to say. "It could've been a lot worse.

"I'm not talking about what I did to you. I'm talking about what happened after you left. And believe me, it *was* worse. A *lot* worse."

"Do you want me to start recording?"

"Yeah.

I fish my mp3 recorder out of my purse and press the red button. I touch my fingertips to his tattooed forearm. "What happened, Connor?"

He whispers so softly the words are nearly inaudible:

"I ruined everything…"

ELECTRA

GRAD NIGHT, 2008.

To my surprise, people aren't as terrible to me tonight as I feared. Maybe it's the fact we all officially graduated a few hours ago and we're putting high school behind us forever. Maybe we're all afraid of our futures and we're too scared to be mean to each other, like we need to band together and face the future as a team. Maybe that's completely ridiculous.

Either way, I've enjoyed the carnival atmosphere since I arrived. I've been on most of the rides with the few people on the school newspaper I can genuinely call my friends, eaten way too much junk food, and generally enjoyed myself, much to my pleasant surprise.

"You really look good in that dress, Electra." Janice Wang smiles at me. "You should totally wear your hair down more often." She's the graphic designer for our school paper and the news website.

"Thanks. Not to change the subject, but I totally have to go to the bathroom. Wanna come with?"

"Yeah, sure." She stands up from the park-style bench where we were sharing a bag of greasy popcorn and drinking Red Bull to keep ourselves awake. It's well past midnight.

We stroll past the Tilt-A-Whirl and head toward the blue portable toilets lined up on the far edge of the field beside the bleachers.

"Yo, Janice!" Some guy yells behind us, running out of a crowd of people lined up for the ferris wheel. It's Steve Washington. He shoots video for the campus news channel.

Janice has a crush on him. Her eyes light up when she sees him, "Hey, Steve!"

"What's up with you two high school graduates?" Steve asks, smiling his usual toothy grin and stuffing his hands in his pockets.

"Just chillin," Janice says. "Want some Red Bull?" She holds up her can.

"Already had four," he chuckles. "What up, Electra?"

"Hey, Steve."

"I hate to bother you guys, but I was wondering…" Steve turns to Janice, "if maybe you wanted to ride the ferris wheel with me, Janice?"

She looks at me, "Oh, Electra and I were just going to the—"

I cut in with a grin, "It's okay. You go." I know Janice has been dying for Steve to make a move all year. "I'll be fine. I'll catch up with you later, okay?"

"You sure?" Janice asks earnestly.

"Yeah. You know me. Tough as nails."

Steve looks at me for approval.

"Go, you two!" I giggle and feel a tad bit jealous as I wave them off. I'm not going to stop Janice from having fun tonight. She deserves it. I'm used to doing things on my own anyway.

Steve grabs Janice's hand and tugs her toward the ferris wheel. She looks back over her shoulder and smiles at me, her eyes wide. She silently mouths, *"O. M. Geeeeee!!"*

I laugh and continue toward the toilets. At the moment, no one is waiting in line, so I step into the first one and lock the door. Light seeps through the vents overhead.

It's pretty dim in here.

And it stinks.

Hovering over the plastic bowl, I pee quickly. Portable toilets are the grossest things ever invented. Why don't they put lights in these things? And why is the toilet paper always so thin it falls apart in your fingers? Finished, I stand and push my dress down and slide the lock, dying for fresh air. Unfortunately, the door is stuck. I jiggle the lock and push again. No luck.

Quiet laughter outside.

"Let me out!" I shout, pounding on the inside of the plastic door.

More brazen laughter.

"We'll let you out if you promise to blow us!"

"Everybody knows AC/DC is a dyke. She won't blow any of us."

Snickering.

"Fuck you guys!" I scream as loud as I can, my voice echoing against the plastic walls. "Let me out, assholes!!!" I lean against the door with my full body weight, but it won't move. I bang my hip into it, but it feels welded shut.

"No one can hear you, Skanklin! The carnival is too loud!"

They're right. Between the sounds of animated conversation, the clanking of all the rides, and that stupid annoying crazy carnival calliope music that is whooping and wheezing loud enough to wake the dead, my voice is lost in the mix.

Damn, I swear the smell in here is getting worse.

The entire toilet suddenly lurches left, then right, accompanied by the gritty honk of plastic sliding across cement.

The contents in the toilet tank slosh wetly. A few droplets jump out of the toilet seat. I wince and slam the lid down. I don't want it splashing on me. "What are you guys doing!"

Laughter. Everything lurches again.

"Stop it! You're going to tip it over!"

One of them hollers, "Enjoy the ride, Vulvage!"

I recognize the voice. "I know that's you, Benjamin Bates! If you guys tip me over, I'm reporting you all to the police for assault! I hope you like jail! Do you think you'll get to play football at USC if they hear about this, Benjamin?!"

More callous laughter.

"Stop!" I scream. "I'm going to kill you guys when I get out of here!"

Crazy cackling as the entire structure starts to tip forward.

I kick at the door with my bowtie flats, but it still won't open. So I brace my hands against the doorframe. "Stop, you guys! Please!" My weight shifts onto my hands as the toilet continues to tip. I brace my feet, ready for impact.

"Sink the bitch," a girl's voice seethes. It sounds like Chelsea Hawkins. "Make her swim in it."

Does everybody in this school hate me?

Tipping...

Tipping...

Tipping...

This is not how grad night was supposed to end.

With mounting horror, I imagine the jolt of smashing into the ground, followed by the sudden soaking I will get when the foul contents of the tank spill all over my white dress.

My outfit will be ruined.

My night will be ruined.

I'll probably get hantavirus *and* the swine flu.

And the very last moment of my high school career will be burned into my brain as the single worst moment in my entire life.

Forever.

"Fuck you all, assholes!!" I scream.

A new voice shouts outside. "What the fuck are you guys doing?!"

The toilet stalls in mid air.

I lean forward at a 45 degree angle, doing a push up against the front wall. Now would be a good time for gravity to show mercy.

"Put that thing back, motherfuckers!" The voice sounds vaguely familiar. It almost sounds like Connor Hughes. But that can't be right. If there's anyone I can imagine as a ring leader for such a stupid prank, it would be him.

Scuffling outside and more laughing and people running.

The Connor voice shouts, "Come back here, you pricks!"

For intolerable seconds, I hang in the balance.

"God damn it!" Grunting from who I think is Connor. "Fuck! Move it, you bitch!"

Is he talking to me? I have no idea what to do. I'm leaning half way over. I can't move or do anything to help.

A long grunting roar from him and the toilet slowly starts to stand up. I feel my weight shift and suddenly *BAM!!* The toilet slams back to standing. The tank contents splorsh ominously, but they don't explode out of the toilet seat like I fear.

Wow, that was *way* too close for comfort.

I push the door open and stare into the azure eyes of my savior.

Connor Hughes.

His brow is dotted with sweat from exertion. "Fuckers ran off and left you hangin. Thing almost fell on me. Good thing you weigh like ten pounds, otherwise it would've crushed me." He winks and offers me his hand. "You okay?"

"Yeah." Without thinking I take it and he helps me step out of the toilet. Not that I need any assistance. But his gentlemanly behavior is somehow irresistible at the moment. "Thanks."

I can't believe I'm thanking *Connor Hughes* for anything.

But I just did.

I guess miracles really *can* happen.

ELECTRA

The ferris wheel spins slowly round and round up and down. I sit next to Connor in one of the seats. We're shoulder to shoulder. The carnival glitters beneath us in the night.

"Sorry about those assholes, Warmoth."

"It's okay," I sigh, staring at my hands which are still shaky.

"Are you all right?"

"I'm fine. But if you hadn't shown up sooner, who knows."

"Good thing I did."

"Did you see who it was? I heard Ben Bates and Chelsea Hawkins, but I think other people were helping."

"I'm not sure. They scattered quick. Want some cotton candy?" He bought it before we got on the ferris wheel.

"No thanks."

"Me neither. I hate this shit." He tosses it over his head.

"Connor!" I twist in the seat and watch the pink puff sail to the grass. Nobody notices.

He chuckles, "Did I kill anybody?"

I sit back down. "Yeah. Some kittens. It was horrible."

"You've got a great imagination, Warmoth. You know that? You could be a great writer someday."

"I want to be a journalist. Journalists don't make things up. They report the truth."

"Well," he grins, "you're good with words. You'll be great at it."

"Thanks, Connor." There I go again. Thanking him. I'm somewhat stunned that Connor has been nothing but nice since saving me. This is a whole new side I never knew he had. To my surprise, I like it. I wish he hadn't waited until the very last hours of our high school career to show it. He might've saved me years worth of misery if he had. But the toilet incident and the rest of my painful past are behind me. I don't want to think about them. The future lies ahead, and that's where I'm focused. The future holds promise. "So, what are *your* plans for after high school?"

"Plans?" He chuckles. "What plans?"

"I'm serious, Connor."

"I don't know. Get a job, I guess. Or maybe I'll just be a gigolo." He winks at me. "You're supposed to do what you're good at, right?"

"You're more than that, Connor. You're smart. You can do anything you want in life. I mean it."

"Have you seen my grades? They had to start using the rest of the alphabet because I didn't even get F's. I got a Z in math all four years."

I giggle. "That's funny." It's weird that I'm sitting shoulder to shoulder in a ferris wheel with my sworn enemy. We should be at each other's throats, not joking like friends. I blame graduating. It does weird things.

"Thanks."

"Maybe you should be a comedian. You're always coming up with funny ways to make fun of me."

"Nobody pays people to be assholes," he scowls.

"You do it for free," I grin. I lean into him for a moment. It feels right. I can't believe it, but it does. "But seriously, Connor. You're clever. This is L.A. People make money writing jokes and stuff for TV shows. You could too."

"Nah. The only way I'm funny is busting your balls."

I wrinkle my nose, "I don't have balls, Connor."

"Are you kidding? You have brass ones, Warmoth. You always have."

"Brass *balls*? I don't think so."

"So you have brass labia."

I grimace, "That sounds weird."

"So call them lady balls."

"*Lady* balls? Did you just make that up?"

"Yeah."

I grimace, "I don't think that's any better."

He chuckles. "Just watch. By 2010, people will be saying lady balls all the time."

"If you say so," I snicker. "But if people do, it's further proof you should go be a stand up comic or whatever."

He grins but says nothing.

We're quiet for a while, enjoying the view as the ferris wheel circles up and down. Between my off-the-shoulder dress and the dewy night air, I start to shiver.

"You cold?" he asks.

"A little."

He puts his arm around me.

"What are you doing, Connor?"

"Keeping you warm?" He's not sure of himself, but his arm stays.

"Why are you being so nice, Connor? It's not like you."

"I don't know. It's the last day of high school, I guess. You deserve at least *one* day off from me harassing you, right?"

I wouldn't be sitting here snuggling against Connor Hughes' side if he hadn't ran off the jerky jocks who tried to tip over the portable toilet. But he did, so here I am.

He flashes his innocent blue eyes at me.

I think he wants to kiss me.

This night can't possibly get any weirder.

ELECTRA

His lips are soft, his tongue polite.

But his kiss is *definitely* doing something to me.

I've never been kissed before. I feel hot all over. I *think* I like it, but I keep wondering why I'm kissing Connor Hughes. I shouldn't be kissing him *or* liking it. But I am. Yes, he's gorgeous. Everyone knows that, even me. But he's my arch-nemesis. I should *not* be doing this.

This is way too confusing and it's making me nervous.

Luckily, the ferris wheel creaks to a stop, ending our kiss. It's our turn to get off the ride. I smile to myself. This will be the only *getting off* Connor gets from me tonight. Like a gentleman, he holds my hand as we step out of the cart onto the damp grass. We exit together through the railing that circles the ride. I'm startled by the face of Ryan Hansen, who stands just outside the fence. Ryan is a good friend of Connor's. I see them together all the time.

Ryan looks furious, his eyes pinned on Connor. "We need to talk.

Now."

"Can't it wait?" Connor says to him.

"No."

"Fuck, man. Can't you see me and Electra are kickin it?"

This suddenly feels very strange. Connor has never called me Electra before. It's always War Mouth or worse. And Ryan's agitation feels somehow... *wrong*.

Ryan smiles crazily and waves his arms in the air. "Fuck. Fine. I don't care. We can talk right here if you want, Hughes. Bates told me what you did."

Is he talking about *Benjamin* Bates? One of the toilet knockers? And what does he mean by what *Connor* did? Connor saved me. Is that bad?

"All right, all right," Connor says nervously. He turns to me. "I'll be right back." He throws his arm around Hansen's shoulders and hurries him off into the shadows behind the Ring The Bell game where a bunch of football players are trying to impress their girlfriends by taking turns swinging the big wooden mallet.

Something's up with Connor and Ryan. I can smell it. Fueled by my natural curiosity as a budding journalist and my feminine intuition, I follow them.

Another football player smacks the mallet against the lever and the metal puck shoots up and hits the bell. *DING!* The crowd of seniors surrounding the guy cheers loudly as I pass by and peer around the back of the booth.

Connor and Ryan stand chest to chest in the shadows like they're going to fight. Should I try and stop them? The investigative reporter in me says that I need to know what they're talking about before I interfere. I try to catch what they're saying, but I can't make out anything over the rowdy football players on the other side of the booth wall. I creep closer, straining to hear. It doesn't help. I take another step, increasingly afraid I'll interrupt Connor and Ryan and not get the inside story.

There's a lull in the action for the Ring The Bell game. Words drift to me. I hold my breath in anticipation.

"Tell her, Connor," Ryan hisses. He looks super pissed off. He's grabbing Connor by the lapels of his leather jacket. "If you don't, so help me I'll tell her myself."

Connor shoves Ryan away with both hands. "Fuck you, man! I'm not telling her shit!"

My intuition says this is the part where I step in. "Tell me what?" I smirk.

Both of them twist to face me. They look guilty as hell.

"Tell me what?" I growl.

Ryan blurts first, "Connor—"

Connor shoves him against the plywood back wall of the Ring The Bell booth. "Shut up, Hansen!"

"I'm telling her, dickhead!"

"I said shut up, Hansen!" Connor grabs Ryan by the shirt and raises a fist like he's going to punch him in the face.

"Stop it!" I bark. "You two assholes are up to something. Tell me what's going on, or so help me I swear I will never speak to either of you ever again." I fold my arms across my chest.

Connor hangs his head and releases his grip on Ryan's shirt.

Ryan frowns at Connor. "Locking you in the toilet was Connor's idea."

DING! Another footballer rings the bell on the other side of the booth's back wall.

Anger swells inside me. My eyes narrow. "Is that true, Connor?"

He runs his hand through his hair. "They weren't *really* gonna do it. I told them just to scare you a bit."

"*Scare* me?" I suddenly put 2 and 2 together. "What, so you could come *save* me?" The very idea disgusts me beyond reason.

"Yeah," he mutters. "I may have been a little bit drunk when I cooked up the idea during graduation earlier."

I narrow my eyes and scowl at him. I don't think I've ever hated him as much as I do right at this moment. He *tricked* me into kissing him on that ferris wheel. I'm ashamed that I fell for his stupid scam. "You really *are* The Con Man, aren't you?"

He chuckles. "It seemed like a foolproof idea at the time."

"Who's the fool now, Con *Scams*?"

He smirks guiltily but says nothing.

"This is a new low, Connor. Even for you. That thing almost tipped over! What if it had! What if it spilled all over me! Did you think about that? You didn't, did you! Oh!!" I stamp my foot. "You are the biggest asshole in history! Do you know that? You just *ruined* grad night for me! I hate you, Connor Hughes! You make me sick!" I spin around and storm off. I don't want to be here anymore.

I'd rather be lonely at home.

I never should've come to grad night.

What a mistake.

Chapter 14

CONNOR

GRAD NIGHT, 2008.

4:00am.

Electra walks fast across the grass toward the parking lot in her sexy ass white dress. The grad night carnival is far behind us.

I run to catch up, right on her heels. "Wait up, Electra! Let me explain!"

She ignores me.

"Please, you gotta give me a chance." I'm begging. I don't care. I know I fucked up. I went too far this time. "Damn it, would you let me explain?!"

She stops suddenly, her back to me. "This better be good, Connor."

I step in front of her.

Even with her braces and her glasses, she's so fuckin beautiful it kills me. Her lips are plump and demand to be sucked. For four years, I tried everything I could think of to be friends with her. She was never interested. She always pushed me away. But I fuckin *need* her. No woman has ever made me crazy like this. No woman has ever consistently blown me off like this either. This is my last chance. It's now or never. "I just, I don't know. I thought if I did something nice for once, you'd talk to me like a normal person instead of your enemy."

"Why didn't you say that in the first place!"

I laugh. "You really think if I'd've asked you to ride the ferris wheel *before* the toilet thing you would've said yes?"

She stares at me.

I have no idea what she's thinking. But I feel any chance I have slipping away. It's written all over her face. "Can we just forget this ever happened and start over?"

"Start *over*? And pretend the last four years of you being an obnoxious ass never happened?" She laughs in my face. "Not on your life."

Her words stab my heart. It hurts so bad my walls go up. I deal the only way I know how. By being cocky as all fuck. I grin at her like us fuckin is the only way outta this moment. It's my go-to move. I've closed every girl I've ever fucked with this grin. Sure, it never worked on Electra before, but I'm desperate. "You totally want me. You've *always* wanted me."

Her face sours, but she's still damn gorgeous. "I've *never* wanted you. *Connor*. You must think I'm pretty stupid if you think I'm going to let myself become yet another notch on your bedpost." She folds her arms across her cute little chest like she always does. Only this time, I can see her delicate collar bones and shoulders in her low cut white dress, and they're the most beautiful things I've ever seen. "The only reason you want me is because you never *had* me, *Connor*. We both know that if I was dumb enough to have sex with you, you'd get what you've wanted all along, and you'd move on. Just like you did with every other unsuspecting girl you've fucked. Tell me I'm wrong."

I want to tell her that if I got her I'd never let go. I want to tell her that the only reason I fucked any other girl is because she wouldn't give me the time of day. More than anything, I want to tell her I *love* her. But that's fuckin stupid. How can I love her? The only time she ever talks to me is when she's yelling at me or cursing me the fuck out. It doesn't make any sense, but I *do* love her. I don't care how stupid it sounds. I *have* to tell her. Here goes nothing. "I—"

The hateful look on her face stops me cold.

I try to get the words out, but they're frozen in my throat.

Fuck. I can't do it. Not when she's this pissed.

She smirks at me. It's the hottest fuckin smirk I've ever seen. "That's what I thought. I'm just another notch for you. But I've got news for you, Connor *Screws*. You will *never* catch me. I will *always* get away. After everything that you've done, I will *never* be one of your notches."

That's when she turns away from me and walks out of my life forever.

And so begins the worst night of my entire life.

I pull my Marlboros out of my leather jacket and jam one in my mouth before lighting it. I'm gonna go find Hansen and beat some sense into that fucknut for ruining my plan. I don't give a shit if we've been friends since first grade.

He just fucked me in the ass on this one.

I'm not gonna take this shit lying down.

CONNOR

The flask I snuck in at the beginning of grad night is almost empty. I wish I hadn't drunk so much of it so early. I was toasty during the graduation ceremony, but now I'm dry. I gulp the last shot's worth of whiskey. It's not enough to get wasted, but that's probably okay. I don't wanna be sloppy when I kick the shit out of Ryan fuckin Hansen. That cock jockey knows how to fight. After I beat his ass, I'll bail on this stupid fuckin carnival and go find more liquor.

I shoulder past a pack of kids laughing in front of the toilets. I hate those blue fuckin toilets.

It takes a half hour of searching to finally find Hansen. He's by himself at one of the game booths, throwing baseballs at metal milk bottles. He looks as miserable as I feel. It doesn't mean I'm gonna show this twat knocker any mercy.

I come up right behind him and shove him against the low counter of the booth. He folds forward and knocks baseballs everywhere.

"What the fuck?!" he shouts.

I barely notice the woman running the booth. She backs away afraid.

When Hansen turns around, I shove his chest and he sits down on the counter. "Why the fuck did you tell her, you dumbfuck?!"

He plants his boot in my crotch, missing my balls by an inch, and kicks back so hard I stumble backward. "Because you're a fucking douchebag. That's why." He stands up.

I regain my footing and notice kids circling us, waiting for a fight. I ignore them. "*I'm* the douchebag?! You fucked up my plan! It worked perfectly! I kissed her on the ferris wheel, for fuck's sake! If you hadn't told her, everything would've been fine!"

"You *kissed* her?"

"Yeah, I fuckin kissed her!" I want to be kicking his ass right now, but he's my best friend. "A better question is, who the fuck told you about my plan? Was it Bates? It *had* to've been Bates. That fuckin tool doesn't know how to keep his fuckin mouth shut." As pissed as I am at Hansen, I'd rather be pissed at Ben Bates than him. Ryan has always been there for me. He was there for me the time I… I block the thought. I can't think about that shit right now.

"You fucking *kissed* her?" Hansen says, missing everything I just said.

That's when I figure it out. I'm suddenly so mad I can't think straight. He fuckin likes her. The idea of my best friend liking the one girl I want more than any other on this planet and then he goes and *sabotages* the *one* shot I had with her after four fuckin years makes me want to murder him and everyone in sight. "You like her, don't you?" My words are angry fists and elbows.

Hansen doesn't answer. He just stares at me.

I get right in his face. "Tell me you don't. TELL ME YOU DON'T FUCKIN LIKE HER!!" I *need* for him not to like her. If he does, I don't know what I'm gonna do. My world is collapsing around me.

He bumps my chest with his. "Fuck you, man. I don't have to tell you shit."

I smash my palm into his shoulder. "TELL ME YOU DON'T FUCKIN LIKE HER!!"

Hansen shakes his head like I'm shit. He backs up a step, not because he's afraid, but because he's figured it all out. "Why do you care, Connor? I thought you hated Electra. All you do is treat her like shit. Why? Why are you so obsessed with her?"

Losing it. "I DON'T GIVE A SHIT ABOUT HER!!"

He snorts a hateful laugh. "Bullshit. You've liked Electra since you saw her freshman year. All you ever talk about is Electra. No matter how many girls you fuck, you talk about Electra. I'm sick of fucking hearing you whine about Electra and then I have to watch you treat her like shit. She doesn't deserve it, man. You had your shot. For four years, I held back because you said she was off limits. Now I know why. If you couldn't have her, you didn't want *anyone* to get her. Guess what? I'm sick of watching you fuck it all up. She deserves someone who won't treat her like shit. She deserves someone who isn't a piece of shit like you, Connor. I don't even know why I'm friends with you. You're a loser. I hope you end up drunk in a ditch somewhere because that's where you're headed. Good luck with your life, dumbfuck."

All the fight has gone out of me. I'm so confused I think I'm going to die. My whole world stopped making sense the second Electra Warmoth walked away. Now my whole world is imploding around me as my best and only true friend gives me the blow off.

"Now if you'll fucking excuse me," Hansen says, "I'm going to find her and apologize for your sorry fucking ass."

My heart stops. Fear drowns me.

Ryan Hansen is a great guy. If anyone has a shot with Electra Warmoth, it's him. Fuck. I'm going to die.

CONNOR

Desperation floods my veins. I sprint after Hansen, who is almost at his car in the school parking lot. "Where the fuck are you going!" I shove him into the back fender of the primer gray '72 Camaro his dad helped him restore last summer. The one *I* helped him restore. I was at his house with him and his dad every fuckin day. Their house was the only place I could go where I wasn't miserable. Right now I hate Ryan and his dad and his house and his fuckin car more than I've ever hated anything.

Ryan recovers, leaning over the trunk of the Camaro. He elbows me in the stomach, knocking the wind out of me.

I shouldn't have drunk any of that whiskey.

He spins around and clocks me in the chin.

I fall on my ass.

"Stay there, you piece of shit," Ryan growls.

I stare at him.

This is the saddest night of my entire life.

No, it's the second saddest…

I'm about to fall to pieces.

Ryan gets in the Camaro and revs the engine before backing out of the space. He rolls his window down. "You should sit there until you sober up and figure out why you're such a complete idiot, Connor. I'm telling you as a friend. Why would you be such a dick to someone you *like*? You need help, man. Get some counseling or something. If you don't, you're gonna ruin every relationship in your life." He drives off.

Speechless, I choke on his exhaust, staring at the back of his car.

All I can think is he's going to steal Electra from me. I stumble to my feet, already running for my motorcycle. I hop on and start the engine, not bothering with my helmet.

If Ryan gets to her first, I'm going to lose it.

His car is way down at the end of the street when I catch air coming out of the parking lot. My bike wobbles when I hit the ground. I almost lay it down, but manage to recover. I've ridden drunk before. I'll be fine. I twist the throttle and rocket after Ryan. I catch him at a stoplight and pull up on his left, between his Camaro and an SUV.

He rolls his window down. "You should park your bike and walk home, dumbass. You're drunk."

"You should turn around and go home, *dumbass*. You don't even know where she lives." I sound like I'm twelve.

"Janice Wang told me."

"Who's Janice Wang?"

Ryan shakes his head. "How can you spend so much fucking time obsessing about a girl and you don't even know who her friends are?"

I panic. "How do you know so much about her? Have you been stalking her? Have you been following her home like a stalker? Are you a fuckin stalker, Hansen? A creeper? A fuckin—"

The car behind him is honking. The light must've already turned green.

"Janice told me, dickhead. I asked her tonight after I told her about your genius plan and how I needed to apologize for *you*, you fucking lunatic. Go home." His Camaro rumbles as he eases up to the speed limit.

I crank my throttle until I catch up and pace beside his window. "Turn around, man!" I yell over the wind.

"Get the fuck off the road! You're drunk and riding without a helmet! Park somewhere until you sober up, you fucking idiot!" He floors it and turns onto the freeway onramp.

I kick my bike into second and goose the throttle. My engine screams. I swing left as the Camaro cuts into the apex of the turn on the right. I clear 60 as I whip through the curve, planning on beating him through it so I can get in front of him and slow down, forcing him to stop. Me and Ryan have watched every *Fast and the Furious* movie multiple times. We both drive like street racers whenever we get in a car. It's a dick thing. Now it's worse. There's pussy on the line.

The Camaro fades left as it begins to exit the turn. I'm in Ryan's blind spot when I realize the racing line he's cutting leaves no room for error. Too bad I'm the error he didn't plan on. He's going to fade all the way left, using every inch of available asphalt at the end of the turn. He'll cut it as close to the cement guard rail as he can. The only problem is there isn't enough room between his car and the rail for me and my bike. Not only am I in his blind spot, my foot peg is nearly scraping the ground as I lean way over.

I'm invisible.

It's too late to do anything. I'm already committed to the turn. If I have to change my line at the last second and stand the bike up too soon or brake suddenly, I'll lose the front end and high side. My bike will flip over and I'll fly through the air and land on the freeway at 60 miles an hour.

Without a helmet.

Or Ryan's 3,500 pound Camaro will crush me against the guard rail.

Only one way out of this without dying.

I honk the bike's nasally horn and hope Ryan hears me with his window rolled down.

He does.

I will regret my actions for the rest of my life.

The Camaro wheels to the right and I squirt past through the narrow gap. I manage to get the bike back to standing. Tires screech behind me. The Camaro swerves wildly right then left, the front bumper scraping against the cement guard rail. The car's nose dives as it cuts back to the right and loses the rear end.

It starts to spin.

The whole time I'm hissing under my breath, "Shit, shit, shit..."

The car glides sideways and 360s on the pavement before sliding right up the safety wedge at the start of the right side guardrail. Sparks explode in an orange spray as the car's frame scrapes across the top. The car slides balanced for a second before tipping off to the right. It spirals down the slope of the dirt shoulder like a football before slamming to a stop against the cement culvert pipe at the end of the ditch. A huge cloud of dirt billows into the air.

I skid to a stop on the side of the freeway and jump off my bike, leaving it to fall over on its side. At four in the morning, the freeway is eerily empty. I run along the patterned concrete wall. I can't see Ryan's car in the ditch until I clear the wall. I stop, grabbing the guardrail. It's a steep drop down to his car. I vault over the edge and slide down the slope, my boots kicking up dirt.

POOMPH!!

A cloud of flame billows up from beneath the car which lies on its left side. It leans so far over the roof rests against the slope. I would pull Ryan out the driver's window, but it's buried in the dirt.

"Ryan!" I shout, not sure what to do.

Flames flicker inside the engine compartment, glowing out from the gaps in the twisted metal. The front windshield is a shattered spiderweb dripping with golden dewdrops of firelight. I can't see inside the car.

I don't even bother calling 911. There isn't time.

I climb on top of the car, which at this angle is the car's right side. I whip out my knife and slam the butt into the passenger side window glass.

The flames in the engine are getting bigger.

I have to get him out.

"I'm gonna kick the window out! Cover your eyes!" I don't even know if he can hear me. I stomp the shattered glass with my boot heel. The window folds in a crumpled sheet of glass and plastic laminate, hanging inside the car. I don't want it falling on Ryan's face but I don't want to slice my fingers open pulling it out. I hesitate for a second before ripping off my leather jacket. I stick my hands in the sleeves like I'm putting it on backward and grab the window glass through the leather. I tear the glass back and fold it over the car door.

POOMPH!!

Another burst of flame.

Ryan screams.

"Fuck, man! I'll get you out! Hold on a second!" I drop my jacket and lean through the window to see how he's lying.

Face first in a puddle of burning gasoline.

Fuck.

I lean through the passenger window up to my waist and grab his arm with both hands. When I pull, I start to fall into the car. I don't have any leverage. I need to hook my legs around something but there's nothing behind me except air.

Ryan screams again.

"Pull your face out of the flames, god damn it!"

He just screams.

— scream-scream-scream-scream —

I lower myself feet first into the car and grab my jacket. I pull on his arm again, trying to stand him up. He moans. He's caught on something. The seatbelt. I whip out my knife and flick the blade open so I can slice it off. It takes me forever to find the belt. I try to reposition Ryan, but it's so tight it won't let go.

The whole time, Ryan's face is cooking in the fire.

By the time I find the belt, the flames are up to my elbows. I can feel the heat hot on my face. I narrow my eyes. I'm not going to have any eyebrows or eyelashes at this rate.

I reach down to get a good grip on Ryan's face so I can lift him up. I hope his neck isn't broken. As soon as I start to lift, I feel flames burning the skin on my hands. I don't care. I pull him to his feet. There's almost no room inside the sideways car. The heat is burning through my leather boots and baking my jeans. "Stand the fuck up!"

Ryan groans and slumps against me. At least his face is out of the fire.

We lean against the sideways bucket seat backs.

The passenger window is as high as the top of my head.

"Can you stand up?"

He groans.

"I have to do a pull up to get out of here. Then I'll pull you out, okay?"

He groans again. His face is a glistening charred mess.

I lean him against the seats. If he can't stand up and he sinks to his feet, I won't be able to reach him.

"Stand the fuck up, Hansen!"

He groans a little more strongly.

I grab the door frame and heave myself out of the car. I lean in and hold my arm out for Ryan. "Grab my hand, Ryan!"

His head lolls against his chest. He's starting to sit down. The flames are up to his waist. I can't even reach him this far away.

"*STAND UP GOD DAMN IT, OR I WILL KICK YOUR FUCKIN ASS!!*"

He lifts his head like it weighs a million pounds. His eyes look like boiled eggs shining out of a blackened chicken sandwich. He struggles back to his feet. But he just stares at me.

I don't know what I'm expecting. He just slammed his Camaro into a cement wall. I'm surprised he's even alive. But I know one thing. I don't want my best friend dead.

"*GRAB MY FUCKIN HAND, YOU WORTHLESS PIECE OF SHIT!! GRAB IT RIGHT THE FUCK NOW!!!!*" If he doesn't take my arm, I can't get him out of the car.

POOMPH!!

Another puff of flames pops up from the dirt near the back wheel.

"*THE FUCKIN TANK IS GOING TO BLOW, DUMBASS!! GIMME YOUR ARM!!*"

He stares at me like he doesn't understand.

I start to weep. "*Damn it, Hansen! I can't lose you, you dumbshit! Gimme your fuckin arm!*"

He stares at me blankly.

I think he's giving up. "Please, man. Gimme your arm. I'm begging you." I'm crying full tilt now. "Please..."

He closes his eyes.

"No! Wake the fuck up!"

His arm slowly rises, his torn up face tightening with effort.

"That's it! Lift it! Gimme your arm, man! I've got it! Come on! There!" I grip it above the elbow and at the wrist. Then I squat down, my boots balanced on the edge of the window frame and I fuckin lift with everything I have. He weighs a fuckin ton. That shit about dead weight is totally true. I'm gonna pop a hernia lifting him. My head pounds, my teeth clench, but the second I have him out up to his waist, I fall back, pulling him as I go.

He drops against the car door.

For a crazy second, I nearly tumble back off the top of the tipped over car but Ryan's weight pulls me back and I lean to the side and drape him over the door. I drop to the ground and pull him over the edge. He falls against me and we drop to the dirt, him all over me. I roll him off and grab him by both wrists and drag him as far down the ditch away from the Camaro as I can get us.

When I lower him into the dirt, the gas tank blows.

I shield Ryan with my back, kneeling over him.

Flames shoot up in a huge greasy cloud of black smoke. Now would be a good time to call 911. But my phone is in my leather jacket and it's somewhere in the burning car.

Ryan groans.

I look down at his messed up face. I don't even recognize him in the faint orange glow of the flames. His crispy skin is peeling off in flakes and there's blood everywhere. But he's not dead. "I left my jacket in your car, you fucknut." I chuckle and smear tears from my face. "You owe me a new one."

His face crackles into a smile, "You owe me a new car, fucknut." His words come out all garbled and he coughs hard and wheezy, his red and black eyelids clamping shut from the pain.

Chapter 15

ELECTRA

PRESENT DAY.

"What happened then?" I ask, still standing on the bright summery North Valley High School field with Connor. "Was Ryan okay?"

Connor is squatting on the grass, twisting a blade he plucked during the story around his finger. The blade of grass is so tight, it makes the tip of his finger blood red. He drops the blade and stands up slowly. "I need to show you something. Come on." He starts walking across the field without looking back.

"Wait, Connor!" I jog on my toes so my two inch heels don't sink into the grass.

He stops, looking at me, his face forlorn.

I've never seen Connor looking like this. Then again, before last week, the last time I ever saw him was *before* Ryan Hansen crashed his Camaro. I can't imagine what Connor has been through over the past seven years. While this recent revelation paints Connor in a whole new light, I can only wonder what happened to Ryan. Maybe I'll never find out.

We walk toward the parking lot in front of the school and climb in my car. Then it hits me.

We're going to a graveyard. My stomach sinks.

Connor directs me to a random suburban neighborhood a few miles from the school.

"Where are we?" I ask.

Connor climbs out of the car without answering. He waits for me on the sidewalk. "Try not to say anything about his face."

"Whose face?" I ask as I follow him up the cement path leading to a modest two-story house.

On the front step, Connor knocks on the door but thumbs the latch before anybody answers and sticks his head inside. He hollers, "Anybody here?" He steps inside.

I reluctantly follow, feeling like an intruder.

A woman old enough to be my or Connor's mom comes walking out of the kitchen with a pair of gardening gloves in one hand. Is this Connor's house? I've never met his parents. I have no idea.

"Oh, hello, Connor," the woman smiles.

"Hey, Mrs. H."

That's when I figure it out.

This is Ryan Hansen's house.

Mrs. Hansen smiles at me. "Who's your friend, Connor?"

I'm about to speak when Connor cuts me off, saying, "This is Lex. She went to school with me and Ryan."

That was weird. Ryan wouldn't know me by the name Lex. Nobody from North Valley would. Whatever. "Hi," I smile at her.

"Well, any friend of Connor's is a friend of ours." Mrs. Hansen seems really nice. "Would you two like anything to drink?"

"I'm okay," I grin.

She says, "Connor, you know where everything is. If you two change your mind about that drink, help yourselves. I'll be out back weeding. I swear, those dandelions have a thing for my rose garden."

"Sure," he mumbles.

"Okay," I say uncertainly.

Mrs. Hansen's brows knit with concern. "Was Ryan expecting… a guest?"

Why does all this feel so awkward?

"Maybe we should come back later," Connor mutters.

"It's okay," Mrs. Hansen says. "Let me just tell him you're here. What was your name again, sweetie?"

Connor doesn't answer. He looks at me like he's seen a ghost.

"Lex," I say to Mrs. Hansen.

She nods. "I'll go upstairs and tell him. Just a sec."

We wait in the living room. It is *super* uncomfortable. An old grandfather clock ticks loudly in the silent room. I have a terrible feeling about what is about to happen. I don't even know what that is, but I'm extremely nervous to the point of nausea.

A voice echoes down the stairs, "I don't remember anyone named Lex, but if Connor knows her, I'm sure I do." The voice must be Ryan, but the words come out in a strange mumbly nasal lisp. Shoes then jeans descend the stairs with a noticeable limp.

My stomach flops before I see his face. His hands and arms are covered in disfiguring burn scars.

Oh my god.

Now I realize why all the curtains are shut in the middle of the day and the house is so dim. I see Ryan before he sees me. The handsome face I remember is now a grotesque mask, the scarred flesh red and puckered and melting. But it's real and thoroughly disturbing. And it's Ryan Hansen. My heart breaks seeing him like this. But I don't want to be rude and stare or let it show that it's affecting me. I try to act normal.

"What up, C," Ryan says when he sees Connor.

I unconsciously take a step back. Not because I'm afraid but because something about this entire situation is horrifying. After all the old memories Connor dredged up about grad night, and what he revealed about what happened after I left, I can only wonder: what the *fuck* was he thinking bringing me here? Does Ryan still think about me? Does he wonder what would've happened between us if he'd found me at home and apologized for Connor? Did Connor tell Ryan that we slept together? What will Ryan say if he finds out? I'm not about to tell him. But what if Connor suddenly blurts it out here and now? This is wrong on so many levels I can't begin to describe it.

"Electra?" Ryan says thoughtfully when our eyes meet. "What are you doing here?"

I don't know what to say. I don't want to say the wrong thing and make this situation worse. I'm frozen with fear.

Ryan glances at Connor. "She's… This *is* Electra, isn't it?"

Connor only nods.

Ryan raises a protective hand to his face and turns away like he wants to hide his disfigurement. "I…"

I feel terrible for him. "I'm sorry, Ryan. I didn't know where we were going when Connor brought me here. It was a complete surprise."

Ryan remains half turned away, his face hidden in shadow. "Why'd you bring her, Connor?" His voice shakes.

Connor sighs heavily. "I don't know."

Now I'm beyond confused. I don't know what to do or say. The room has suddenly grown so uncomfortable, I want to run out the front door, but I won't, out of respect for Ryan. I also want to slap Connor upside the head and shout at him, *What the hell were you thinking?!* But I know that isn't the right thing to do either. I feel awful.

We all stand in the dim living room in silence for a long time.

The grandfather clock ticks and ticks and ticks.

Should we leave?

"Why didn't you at least tell me you were bringing her, man?" Ryan asks in his lispy voice. He sounds heartbroken.

Does Ryan still like me?

I'm horrible by association.

"Fah-*fuck*," Connor hisses, his breath hitching in his throat. "This was stupid. Sorry, man. Sorry. I'm a fuckin idiot." His voice is quiet and obviously near tears. He strides to the front door of the house and rips it open. I expect him to slam it behind him as he walks outside, but he doesn't. The latch clicks gently and he's gone.

Now it's just me and Ryan Hansen all alone in his living room. I haven't spoken to him once in the seven years that have passed since his face was ruined by the car fire.

Oh, fuck.

This just got a billion times more awkward.

CONNOR

I sit on the curb outside Ryan's house.

There's no way I can be with Electra.

The look on Ryan's face said it all. It will kill him if he knows I'm with her. After all he's been through, the broken bones, the surgeries, the titanium pins and rods, the skin grafts, the recovery, the pain every single day, all because of me, I can't do this to him. He'll never have Electra or anyone like her. So why should I be happy if he can't? Why should I have an amazing woman in my life if he has to hide his face so people don't stare at him like he's a fuckin monster? I shouldn't.

Because I'm the fuckin monster.

If it wasn't for me, Ryan would have the same damn face he was born with. Not the one I caused. He would be chasin chicks like I do. We would be trading stories about all the hotties we banged instead of me hiding all of it from Ryan so he doesn't have to be any more miserable than he already is.

That's why I have to finish this interview with Electra as quick as I can and say goodbye to her forever.

My guts are in knots.

I pull out my phone and turn it over in my hand, thinking.

This is a fuckin mess. I should've told her to turn around and go home the second I saw her at that fuckin convention. But that's not how I operate. I take something good and turn it into shit.

I hang my head.

Fuck me.

I should be dead.

I wait for my heart to stop, but it doesn't.

A car drives slowly by in front of Ryan's house. Some little brown bird flaps its wings and flies from a telephone wire and lands on someone's front lawn, looking for worms.

I remember my phone in my hand and play the voicemail.

"It's your dad again."

"*Hiiii*, Connor!" My mom's voice cheers in the background.

"Sorry we didn't call sooner. The east coast was a zoo. Never drive an RV through New York City."

My mom chimes in. "They gave your father a parking ticket because he drove so slow. He was afraid to go the speed limit! Can you imagine that?"

"I went the speed limit!" Dad protests with a laugh. "But I'll tell you, son: parking is impossible in New York and traffic is a pain in my ass. They should call that place The Big Hemorrhoid, not The Big Apple."

I chuckle to myself through tears.

Mom laughs. "That's disgusting, Finn!"

"What? If you think about it, the *bottom* of an apple looks a lot like a big red hemorrhoid."

I snicker and blow snot from my nose, crying hard.

"Ohmygod, Finn! I'm going to throw up! You just *ruined* apples forever!"

I definitely got my Dad's sense of humor.

"What?" he says. "Apples don't taste like hemorrhoids. They're sweet and crunchy. *Nothing* like a hemorrhoid. What's the problem?"

"Shut *up*, Finn!"

"All right, Kell. I'll stop," he sighs apologetically.

"Thank goodness," she laughs.

"One question for you, Kelly Hughes," Dad says seriously.

"It better not be about hemorrhoids."

"What do you want for dessert tonight? Apple *pie* or apple *sauce*?"

"Finn!" Mom laughs like it's the funniest thing ever said in the history of talking.

Hanging my head, I watch my tears drip onto the cement gutter beneath my boots.

There's a sound of fumbling with the phone, then my mom has it. "I hate to break it to you, Connor, but your father is *not your father*. I was impregnated by a much nicer man with manners."

Dad barks a laugh and he's holding the phone again. "She's right, son. Anyway, we just wanted to say hello. We'll call you again soon.

Probably when we get to Philadelphia. I hear the City of Brotherly Love is also the city where that old folktale about Johnny Appleseed got started."

"That's not true," Mom snorts.

"All that brotherly love led to a bunch of guys with over-used butts getting hemorrhoids."

"Finn!" She's screeching with laughs.

"The story used to be called Johnny Apple Ass, but they changed it for the sake of the children."

"*Finn!!!!*" Mom screams.

The phone drops and there's a bunch of laughing and random noises before the message ends.

I save the voicemail and hang my head between my knees. It takes a second. It's almost nothing at first, but the sobbing starts and my body shakes as the pain and sadness knocks me out.

Everything turns upside down.

ELECTRA

"Did Connor tell you he bumped into me at the convention?" I ask, sitting across from Ryan on his living room couch.

"No. He just said he was doing some signing thing downtown."

"Do you know about his book covers?" I'm careful with my questions, not wanting to spill any beans I shouldn't be spilling. But this topic seems safe if Connor and Ryan are close enough that Connor can walk in Ryan's house without knocking.

"Yeah. I've even got one of his books upstairs. *Stepbrother Obsessed*? Have you read it?"

"No," I grin. "But I saw the cover at the convention."

"I did." Ryan laughs. "I don't know how women read that romance shit. Guys don't act like that."

I'm surprised by his laughter. I smile. "I imagine it's a fantasy. Women like to read that sort of thing."

"Do *you* read romance?"

"Well, no, but—"

"See? It's trash! Give me a good car chase or a gun fight any day. I'd rather watch *How It's Made* than read a romance."

"I'm with you," I chuckle. I'm surprised Ryan is so relaxed around me. It helps that the living room curtains are drawn, blocking out nearly all the light. And he's in the corner easy chair, lost in deep shadow. I imagine he sat there on purpose. "So, you've been friends with Connor since—I mean, for all this time?" I almost said *since the accident* but I want to avoid that hot button. Why did I think the word hot? It reminds me of car fires. Wow, I'm glad I'm not saying all this out loud. This is really uncomfortable. Ryan deserves my respect. I take a deep breath, trying to calm myself.

"Yeah. Connor comes by almost every day. He always has."

I want to ask more, but I don't want to invade his privacy.

"You want to know about my accident, don't you?"

I wince.

"People always want to know. Did Connor tell you anything?"

"He, um, told me *how* it happened but that's it."

"Don't let his asshole attitude fool you. He was at the hospital and then the burn center every day. I was in and out of consciousness for weeks because of all the pain meds, but he was the first person I saw. Well, him and my parents. But Connor was there helping me through all of it."

"He was?"

He snorts a laugh. "Hard to believe, right? Connor Hughes having aaaa... what do they call it? A bedside manner."

"I guess you had a different relationship with Connor than I did."

"We've been best friends since first grade." There's pride in his voice.

I'm slightly envious. The only people I've known since first grade still in my life are my parents, and I don't see them much. I really ought to drive out to their walnut farm soon.

"Even when the doctors told me my scar contractures needed more surgery, and I was ready to off myself, Connor was there for me long after my other *friends* faded into the woodwork."

That was a lot to take in all at once. I start with the obvious. "What's a contracture?"

"That's when the skin tightens up after the burn heals. It restricts your movement and can ruin your joints and do all kinds of crazy bad shit to your body over time. In my case, I couldn't close my eyelids all the way. Talking and chewing made it worse. Every time I opened my mouth, my whole face pulled my *eyes* open. Can you believe that shit? It even hurt to smile. So I never smiled at anybody, and it got to where I hated opening my mouth to talk or eat because of what it did to my *eyelids*. I got pink eye all the time. When I started getting corneal ulcerations—which hurt like fuck, by the way—my doctor told me I could go blind without surgery. By that point, I didn't want to go through any more fucking surgeries. I was over it. The pain, the hospital visits, the staring from strangers, the stupid ass questions about my face, knowing nobody would ever look at me like a normal person ever again. The last thing I wanted was another skin graft and all *that* pain. I already had enough fucking pain. *Emotional* pain. But the doctors and my parents insisted. At one point, I was ready to throw it in and jump off the nearest bridge. I told Connor how I felt and all he did was tell me we'd get through it together, and if I gave up, he'd shit on my grave every weekend for the rest of his life." Ryan chuckles with amusement. "I remember telling him to go for it because it would keep the grass green." He shakes his head, lost in the memory. "If it wasn't for him, I really *might* have swallowed a bullet."

I smile. "Wow. Just, *wow*."

"Connor's a good person. Don't let him fool you otherwise."

If anyone else said that to me, I would laugh in their face. Coming from Ryan, I take it in. But I have to ask: "Are you sure?" I quip, "Because Connor has pretty much been acting like the Connor I remember from high school since I ran into him."

"Don't get me wrong. He'll always be a dick," he laughs. "But that's just an act. I mean *fuck*, that bastard even helped my parents with some of the medical bills when they got out of hand."

Mrs. Hansen comes walking into the living room. "Oh! You're still here. Was it Lex?"

"Yeah," I nod.

"Is Connor still here?"

"He's outside," Ryan says confidently.

I don't know how he knows.

"Is anybody hungry?" she asks. "I can make a snack." She walks to the front door and opens it. Blinding light pours into the room. I don't want to stare at Ryan, so I watch Mrs. Hansen. She hollers outside. "Connor? Do you want a snack? ... Okay. I'll make enough for everybody." She closes the door and walks into the kitchen.

The family quality that exists between Ryan, his mom, *and* Connor is unmistakeable. His presence is assumed.

"Does chips and salsa sound good?" Mrs. Hansen calls from the kitchen.

"That would be great," I answer.

"Thanks, Mom!" Ryan calls.

The front door opens.

Connor stands in the door frame and stares at me. Remorse weighs on his face. It's almost like he's afraid to step inside.

Once again, I don't know what to say.

"Are you gonna stand there all day?" Ryan jabs. "It's hot as hell outside. Close the door, dumbass."

Connor's face relaxes. A faint grin appears. He closes the door behind him and sits in the easy chair across from me, keeping the coffee table between the two of us.

I imagine he would have the courtesy to sit beside me after we just had sex six ways to Tuesday—in my workplace, no less—but I get it. There is an elephant in the middle of the room and neither I nor Connor are going to talk about it in front of Ryan, for good reason.

"You guys still like each other, don't you?" Ryan asks.

My eyes pop and flick sidewise at Connor. I sit up as straight as possible.

Connor guffaws. "I never liked Warmoth and you know it."

Hearing him say it doesn't stab my heart like it did in the conference room at *Trending Magazine*. Things became infinitely more complicated since we walked in Ryan's front door.

Ryan's face wrinkles, "Gimme a fucking break, Connor. You talked about her every day for four years. You think I forgot when you stopped talking about her after graduation?"

Connor barks, "Bullshit, man! The only thing I liked to do was harass her. You know that."

"Yeah, right," Ryan chuckles.

Not even I believe Connor.

Mrs. Hansen walks into the room with a plate of tortilla chips, a bowl of salsa, and napkins, followed by a pitcher of ice water and glasses. "Here you go. Enjoy. Holler if you need anything."

Ryan leans forward for chips, as does Connor. They fight over them like brothers, spooning out globs of salsa with the chips like they're going out of style.

All I can wonder is if they're going to fight over me, and not in a good way. At that exact moment, I resign myself to letting go of Connor. I won't come between him and his dear friend. *They* need each other more than I need Connor. I stand up. "I should probably go."

Connor stares at me, jawing on a mouthful. His eyes are sad.

"Sit down, Warmoth," Ryan says. "Have some chips."

Why does this feel like one of those mafia movies where the boss plays nice with his henchmen right up until the moment he shoots them all in cold blood? "I guess I have a few minutes." I smooth my skirt and plop back onto the couch cushions and grab a chip and dip it.

Ryan wipes his hands on a napkin. "I haven't heard much from Connor since he went to that book signing thing."

"It was a romance convention," Connor offers. "Rom Com Con."

Ryan snorts, "That's a stupid name. Anyway, what have you two been doing since then? Don't pretend you haven't been seeing each other. The way you two went at each other in high school, it was obvious you liked each other."

"Okay," I laugh. "Hold on. You're joking, right?"

Ryan laughs, "Don't play dumb, Electra."

And like that, I forget all the weirdness of being here. "You're insane, Ryan. The only feelings I had for Connor were hate. Hate, hate, and more hate. Connor is the biggest asshole I've ever met!" I'm giggling as I say it.

Connor grins sheepishly. "Still am."

"See?!" I motion at Connor with both palms turned upward. "Who dubbed me Lightning Dolt? Or Brown Out? Or High Vulvage?"

Both of them are snickering.

"Or Benjamin Skanklin?"

"That was Chelsea Hawkins," Ryan says confidently.

"Whatever!" I roll my eyes. "Connor called me that and everything else every single day! Or did you guys forget all that?"

"Don't look at me," Connor says cagily, reaching for another chip.

"You guys are worse than climate change deniers. It *happened*. People at North Valley were *horrible* to me! Well, you weren't, Ryan. But Connor was! Geesh! You weren't there when he tipped over the stupid portable toilet!"

"Yeah I was," Ryan says.

"What?"

"I was there to make sure it *didn't* tip all the way over. Do you think Connor stood that thing back up by himself?"

"Are you serious?"

He nods. "Those things weigh hundreds of pounds *empty*. With you in it and a full tank, it must've weighed over 700 pounds. Connor couldn't lift that much all by himself."

"I didn't need your help," Connor scoffs.

"You wish," Ryan chuckles. He looks at me. "I *made* him let me help when he told me his plan during the graduation ceremony."

Wow. Everyone really *was* an asshole to me in high school. Even Ryan. If the bombshell of being in Ryan's house wasn't still the smoking crater of surprise that it is, I would be furious at both of them. What Connor and everyone else did to me was terrible. I guess I got over it, but it still hurts to this day whenever I think about it. At that moment, Ryan leans forward for another chip, coming into the light. I get a clear view of his disfigured face. I can only imagine that the pain

Ryan carries makes mine look insignificant.

"Let it go, Electra," Ryan says. "I did." He leans over and grabs Connor by the knee. "If it wasn't for this asshole, I would've died in that fire."

All I can think is that if it wasn't for stupid Connor, he wouldn't have *crashed his car* in the first place.

Connor looks guilty as hell.

Ryan sits back in his chair. "You guys need to be together. It's obvious."

"What the fuck?" Connor blurts. "What did you do with Ryan Hansen? And what the fuck happened to me not telling you about whoever I was bangin because it made you sad, you big baby?"

Ouch. I can't believe Connor revealed something so personal about Ryan right in front of me.

"It's time I come clean," Ryan says, his face wrinkling into a dented smile.

"About what?" Connor chuckles. "Are you gay or some shit?"

"No, dumbass. I met someone."

"What?!" Connor is shocked. "When? Who? Why the fuck haven't you told me?"

"Because I didn't want to jinx it."

Connor jumps up from the easy chair. "Well fuckin tell me, Hansen! When do I get to meet her?"

"Soon. I hope. She's French. She lives in France. Her name is Cecile. She's also a burn survivor. We've been talking on Skype for six months. My high school French is coming back to me. She can cover her burns with a scarf, so she's going to fly out for Christmas. I was gonna wait until then to tell you. She's beautiful, Connor."

"No fuckin way! Do you have any pics?"

I've never seen Connor this boyishly excited. None of his cocky macho artifice. This is the *real* Connor Hughes. The one I've never seen before.

Ryan nods. "I'll show you. Come on."

We follow Ryan upstairs to his bedroom. It looks like any other high school boy's bedroom. Ryan may be our age, but I imagine his life has worked out very differently than your average 25 year old's. Unlike downstairs, the curtains are open and cool light pours into the room. He wakes up his laptop and opens some screenshots of a young woman sitting behind a computer in a different bedroom. Her face is flawless and genuinely beautiful on the left side, but savage burn scars twist up her neck and finger over her crooked jawline and up past her cheekbone on the right. Based on her radiant smile, you wouldn't think the scars bothered her at all.

"That's her?" Connor asks.

"Yeah. From talking Saturday."

"She's a fuckin fox, Ryan!"

"I know, right?" Ryan grins.

"When are you gonna bang her?" Connor quips.

"Fuck, C. Is that all you think about?"

"When I see a hottie it is."

I can't decide if Connor means it or if he's trying to make Ryan feel normal about himself. I realize it doesn't matter. The interaction between Connor and Ryan is perfectly normal. And that is a miracle. "She's beautiful, Ryan. I'm so excited for you." I mean it and look him right in the eyes, which are a sparkling green gold in this light. His beauty shines from his face.

"Thanks," he grins.

Connor chuckles. "I'll buy you a case full of condoms for your Christmas present."

"Connor!" I blurt.

"What? His dick still works. Oh, shit. Her vag isn't burned, is it?"

I grimace, but just as quickly remember how *normal* all this is.

"Yes, Cecile has a working vag," Ryan groans.

Connor grins at me. "See? He already asked her about her vag! This is awesome, Ryan. I'm so fuckin happy for you, bro."

Ryan glances at the photo of Cecile on the computer screen. "Yeah. Me too." He turns to Connor and they share a long look, both of their faces completely open and vulnerable.

I shudder, holding in tears.

ELECTRA

"That's so awesome Ryan met someone," Connor muses, sitting beside me in my car.

I'm driving around aimlessly. I don't know what else to do at the moment. "I know, right? If it wasn't for the internet, he probably never would've met her."

Connor sighs, "Amazing shit, technology."

"Can I ask you something?"

"Shit. You need your interview, don't you?"

"Yeah, but I was thinking about something else."

"What?" Connor has a huge grin on his face.

I'm not used to it. I don't know if I've ever seen it before today. "Earlier, when you said we could never be boyfriend and girlfriend, was it because of Ryan?"

His grin is gone.

I pull the car over to the sidewalk and park so I can look at him. "Please tell me, Connor."

He stares out the window for a long time.

"I know this is hard. I can't imagine what it's been like with Ryan all these years. I don't pretend to understand what he or you went through, but—"

He whips his face around, furious. "That's right! You don't understand shit, Warmoth!" He kicks the door open and jumps out, barreling down the sidewalk in the opposite direction my car is pointing.

Am I missing something?

Obviously.

But I'm not missing the way my heart races and my hands shake. I fold my arms against my chest and try to hold everything in.

What the hell is wrong with Connor? Is he crazy? Why would he act that way? Ryan basically gave us permission to date. But apparently, Connor only wants sex. Only that seems too simple. There's something I'm missing here. But I can't think of what it might be.

Then again, maybe I'm not missing anything.

Is it possible that Connor Hughes is a basket case and I'd be foolish to pursue anything with him? Something tells me I would be asking for heartbreak if I opened up to him. I don't want to go through that again. Once was enough. Dylan Montgomery nearly ruined me.

I lean my forehead against the steering wheel and sigh.

One thing is for sure.

Connor Hughes makes me miserable.

That fact hasn't changed one bit since day one.

In the mean time, I have mere hours to finish this godforsaken interview. If Connor isn't going to help, then I'll have to figure something else out.

But what?

I've got it.

I put the car in gear and make a U-turn.

I have a plan.

Chapter 16

CONNOR

I'm fuckin miserable.

I go out drinking every night for two weeks straight. Tons of chicks throw themselves at me. All I manage to do is throw up on one or two of them. I don't care. I don't want to hook up with any of them anyway. I can't even get a hard on.

But that's okay. When I get tired of this booze bender, I'll get it up in no time and go on a pussy bender. Then I can make up for all the fuckin I've missed. The only problem with being sober is the nightmares always come back. I hate that shit. No wonder I used to drink so much back in the day. Drinking kept a smile on my face. I didn't want Ryan knowing how miserable I felt about everything. Shit, *I* didn't want to know how miserable I felt. If Gloria hadn't come along and pulled me out of the gutter, I'd probably be dead already. Too bad she turned into a possessive money-hungry bitch.

Man, I don't want to think about all this shit.

I need to get back to either some serious drinkin or some serious fuckin ASAP.

I haven't gotten a single text from Lex since taking her to Ryan's house. It's for the best. Her and I are a bad idea. I'm better off fuckin randoms. That's the life for me. Not knowing any women for more than a screw or two.

The only problem is that people are starting to recognize me. I blame *TMZ*. And L.A. People in this town are more obsessed with celebrity and fame-whoring than any place else I've been. I don't want anything to do with it.

I avoid Ryan's house. I don't know why. I should be happy for him. Shit, I *am* happy for him. But I'm not happy for me. And I don't want to bother him with my shit. He has enough of his own. Just because he has a girlfriend in France doesn't mean he can walk out of the house without people staring at him.

Why should my life be any easier?

So I hole up in my apartment and let the world pass by.

Gloria has called a bunch of times and left messages. I won't answer the phone, and I won't answer the door when she comes by. But I listen to the voicemails. She has work for me. Not just more book covers. Now that people have seen my face, I guess I'm the next new thing. *Men's Fitness* wants me on the next cover. So does *Men's Health*. I don't give a shit. They'll stop calling eventually. I don't want my face out there any more than it already is.

I never bothered to call Xavier Soto at Torrent Films because: *why?* I'm not an actor. I don't wanna do a fuckin movie.

There's more important things than being famous or making money.

I don't really know what happened with the *Trending Magazine* interview. Maybe Lex got enough from our conversations to put something together to keep her boss happy. Good for her. I don't want to bring her down too.

I drag myself out of bed where I've been staring at the ceiling for the last two hours and open my fridge. Shit. No more beer. I'll have to go buy some. It's almost dinner time.

A sixer of micro brew stout hangs from one hand as I walk back from the grocery store. I tip one of the open bottles to my mouth and swallow creamy brown beer. I love this shit. And I don't give a shit that I'm not supposed to be drinkin in public. There are never cops around this part of L.A. anyway.

When I get back to my apartment, my phone is blinking. A text from Lex.

Can you be at a photo shoot tomorrow at 11am? It's for the *Trending* cover. Ryan will be there. Here's the address...

What the fuck?

Is she serious?

Ryan at a *photo* shoot?

I blurt a laugh that echoes in my empty apartment.

Why the fuck not?

CONNOR

The photo studio is a brick building in Hollywood. I buzz the intercom and give my name and they buzz me in. The chick at the front desk walks me to the big back room. It's set up with studio lights and a gray backdrop. People mill about getting shit ready.

Ryan stands in a corner talking to a random dude who nods at everything Ryan says. He's wearing mirrored shades, the L.A. Dodgers cap I gave him two years ago, and a black bandana over his face.

I walk up, smiling. "Dude, you look like an outlaw tagger. Where's your can of spray paint?"

"Hey, man. I wasn't sure if you were coming."

"I figured I had to run interference for you if anyone got out of hand. What the fuck is going on?"

"We're doing a cover shoot."

"*We*? What the fuck are you talking about, Rye?"

"It was Electra's idea. She wants me on the cover too."

"Like this? In a fuckin mask? Fuck that shit, man." I'm pissed. What was she thinking? Did she trick him into doing this? Into wearing a fuckin Halloween costume instead of showing his face? What kind of shallow shit is that?

"No, man. I just wore this for the ride over. I left it on so nobody would stare at me."

I snort, "You look like a fuckin criminal and you think no one is going to stare?"

"Not in Hollywood," he laughs.

"You're right about that shit. Did anyone ask for an autograph thinkin you were Banksy or some shit?"

"No. But I should tell people I am. Or say I'm that Shepard Fairey guy. I think he lives around here somewhere."

"You're a goon, Hansen," I snicker and nudge his arm with my elbow, but not too hard. His scars still bother him after seven years. He's always putting lotion on to keep them from drying out. "Are your parents here?"

"Yeah. I told them I needed a chauffeur since I was going to be a big star now."

"In your own mind, Hansen," I joke and look around the room. I spot his parents at the craft services table pouring coffee for themselves. I wave, "Hey, Mr. and Mrs. H!"

They wave back and his mom says, "Hi, Connor!"

I'm about to go talk to them when the sound of clicking heels on concrete stops me.

"Hey, Connor!" Lex comes walking up, rockin the tight skirt and glasses, looking hot as fuckin hell.

"How did you talk him into this shit, Warmoth?" It's good to see her, but I'm not gonna act like it.

"It was really *both* our ideas." She smiles at Ryan. "I mentioned to Ryan that I was, um, *touched* by the interaction between you two. Since you told me *your* side of the story, I asked Ryan if he wouldn't mind telling his."

I'm blown the fuck away. "Are your parents okay with this, Rye?" They're very protective of him.

He shrugs. "I'm twenty-five. They can suck it."

I smirk, "Are you sure you're up for this, bro?"

He nods, "I keep seeing that Caitlyn Jenner thing on TV and all I can think is that guy is a fucking weirdo. But you know what? I'm just like him. Bruce Jenner was a guy who got up every morning and saw a face in the mirror he didn't want. How am I any different? People stare at me every time I walk out my front door. Same thing for Jenner. But he's not afraid to show the world how weird he is. He, I mean *she*, is risking her life putting it out there. But she's normalizing it. Maybe burn survivors need someone like me to put my face out in public with no apologies. If people see burn survivors all the time, they'll get used to it. Ever since Jenner outed himself, and you got the balls to show your face at that Rom Com Con thing, I thought maybe it was time I grew a sack and did it too." He puts his arm around me. "And what better way to get my message out there than by riding your coattails, C? I like the idea of having your ugly mug next to mine."

"Why?"

"To make *me* look better, dumbass!"

I grin at him.

Lex smiles at me hopefully.

I want to fuckin cry.

I'm so proud of Ryan, I start to fuckin tear up in front of both of them.

"What do you think?" Lex asks like she's asking *my* permission to do the shoot.

"Yeah." I'm all choked up. "Let's do it."

ELECTRA

"Check that shit out," Connor says appreciatively, admiring the finished cover of *Trending Magazine* while leaning his muscled tattooed forearms on the coffee shop table beside me. The upcoming issue featuring Connor and Ryan on the cover and my in-depth interview with both of them won't hit the stands for another week, but I got an advanced copy from Vince today.

The cover line reads: *SCARS*. Below that in smaller type, the pull reads: *That Heal The Heart*.

We sit outside at a sidewalk cafe in Beverly Hills near Rodeo Drive, enjoying the end of summer weather while people in expensive clothes with expensive hair and expensive plastic surgery stroll by with expensive designer shopping bags on their arms. Every few minutes, a priceless sports car rumbles by. Business as usual in upscale 90210.

My arm presses against Connor's. "You guys look great together. I can't believe how well the photos turned out."

"Ryan was right. I look ugly next to him," Connor jokes.

"You look great, Connor. Look at that smile."

In the photo, Connor is shirtless and pumped. His romance cover physique is as delicious as always, but this time, instead of having his tattooed arm around the wasp waist of a beautiful faceless woman, it's thrown over Ryan's shoulders. Ryan wears a T-shirt and jeans but nothing covering his face. His burn scars are impossible to miss. They were not touched up in Photoshop in any way. He insisted on it.

During the photo shoot, the saucy camaraderie between Connor and Ryan quickly took over the room. Those two busted each other's balls like the lifelong friends that they are. Their energy was contagious. Everyone at the shoot was laughing at their jokes like they were at a comedy club. When Connor and Ryan get on a roll, they're incredibly funny. Any self-consciousness Ryan may have had walking into the shoot disappeared entirely by the end. And all that relaxed fun energy made it into the photos. The shot Vince Pitts selected for the final image shows Ryan and Connor in the middle of laughter. Despite Ryan's scars, the first thing you notice about the photo is how much fun he and Connor are having together. The cover couldn't have come out any better.

"I can't wait to show this to Rye," Connor says softly, his voice raspy.

I squeeze his hand. "We can bring it over later."

I've spent a lot of time at the Hansen house in the past two months getting to know the family's story. In that time, Ryan's burn scars have become almost completely normal to me. Ryan was right. You eventually get past the shock of seeing it. Connor helped with that. All he sees is his best friend. He truly doesn't notice Ryan's scars. You quickly realize there's an intelligent, funny, charming human being underneath the disfiguring scars, a person with hopes and dreams and feelings like everybody else.

Connor skims his fingers across the magazine cover and smiles at me, his face a mixture of profound emotions. "It's perfect, Lex. I can't thank you enough for everything you've done for Ryan. I've never seen him so relaxed around so many strangers. He had a blast that day at the shoot."

I never would've believed that Connor Hughes had a soft spot anywhere under all those hard muscles and sharp-edged tattoos and his smart mouth, but he does. He's not an asshole. He's a wonderful man with a huge heart. "Thanks to you," I smile. "If you hadn't introduced me to Ryan, all I would've had was a shallow exposé about a muscled manwhore."

He chuckles. "How is that bad? You know women can never get enough of that shit." He winks at me and swallows a big gulp of his iced coffee. "You especially."

I smirk. "Me? You know I *hate* manwhores." I elbow him in the bulging bicep.

"Uh huh. That's why you spend so much time with me."

He's right. Connor and I have spent plenty of time together since our unexpected reunion at Rom Com Con. "Off the subject, but you know what I found out?"

"That you can't stop thinking about me for more than half a second?"

"You wish," I giggle. "But, no. Remember that guy Romeo Fabiano? The one helping us out at the convention?"

"Yeah. What about him?"

"I looked him up on Facebook and found out *he* went to North Valley too."

"No shit?"

"Yep. He started in 2009, a year after we graduated."

"Small world, huh?"

"*Soooo* THIS is the *little* bitch," a strange voice chortles with dripping judgement.

I look up into the eyes of an attractive woman in a tight tailored navy business suit. Her straight ink black hair cascades over fine features, full lips, and tan skin. She holds a paper to-go cup in one hand and her iPhone in the other. Her nails are an expensive French manicure with a classy hint of glitter. I have no idea who she is. But she's smirking at me like she knows me.

I shake my head. "I'm sorry, I don't…"

Connor grunts. "Gloria."

I mutter to him, "Who is she?"

Gloria cuts in, "I'm his agent. *And* his girlfriend. Is he fucking you too, sweetie?"

Girlfriend? I glare at Connor, instantly furious. I should've known. I shake my head, stunned. I *really* should've known! Just because Connor is friends with Ryan doesn't change the fact he screws lots of women. People don't change. I am an idiot. And I have no one to blame but myself.

Gloria smiles victoriously. "He didn't tell you about me, did he? Oh, *thaaat's* right. He and I have a *Don't Ask, Don't Tell* policy. I suppose that applies to you too. Did he not tell you that?"

I shift my seat away from Connor so we're no longer hip to hip. "What's going on, Connor?"

Connor's face is a dark mess. He stares at Gloria with rancid hatred.

"Well?" I press.

"She's my agent. And…"

I wince, waiting for the knockout blow that will put me on the canvas.

Connor shifts forward, leaning his arms on the table again. "She's *not* my girlfriend. She was *never* my girlfriend."

"Oh, *really*?" she scoffs. "Who found you that apartment of yours? Who bought your dining room set? Who picked out your curtains?"

Connor smirks, "I *let* you do that shit because you're a bossy bitch."

"Damn right I am," she chuckles. "And I'm also the bossy bitch who is FUCKING—" she jabs her finger at him "—YOU." She jabs again.

Connor shakes his head, disgusted. "Not so loud, Gloria. One of your *other* boyfriends might hear you."

I stand up, irritated with both of them. "I think the two of you need to have a talk. *Without* me." I pull out my chair for Gloria. "Here. Be my guest." I turn to walk away.

"Wow, Connor," she smiles at him and chuckles as she slips into my chair. "This one is a *pushover*. I thought you liked your sluts on the side with a little more attitude."

I spin around and—*CRACK!!*—slap her across the jaw.

She tumbles out of the chair.

"I'm nobody's *slut*," I growl.

"Oh shit!" Connor gasps. "*That* happened!"

That also felt really good.

"Help me up, Connor!" Gloria barks, her ass on the sidewalk cement and both red-soled Louboutins flailing above the seat of the chair like a helpless turtle. She grabs the chair back with one hand and waves at him with the other, completely unable to stand on her own.

I notice her nude shoes have stiletto heels that are wavy and actually quite cute. They've been all the rage in L.A. this summer. They also cost $1,000 and I could never afford them. "*Love* the shoes," I smirk sarcastically.

"Connor!' she growls.

Connor stands up, grabbing the magazine off the table. He smiles at me, "You know, I've been wanting to do that for five years. But I would never hit a woman. Doesn't mean *you* can't." He winks at me.

I laugh.

Gloria screams. "I'm going to sue your ass off, you little bitch!"

I shrug. "Sue away. I don't have any money anyway."

Gloria screeches. "Don't worry, you little *slut*. My lawyer—"

Connor cuts in, "Are you sure you want to call her a slut again? After she dropped you like that?"

Gloria growls at him and tries to stand up. But she can't because her tailored skirt is so tight and her back is right up against the brick wall of the cafe. The woman sitting beside her stares down like Gloria is a rabid wolverine. Realizing no one is going to help her, Gloria kicks at the metal chair and it rattles loudly against the metal table. The other customers all stare, as do the expensively dressed shoppers walking by. "You bitch! The second I call my lawyer, he'll—"

I roll my eyes. "You don't even know my name. Let's go, Connor." I'm surprised I say it, but after slapping Gloria and her bitchy tirade that followed, I at least want to hear him out before jumping to conclusions. And yes, I'm gloating. There's a certain satisfaction to walking away with Connor by my side when Gloria so obviously wants him.

"Don't worry!" Gloria hollers as we walk down the wide sidewalk, "I know where to find you. Electra *Warmoth*."

I almost stop.

"Ignore her," Connor mutters, moving me along by the elbow. "She's all talk."

"It was nice knowing you, Connor!" she shouts. "Good luck finding another agent willing to put up with your bullshit!"

"Maybe you should talk to her?" I suggest, concerned. I don't want to cause career trouble for Connor. In this town, a good agent can mean the difference between starving and thriving.

"Fuck her," he grunts.

"You already did," I quip sourly.

"Don't remind me. I was a stupid confused kid when she found me.

I've grown a lot since then. Let's go. I don't need Gloria fuckin Powers in my life anyway."

"Are you sure?"

"Yeah." He gives me a cocky grin. "I don't need *her*."

I search his eyes. Was he just implying he doesn't need *her* but he needs *me*? I don't know. I'm probably reading too much into it. Who am I kidding? I don't *really* want Connor anyway.

Do I?

Chapter 17

ELECTRA

"You totally fuckin want me," Connor mutters, nuzzling against me in the candlelit booth at ReaXion two weeks later.

"So did Gloria," I grumble.

"So does every other woman in this restaurant."

He's right. Ever since we walked into the trendy restaurant on Melrose to get dinner, the women here have *all* been checking him out. In fact, *before* we walked in, they were checking him out too. There are lots of cute young things on Melrose shopping and bar hopping this time of night, and they couldn't keep their eyes off Connor. I should be used to it by now, but I'm not. I glare at him, "Have I ever told you how cocky you are?"

"Once or twice," he grins.

If his masculine scent wasn't so intoxicating, and if his rugged beauty wasn't so irresistible, I would have walked away from whatever this thing is we have going *weeks* ago. But I can't resist him.

He leans in and breathes in my ear, "Do you have any idea how cocky I am right now?" He grabs my hand and places it on his crotch beneath the table.

He's cocky all right. I can feel him straining against his jeans.

"Does your hard on ever go away?" I titter.

"Not when you're around, Lex..."

I never get tired of him calling me that. It's something that helps me distance myself from thousands of painful high school memories involving Connor. I do my best never to think about those dreary years when we're together.

Are we dating? Not officially. We're having a lot of sex. Ever since my article hit the stands, we have no real reason to see each other. Any pretext that I need to interview him further or clarify some little detail or get his approval on something or other is gone. But he keeps calling me, I keep taking his calls, and we keep sleeping together. Correction, having sex and him going home afterward. What happened to me being the one who walked out first? I guess since I was the one who established that precedent our first night together in his room at the Beverly Hills Resort, I can hardly blame him. One of these days we might actually discuss our official relationship status. For now, I don't want to think about it because his hand has worked its way under the hem of my slinky red sundress.

He mutters in my ear. "Are you ever not hot and wet when I'm around?"

I part my thighs and slouch slightly, giving him better access. "I blame you for that," I giggle. "You've turned me into a sex vampire."

"Fuck, woman. I can't find any panties." His fingers tease me.

I smirk smugly at him. "Again, your *faulllllllt*..." I moan when I feel his fingers sliding up and down my wet cleft. I admit it. Connor sparked my sex binge. I'm making up for years of dry spell. If things don't last, does it really matter? I deserve at least another seven hundred orgasms before I go back into sex retirement to focus on my career. "*Connor*..." I moan.

Our perky waitress suddenly interrupts. "Would you two like any dessert?"

Good thing this place has tablecloths. Otherwise she'd see my wide open thighs, my red sundress hiked up to my hips, and Connor's fingers *invading* my nakedness.

While working some kind of hand magic on my clit, Connor smirks at her, "Do you have any of those cream filled cannolis? I think she wants one. A really *big* one..."

If I wasn't on the verge of coming, I might say something snappy to Connor followed by an apology to our waitress for his rudeness. But I can barely keep my eyes open as waves of pleasure radiate out from my sweet center.

"I'm sorry," Perky smiles, "We don't." She looks me right in the eyes, ignoring Connor. "But we do have a super delicious strawberry whipped cream cake. The strawberries are fresh and *that* has whipped cream. How does that sound?" She's staring straight at me, waiting for an honest answer.

I can't answer her because anything I say will come out in a moan. Maybe she'll think I'm high or drunk. It's a plausible explanation here on Melrose.

She's waiting.

Connor is stroking my pussy.

Stroke stroke stroke.

I have to say *something*. But the only thing that comes out of my mouth as I sink further into the cushioned booth is, *"Aaaahhhh…"* What did you expect I would say? That I wanted extra whipped *cream*? The kind that *comes* in a can so you can shoot it down your throat? I repress another moan. I'm going to lose it right in front of her. I don't care if she *does* watch me come. It won't make any difference to me because my eyes are now nearly clamped shut, blocking out everything except what Connor's fingers are doing. Oh, gawd. The sensation of him sliding inside me nearly sends me over the edge.

Perky blinks several times, her hands folded politely together in front of her, waiting.

I feel bad for her she has to endure this. Me on the other hand? I feel wonderful.

Connor says, "I think we could use a minute. Or do you need *longer*?" He looks at me pointedly.

Stroke stroke stroke.

"I…" Can't speak.

"It's a *hard* decision, I know," he jokes.

Stroke stroke stroke.

I'm about to tell him to *fuck off*, but I really just want to tell him to *fuck me*. For Perky's sake, I don't say anything. Instead I squeeze Connor's jeans-sheathed hardness, which has been in my hand this whole time.

"Yeah," Connor grunts. "Give us a minute."

Perky giggles nervously. "I'll leave the dessert menu with you. Take your time." She sets the menu on the table like she's afraid she'll catch something if she get's too close before hurrying off.

Are people watching us? I don't care. But I am aware of the sounds of conversation and clinking silverware all around us.

Like I said, I *really* don't care.

I unbuckle Connor's belt with one hand. It's awkward, and he has to help, but we get it done. He shifts so I can unbutton his fly and zip it down. His cock nearly jumps out. If he wasn't slouching in the booth like I am, his big hard dick would be poking above the table cloth like a purple periscope.

Again, I don't care.

Because the thrill sizzling between my legs has made me come dumb.

I start to stroke Connor's cock, keeping it against his hard abs. He lifts the hem of his shirt and drapes it over my hand so it's *sort of* covering things.

He snickers, "We're totally gonna get thrown out for this. Our waitress is probably telling her manager right now."

"I don't care," I moan, swirling my thumb around the tip of his cock, skimming across a drop of pre-cum that I use to slicken him.

"Me neither." He drops his head against the booth cushions and hisses, "Fuck, Lex. Like that."

My cheek squishes against his muscled shoulder. I'm half tempted to go down on him. But I peer through a slit in my eyelid and I'm very aware of the dozens of people who would definitely notice. "This is so wrong," I whisper. But it feels so right. So does his cock in my hand. I pump the shaft and work the head as best I can with one hand. It's hard to concentrate because of what he's doing with *his* hand.

"You're starting to come, I can feel it."

This is the dirtiest thing I've *ever* done.

The waitress is going to be back any second. She's going to ask if we've decided on a dessert, and I'm going to look her in the eye as I come. Because Connor isn't giving me any other choice. Thankfully, because that would just be *weird*, I start to come right now.

"Oh, Connor," I mutter. I forget all about his cock as I come on his hand. I don't even know if I'm still holding *him* because all I can think about is the hard orgasm hammering through me.

"Fuck," he grunts. "Fuck, fuck, fuck."

That's when I realize he's coming too, shooting hot cum up under his shirt. I cup my fingers around the head of his cock, wanting to catch it. It's hot and sticky in my hand. His cock throbs and pulses with each spurt as he squirms in his seat.

I *really* hope nobody notices us now.

The white noise of everyone in the restaurant becomes piercingly loud as I come down from my orgasm.

Nobody is staring at us. I don't see Perky anywhere, which is good, because I have a handful of hot cum.

Breathless, my eyes still fluttering half closed, I say, "I guess she was wrong about those cream filled cannolis."

Connor represses a snorting laugh and leans his head against mine. "What am I gonna do with you, Warmoth?"

I can think of a thousand things...

CONNOR

"I can't believe you smeared my load all over my abs," I laugh as we stumble out of ReaXion and onto Melrose, which is packed with people on a warm summer night like this.

"Me neither," Lex giggles, holding onto my elbow, both of us fuck drunk from coming together. "But I couldn't think where else to put it."

"I can think of a place." I slap her on the ass and she jumps.

"I bet you can." She tosses her hair, which is down for once, and gives me this sex kitten look over her shoulder as we walk.

The red fuck-me sundress she's wearing is killing me. I was starting to think she didn't own anything other than tight skirts and blouses—not that that's a bad thing—and she surprises me this afternoon wearing this thing. It barely covers her ass when she walks. Her auburn hair flows over her shoulders like a mahogany breeze. The brown cowboy boots add up to her being so ridiculously hot every guy on the sidewalk is turning heads to stare at her. She has *no* idea how fine she is. But I do. She looks like a fuckin supermodel. Knowing she's got no panties on under the dress makes her *illegally* hot. I keep waiting for the dress to catch air so I can see the crack of her impossibly tight ass. My nuts tighten at the thought.

Fuck, I'm hard again. I need to be inside her sometime in the next ten minutes or my balls are going to explode.

I don't know what it is about Lex, but she's the sexiest woman I've ever met. It's not just her looks. The way she slapped Gloria the other day? I smile every time I think about it. I don't give a fuck that Gloria tore up my contract with her. I needed a reason to move on anyway. She definitely did a lot for my career, and the sex was good in the beginning. But she became such a pain in my ass, not even her cutthroat agenting was worth the bullshit she put me through. And now that my face is out there, who knows? Maybe I'll get high profile work. I don't care either way. Right now I'm happy hangin with Lex. She's all I need. I fuckin *hope* she feels the same way, but I doubt it. She's going to get bored of me sooner or later. At the end of the day, I'm just a fuckin brainless model. She's the one with a good head on her shoulders.

"What's on your mind?" She asks as we walk up a side street to where her car is parked.

"Nothin." I grin at her. I don't know how to talk about this kind of shit. Relationship shit. I've never talked to any women about anything except how I'm going to fuck them. Speaking of which, the way her red sundress is bouncing around her ass pulls my thoughts right back to what I'm gonna do to it the second I get my hands on her. "I'm gonna fuck you in that dress."

"Who says I'm going to let you?" She winks at me, her hair flying everywhere.

Kill me now. I'm already in heaven looking at her.

When we get to where her Honda is parked on a neighborhood side street, I push her up against the driver's side door, her ass facing me, and pin her there with my crotch. I don't waste any time hooking my hand under that red fuckin dress so I can feel the heat of her pussy. It practically burns my fingers, it's so god damn hot and wet. "You want me to fuck you right here, don't you? You want me to peel this dress over your ass and stick my dick in you and fuck the shit out of you while the whole neighborhood watches and hears you moan, don't you?"

"You're crazy, Connor," she moans, pushing her ass against my dick.

I almost fuckin come right then. But I don't because a mom in jogging clothes following a boy and a girl on bikes with training wheels and those cute little helmets and all the pink and blue bike gear come pedaling by. The two kids stop and stare at us, their feet on the ground and their hands on the handlebars.

I hide my hands behind my back like a guilty fuck.

Lex shoves her dress down.

The mom scowls at us.

All curious, the little girl says, "Mommy, what are they doing?"

The boy just fuckin stares at Lex. I can't blame him.

Good thing Lex's Honda is between us and them.

"Don't pay any attention to them, you two," the mom growls, hustling the kids along.

I call out, "Her door was stuck. I was helping her unlock it." I feel like a fuckin tool. The second after the kids pass by, I whisper in Lex's ear, "Gimme your keys."

"Why?"

"I'm taking you home. We need to get there before my balls blow, so I'm driving."

"No you're not," she scoffs. "*I'm* driving. You probably can't see straight without any blood in your brain."

I chuckle, "Didn't anyone ever tell you I'm the one who calls the shots?"

"Didn't anyone ever tell you your dick isn't a magic wand that can make women do anything you want?" She winks at me, jingling her car keys in front of me.

I laugh and she laughs with me.

She pins me with her eyes. Magic eyes. Eyes that do shit to me that makes me really fuckin uncomfortable. Eyes that make me forget how totally fuckable she is and think only about how much I… "Fuck, Lex. I —" I can't say it. I can't tell her how I feel.

"What?"

I close my eyes hard. "Nothin."

"What, Connor?"

"Never mind. Let's just go." I gently take her car keys from her hand and unlock her door. "Get in. You can drive."

She climbs in the car and I close the door and hand her the keys and walk around to the passenger side. She leans over and opens the door for me and I drop into the seat. "What was that about, Connor?"

"I don't know." I'm all quiet.

"If you want to talk, Connor, I'm here. Say whatever is on your mind. It's okay. I won't judge." She means it.

I want to tell her everything. Finally get it all off my chest. I look at her for a long time. I *want* to tell her. But I don't want to talk about *it*. I *hate* fuckin talking about *it*. I never bring it up with anybody. Not even Ryan. He knows what it does to me.

"Please, Connor. Tell me."

I stare out the front window, white-knuckling the suicide handle above the door like we're driving off a fuckin cliff. The idea of talking about *it* makes me feel like I'm *already* falling over a cliff that has no fuckin bottom. I can't do it. "We should go."

She sighs hard. "What are we doing, Connor?"

"Driving home."

"No. I mean us. What are we doing?"

"You tell me."

"Damn it, Connor! Can't you say more than that? Something is on your mind. Why won't you tell me?" She's getting annoyed.

It pisses me off. Nobody makes me talk about shit I don't wanna talk about. I open the car door and climb out.

"Connor! Where are you going!" There's a desperate quality to her voice that makes me want to hurt her feelings.

I'm a dick. I don't care. She should know that by now. But I'm not gonna say anything right now because I don't know what the fuck will spill out my mouth. So I walk up the fuckin sidewalk by myself. I'm a big boy and I can fuckin walk home if I have to. Two blocks and two turns later, I'm all alone, walking past the rich homes north of Melrose.

I pull my phone out of my pocket and listen to another voicemail.

"Bad news, son," my dad says. "Your mom gambled away your entire inheritance in Vegas. Can you believe she blew it all on nickel slots?"

"I didn't blow it *all*. I only lost a hundred dollars, Finn," my mom laughs. "And we don't have an inheritance anyway."

Dad starts laughing. "What do you mean, Kell? We have the RV. We can give it to Connor after our trip. He can live in this thing like a king!"

"He won't want to live in an RV," Mom chuckles dismissively. "He needs his space, isn't that right, Connor?"

She's wrong about that. I know guys who live in their RVs. It's not a bad way to go. You can park at the beach and enjoy the view all up and down the west coast. Seattle in the summer when it's hot, San Diego in the winter when it's cold. I'd just need a trailer to tow my bike and I'd be golden. Maybe that's exactly what I need to do with my life. Get the fuck out of L.A. and never look back. Maybe Ryan can come with me and we can rob banks like fuckin Butch Cassidy and the Sundance Kid. There's worse ways to live.

"The good news is," Dad says, "if you don't want the RV, we can help you out with a down payment on your first mansion. Would you believe your old man won six hundred bucks on dollar blackjack?"

"He did, Connor! Your dad was like Dustin Hoffman in Rain Man last night! Six hundred dollars! I made him take me out to a fancy dinner."

"And afterward I took her back to the RV and I was *all* Tom Cruise *all* night long."

I grin. Fuckin Dad.

"That's awful, Finn," Mom groans while laughing. "Connor doesn't even know what Rain Man is."

"Oh, I almost forgot! We saw the Grand Canyon. It was magnificent, son. You really need to go someday. It really is one of the seven wonders of the world."

"But would you believe it's not as large as your father's mouth?" Mom giggles.

"Too true," Dad laughs. "I asked your mom if she wanted to take a donkey ride down to the bottom of the canyon, but she said she already rides *my* ass enough as it is." He laughs to himself. "Anyway, son. Our cross country adventure is almost over and we're almost home. We've had a great time, but we both miss you like crazy and we'll see you soon."

"Bye, Connor! Say hi to Ryan and his parents for us! We love you!" Mom makes kissing noises before Dad ends the call.

I stop on the sidewalk and hang my head, ready to fuckin cry right here.

"Who were you talking to?" Lex asks, leaning over to look out her passenger window at me. She must've just driven up. Fuckin Hondas. Quietest cars on the road.

"Were you following me?" I growl, instantly angry.

"Yes." She smiles.

"Don't be such a fuckin stalker, Warmoth." I turn around and fast walk the other way. I sounded like a dick, but she shouldn't be invading my privacy like that.

Her car door opens and closes and cowboy boots click behind me. "What the hell is wrong with you, Connor?!"

I slow, but don't stop. I almost stop. Fuck. I keep walking.

"Connor! Stop! Please!"

"Fuck! What?!" I turn around and glare at her. "What do you want, Warmoth?!"

She frowns, her face hardening. "You're an asshole, Connor."

I'm not arguing.

"I don't know why I bothered with you. You're no different now than you were in high school. Having sex with you was a big mistake."

I know. "What were you expecting? Prince Fuckin Charming? I'm just the cover model, Warmoth. I'm not the guy who buys roses and rings so you can take me home to your parents." Fuck, it hurts to say it. But it's true.

She stares at me.

This is the part of the story where she turns around, jumps back in her car, and drives off and I'm supposed to chase her and shit. I know. I've read a few of those corny ass books I've done covers for. But guess what? I don't play that shit. "Fuck off, Warmoth. Don't call me."

I turn around and keep walking.

ELECTRA

"Come back here, asshole!" I shout as I run after him.

He doesn't stop.

"You owe me an explanation!" I scream. You would think he would stop or at least slow down or *something*. But *nooo*, Connor keeps going. I finally catch up and grab him by the back of his shirt. "Stop already!"

He spins around, yanking his shirt free. "Go the fuck away, *Brown Out*."

"Don't call me that, Connor *Stupid!*"

"Fine, *Skanklin*. Back the fuck off and leave me the fuck alone." He's totally serious.

"What is wrong with you, Connor?"

He grinds his jaw and stares at the night sky. "I'm not going to be your fuckin boyfriend."

"Who said anything about being my boyfriend? I just asked what was on your mind and you flipped out like a crazy person!"

"Yeah, well maybe I am fuckin crazy. You should take that as a hint and move on."

"No, Connor! I'm not moving on!"

"I am." He turns to walk away.

I grab the back of his shirt again and pull as hard as I can. "Tell me what the hell is going on, Connor!"

"Would you let fuckin go, Warmoth?" He doesn't turn around but he stops.

"No! Not until you tell me what's wrong!"

He sighs heavily and rakes his hand through his hair.

I'm afraid to say anything. I don't want to spark his anger again. Instead, I place my palm gently against his back.

He winces but doesn't move away.

After a minute, he turns slowly, reaches into his pocket and pulls out his phone. He punches buttons and puts it on speaker. A voicemail from his parents plays. It sounds like they're on an RV trip in Vegas. I laugh at his dad's joke about Tom Cruise. When the message ends, he puts the phone away.

"Your parents are funny," I grin. "How come you keep them hidden away?"

"Because they're dead," he says grimly.

"What? They said they'll be home soon. Vegas is like four hours from here. They'll be in L.A. just after midnight."

"They're dead, Warmoth."

"What are you talking about?" I don't know anything about Connor's family. In high school, the only things I knew about him were what I saw in school. I have no idea what his home life was like. Or Ryan Hansen's, for that matter. We weren't friends. Now, I know all kinds of things about Ryan and his family. Thinking about it, none of them ever mentioned the first thing about Connor's parents in all the times I visited. Mr. and Mrs. Hansen never asked about Mr. and Mrs. Hughes. You'd think they would have, considering how close Connor is to them. Unless they had some kind of weird feud because of Ryan's accident? "This doesn't make any sense, Connor."

"They're dead. They died when I was twelve. My uncle raised me after that."

"Oh my god." I gasp and cover my mouth. "Are you serious?"

His voice turns robotic. "Yeah. He didn't *want* to raise me. My uncle never had any kids. He thought having a kid meant you didn't get laid anymore, so he never wanted any. And he never got married. Just had a string of girlfriends. One after the other. Always had them over at the house. Fucked them in his bedroom." He smiles morosely. "Maybe that's when I decided to start chasing girls. If it could chase away my uncle's pain, it could chase mine, I guess."

I'm still in shock. It's hard to take this all in. "I'm so sorry, Connor."

"My uncle told me straight up I was the reason for his brother's death, my dad. My parents went on that road trip because their marriage was having problems. My uncle told me they wouldn't've had any problems in the first place if I wasn't around fuckin things up for them."

"What a jerk," I mumble.

"I don't know if that part is true or not, but I do know they needed some time away from everything. They were arguing all the time for the whole year before the trip. They needed a real vacation to work things out and rekindle their romance or whatever. So they drove their RV across the country and died right before they got home."

"How? I mean, you don't have to tell me if you don't want to, but this is all so confusing." I feel guilty and awful for asking.

"Their RV had a blowout on a long downhill grade on the 15. My dad was trying to avoid hitting a fuckin *washing machine* that fell off the back of a pickup truck. The dumbshits driving it *didn't tie it down*. The CHP officer told me and my uncle that Mom and Dad's RV popped a front tire and landed on its side because of god damn *washing machine* debris. And because of the downhill, an 18-wheeler plowed into the roof of the RV's cab before it could stop, killing my parents instantly." His face is tortured and haunted.

"Oh my god, Connor. That's terrible. I'm so sorry."

"The funny thing is," he's not smiling when he says it, "if my parents' marriage *hadn't* been having problems, I would've been in that RV with them. Then we all would've died *together*. My uncle wouldn't have had to raise me. I wouldn't have had to deal with him hating my ass and me hating his, or wondering every fuckin day why my parents had to die without me." His eyes shimmer with profound sorrow.

And like that, the last piece of the puzzle that is Connor Hughes falls into place. I can't begin to imagine what his life was like after his parents' death. I don't *want* to imagine it. The guilt, the heartbreak, the misery. I can gather everything I need to know from the broken look on his face. Inside Connor's ruggedly muscled manly body is a broken little boy. My heart aches for him. "Oh, Connor. I'm so, *so* sorry." I take one of his hands in mine and hold it gently.

"Now that you know, please never ask me to talk about this again. Okay?" His face is raw and sad and infinitely heavy.

I nod slowly, my own voice shaky. "Oh—okay." Something tells me holding it all in isn't the way to go, but I'm too overwhelmed to argue and I don't think saying anything now could possibly fix this. It could take a lifetime to heal the damage he's suffered. If it can be healed at all. "Whatever you want, whatever you need, I'm here for you, Connor."

"I need to fuck you, Lex."

I'm shocked by his request. It comes from left field. I'm no grief counselor, but something tells me this isn't the healthiest way to deal with grief.

"Please," he whispers.

"What, here?" I look around the upscale neighborhood. Lights are on in the houses, cars are parked all up and down both sides of the street beneath the orange glow of the street lamps. Some shirtless guy with shaggy hair bouncing out of his headband runs by with a big dog on a leash. At least it's not little kids this time.

"Yeah." His voice is hoarse.

I consider suggesting we drive back to his place or mine, but this moment seems as fragile as Connor. I don't want to break him or it or us and risk never seeing him again. "Okay. Should we, uh, use my car?"

He nods.

For a second, I hesitate. I'm afraid Connor is using me by making this request, but maybe he isn't. My own powerful emotions coarse through my chest. Something incredible is happening between us and I know it. It's unexplainable, beyond words or any rational sense, but I *feel* the rightness of it.

We climb in the back seat. I roll up the windows and close the doors. The second I do, the outside world disappears.

We fight and fumble and kiss passionately in the back of the shadowy car, him heavy on top of me, me beneath him on the bench seat, my red sundress already above my waist. I'm still wet from the restaurant. I pull my arms out of my short sleeves and push the thin dress down into a red ribbon around my waist. He peels his shirt off and lays against me, his stomach still sticky with cum. I barely notice.

My cowboy boots are hooked around his ass as I undo his belt and pull him out.

He's rock hard.

I'm soaking wet.

"Fuck." He grunts. "I don't have any condoms. I forgot to put more in my wallet after last night."

"I'm on the pill," I gasp, breathless from kissing.

"Since when?"

"Since weeks ago. We're safe."

He stops. "Did you start the pill for me, Lex?"

"I guess so. The question is, are *you* safe?" I wince, afraid I'm ruining this moment for him and me and us.

"My uncle told me a million times to wear a rubber so I wouldn't get anybody pregnant. I guess I listened. I've never had sex without a condom. And I get tested every six months. Just in case."

I sigh softly and smile at him in the faint light, pushing a lock of hair out of his eyes.

He removes my glasses with infinite care and sets them on the center console between the front seats.

He lowers his lips to mine and we kiss softly.

He sinks into me, hot and hard.

I am ready for him, wet and aching.

The sex is slow, quiet, and intense. Every cell in my body tingles with feeling for this man. It is the best sex I've ever had, and I haven't even had an orgasm yet. We say nothing, never breaking our kiss, but our bodies say everything. I have multiple orgasms, each one building off the last. During orgasm number six, it's so damn delicious I close my eyes and see stars. My core clenches so hard, I think I'm going to tear his cock off. But he drives into me incessantly, throbbing inside me with every thrust, building toward his own intense orgasm. I feel him start to come, his cock growing impossibly large at the last moment before his own release.

As he falls into me, he breaks our kiss and buries his face between the seat cushion and my ear. His voice is raspy, tight, and afraid. *"Don't leave me, Lex."* He's crying as he orgasms, emptying himself inside me. *"Don't fuckin leave me. Please…"*

His words stir my heart, touching me more deeply than I ever thought possible. This is beyond sex, this is… *everything*. My body launches into a final life-altering seventh orgasm as his seed pours into me. I gasp and scream and nearly die as my entire body shakes beneath his.

As our orgasms fade and the silent pounding of our hearts fills the car, I whisper.

"I'm here, Connor. I'm right here."

Epilogue

ELECTRA

ONE YEAR LATER…

Dust kicks up behind the RV as we drive down the long dirt road leading to my parents' farm house at the back of their walnut farm. We pass row after row of leafy green walnut trees.

"This place is beautiful," Connor says, at the wheel of the RV.

To my complete surprise, Connor Hughes is still in my life. To be honest, I thought after he told me about his parents, things between us would implode in a matter of weeks or even days. The way Connor stuffs everything down, whether it's about his parents, being raised by his uncle, even how he deals with the aftermath of Ryan's accident, *screams* hot mess. I kept waiting for Connor to have a meltdown and run away again. But he didn't.

Are we dating?

I'm not really sure what we're doing. But we see each other almost every day. We don't live together and I don't know if we ever will, but I try to stay focused on the present moment. I learned that novel concept from my hippie parents.

I also see Ryan Hansen and his family all the time. They're very much Connor's family, and we've all become very close since my article about Connor and Ryan went public.

As promised, Cecile flew out for Christmas. She and Ryan are officially a couple. It's a long distance thing for now, but I think those two will go the distance. Their biggest struggle is where to live. Cecile wants to move to the U.S. Ryan wants to move to France. Go figure.

So here I am with Connor, visiting my *parents*. I never thought *that* would happen. But I've spent so much time with Connor's extended family (the Hansens), I decided it was time I introduce him to mine.

We pass a wooden sign nailed to the rustic ranch fence that runs between the orchard and the house.

He chuckles. "Warmoth Walnuts?"

I scoff, "I didn't name it." I'm nervous about bringing Connor to my parents' ramshackle hippie paradise, but he insisted we stop here. "This farm and the farm house are *literally* a hundred years old." I groan. "I hope you don't mind using an outhouse, because that's all they have."

"This place has an *outhouse*?" He wheels the RV into a dirt area beside the farm house, parking in the shade of the trees.

"I told you it was old." It's embarrassing to say it, but my parents have never had any money. It's sad that this RV has better plumbing than my parents' *house*. They should've stayed in the apartment we had in high school. "I *hate* that smelly outhouse. Getting up to pee in the middle of the night is the *worst*. Especially when it's cold out. Your butt freezes to the seat if you don't hover. Hover-peeing while you're half asleep is *really* annoying." I glare at him. "And don't you even *think* about trying to tip it over when I'm in it."

"Awww, I would *never* do that," he winks.

"You better not. If you do, I'll lock you in there with the nearest skunk."

"Are there skunks out here?"

"Yes. And they *hate* practical jokers like you and will spray you on sight."

He shuts off the engine. The silence of the remote farm is immediate. "I can't get over how quiet it is out here. You wouldn't know L.A. was only an hour away."

"Trust me, sometimes it can get *too* quiet out here."

We step out of the RV and look around. The screen door on the covered porch of the farm house opens and my mom and dad walk down the steps.

I smirk, "See? I told you they were hippies."

"They look like farmers to me."

"Fine. But they're *hippie* farmers. Don't let their lack of paisley and tie-dye fool you." I'm a little bit worried how my parents will treat Connor. After all, they knew about how he treated *me* in high school.

Dad walks up to Connor and hugs him without shaking hands. "I'm Gerry Warmoth. You can call me Gerry." He wraps his arms around me, his eyes wet. "So good to see you, Sunshine."

I hug back. "Good to see you too, Dad. I mean, Gerry."

He chuckles, still weepy.

"I'm Sage," Mom smiles her sunflower smile and hugs Connor like he's her long lost son, patting him on the back. "So good to finally meet you. Are you two ready for some lunch?"

"I'm starving," Connor smiles.

Mom serves walnut butter and fig sandwiches. We sit at the picnic-style table on the screened off front porch, eating in the warm summer breeze. For dessert, Mom serves walnut maple pie. Our conversation covers an abbreviated version of what's been happening over the past year.

My parents have turned Warmoth Walnuts into a burgeoning business. They now have their organic certification and ship their walnuts all over the U.S. and Canada, and are working on a contract with a major distributor in the U.K. Mom has developed her own line of flavored walnuts that sells in all the health food stores, and she's trying to get them into Whole Foods. With the money they've made, they put in two bathrooms in the old farm house. No more late night trips to the outhouse!

Connor completely cut ties with Gloria and found a new agent at CAA, one of the biggest talent agencies in Hollywood. He also did that screen test for Xavier Soto and Torrent Films. To his surprise, they cast him in the movie. Not a big budget feature film, but it's still an actual movie that will air on the Lifetime Movie Network this fall. Connor isn't a Hugh Jackman or a Channing Tatum. Yet. But, with Connor's natural abilities as an actor and his incredible looks, the sky is the limit.

As for me, I still haven't won the Pulitzer Prize, but I was lucky enough to be officially nominated in the feature writing category. Late last year, Vince Pitts saw to it that my article about Connor and Ryan was excerpted in the L.A. Times and he secretly submitted it for consideration to the Pulitzer Board, if you can believe that. Now I get to put *Pulitzer Nominated* on all my bylines.

"Do you two have plans with that RV of yours?" Dad asks. "Or did you just drive it out so Sunshine wouldn't have to use the old outhouse?"

I shake my head and snort. Ugh. Appreciating my parents and their hippie ways will take some work.

"We're going on a cross country road trip," Connor says. "To see all the famous American destinations." He smiles at me. "The Grand Canyon. The Mile High City. The Windy City. The Big *Ass*pple." He smirks at me.

"The big *what*?" Dad asks.

"The Big *Apple*," I grin, rolling my eyes.

Dad lifts his eyebrows. "You mean New York?"

"Yeah," Connor smiles.

"That sounds like a fun trip," Mom says. "I'm sure it will bring you two closer together."

Connor gives me a strange look.

I smile at him for a moment.

Suddenly uncomfortable, I look out the porch screens at the endless rows of walnut trees surrounding the farm house. It's getting close to harvest time. The green-hulled nuts are already falling from the trees.

I can't escape the feeling that this road trip is the beginning of the end for Connor and I. Not that something tragic will happen. Well, not like we'll die. But I can't escape the feeling that after the trip, Connor and I won't last once the sex eventually gets old (which seems impossible) or his career takes off and he gets too busy for me or who knows what.

Dad stands up from his chair, finished with his walnut pie. "Want a tour of the farm, Connor?"

"Sure," he smiles. "You coming, Lex?"

"I've already seen it," I smile. "Don't let him put you to work."

Connor chuckles, "I won't mind. I've got a belly full of walnut sandwiches to keep me going."

Dad pats him on the back and they walk down the porch steps together.

ELECTRA

I help Mom clean up in the kitchen.

"He sure is *cute*, Elle."

"I know," I smirk, sponging a soapy plate in the sink. "Don't let him hear you say that. His ego is already big enough."

"How are things between you two?"

I sigh. "It's complicated."

"Love is *always* complicated, Elle."

"I don't know if I'd call it love."

"It looks like love to me."

"Well, he's never *told* me he loves me."

Mom looks thoughtful. "Never?"

I shake my head.

"Are you sure? Maybe he said it and you forgot."

I level a look at her. "I think I'd remember, Mom."

"Do you love him?

"I guess." I hate to say it out loud. It feels like I'm opening myself up for disaster.

"Have *you* told him you love him?"

"No, but…" I roll my eyes. "Isn't the guy supposed to say it first?"

"Does it really matter *who* says it?"

"Ugh! Mom! Why do you always have to be so annoying?"

She chuckles to herself while setting a freshly rinsed plate in the dish rack. "If you love him, you should tell him, Elle."

"Do you remember what happened with Dylan Montgomery at UCLA?"

"That was a few years ago, honey. Remind me."

I huff, "I told Dylan I loved him after three months. Three months *later*, I found out he'd been a cheating bastard the whole time we were going out! I swore I'd never tell another guy I loved him after that."

"Maybe it's time you reconsidered your vow," she smiles. "I have a good feeling about Connor."

"You and your feelings. What if they're wrong?"

"The only way you'll find out is by taking a risk with your heart. Love is *always* a risk. That's why it's important."

"If you say so," I groan.

ELECTRA

After dinner that evening, the four of us play Scrabble on the porch under the soft light of an old Coleman lantern. I kick ass. Connor and my parents try to compete, but nobody knows the two-letter words as well as I do.

Despite my protests, Connor convinces me to sleep in the guest bedroom instead of the RV. Mom and Dad are of course pleased. I have to admit, they've fixed up the farm house nicely. It now has a charming country style that is very homey. They sure have turned this place around.

"Can you help me get this window open?" I snarl at Connor as I fight with it in the moonlit bedroom. "It's glued shut and this place is an oven."

"Give it some muscle, Warmoth," Connor chuckles, lying on the bed naked.

"*You* give it some muscle, Connor Huge." I giggle.

He comes up behind me, pressing his naked hard on against my granny panties.

"Back off, buster. Not in my parents' house," I bark. He apparently didn't read the rulebook before coming here. "If you try anything, I'll have to school you like I did at Scrabble."

"You can school me in the bedroom all you want."

"I'm talking about the kind of school where you study books and take exams and get detention. The un-fun kind."

"As long as you're the teacher, I'm game," he grins, easily opening the old window. He gazes out at the full moon.

I stare at *his* full moon. "Would you get away from the window? You're totally naked."

"The only people watching are the walnut trees."

"You never know with my parents around. They could be outside naked moon bathing," I snicker.

He turns around, his cock staring straight at me. He arches an eyebrow.

"No, Connor," I hiss, irritated. "I don't want to have sex in my parents' house! It's weird. They'd probably tell us tomorrow over breakfast that they heard us, but *'that's okay'* and it's *'totally natural'* and we *'shouldn't be ashamed of our bodies'*. Do you want to have that conversation with them over walnut pancakes? I sure don't."

He smiles and climbs into bed next to me. "All right, but I can't guarantee I won't fuck you in your sleep."

"That's ridiculous. Nobody does that." Strangely, I would very much like to find out what it feels like…

He shrugs, lacing his fingers behind his head on the pillow. "What do you expect, Lex? You think those granny panties make you *less* hot?"

"Yes."

"You are sadly mistaken. And in a few hours, you will also find out what it feels like to wake up to an orgasm."

I'm speechless. But the idea he might *really* do it secretly thrills me and I'm suddenly very aware of the cotton of my t-shirt rubbing against my tightening nipples.

"You're getting turned on just thinking about it, aren't you? I bet your pussy is already tingling…"

"Shut up!" I hiss and pull the sheet up to my neck. "I'm going to sleep."

"You just want to get to the part where I wake you with an orgasm quicker, don't you?"

Guilty, I say nothing.

"I'll wait until I know you're out like a light. Then I'll touch your pussy so softly with my fingers, you won't even know it's happening. Lightly across your lips at first, until you're turned on and totally wet, but you'll still be asleep. I'll work your clit for awhile. Nothing intense, just enough to relax you even more. Then I'll slide my finger inside you. An inch at a time. Maybe you'll start having sex dreams, not even knowing it's me. When you're good and ready, I'll spoon up behind you, just touching the tip of my dick against your—"

"Okay! Parents' house! Can we go to sleep now?!"

He chuckles but says nothing more.

We lie in bed together for who knows how long, listening to the quiet night sounds of the remote farm. There's no way I'm getting to sleep now. But there's also no way I'm having sex in my parents' guest bedroom. Unless of course Connor tricks me into it…

"I really like your parents," he whispers, startling me.

"Thanks. I guess they're not the *worst* parents ever. But I will never be a hippie like them. Or live on a farm."

"How about in an RV?"

"As long as we spend half our time in the city, you've got yourself a deal," I joke. I don't know if I mean it. Living in an RV was never in my life plans. I don't think he means it either.

Eventually I start to drift off to sleep, only half wondering if he'll wake me with that orgasm he promised.

Out of the blue, he mutters, "I love you, Lex," saying it almost like he's talking to himself. "I think I always have." His voice has a fragility and a softness I'm not used to. It reminds me of how he sounded the night he told me about losing his parents. "And I know I always will."

I stare at the ceiling for a long time.

Crickets chirp outside. A summer breeze billows the sheer curtains into the room like angel's wings.

My voice is tight when I whisper, "I love you too, Connor Hughes."

He reaches for my fingers under the covers and squeezes my hand. Something sharp presses into my palm. "Ouch, Connor! What is that?"

He stares at me in the moonlit darkness. "Marry me."

I lift my hand and examine a sparkling engagement ring in a beam of moonlight.

"Your dad said it was okay."

I'm dumbfounded. "You asked him?"

"Yeah. When he showed me the farm. I'm sorry for always being a jerk to you. Marry me, Lex." The way he puts it is awkward and annoying and 100% Connor Crude.

I sniffle and start to cry. "Okay."

For the first time in probably ten years, since that first day of high school freshman year, when Connor Hughes saw me in the hallway for the first time and he made fun of me and called me Power Pole and made me cry, and I *swore* I would *never* cry again, not for him or *anyone*, I cry silently.

I cry and my body shakes with feeble sobs.

But the tears flow.

Happy tears.

Connor pulls me into his arms and holds me forever.

Four hours later, I wake up to the craziest, most intense orgasm ever as Connor comes inside me…

THE END

Still wondering what Dylan Montgomery did to break Electra's heart in college? Sign up for my mailing list, and you'll find out! You'll receive a short novella that reveals all the dirt, and you'll also meet a familiar character before he starred in one of my other novels.

Sign up here: **http://eepurl.com/B7crf**

or go to **devonhartford.com**

and **click** the **blue SIGN UP button**

IF YOU ARE ALREADY ON MY MAILING LIST, CHECK YOUR INBOX ON AUGUST 21st, 2015!

I only send out emails to announce new books or give you freebies like Electra's novella.

Personal thanks from Devon Hartford:

Thank you so much for taking the time to live with Connor and Electra for a while! If you enjoyed *Cover Model*, please leave a review wherever you purchased this ebook, on Goodreads, or any book blogs you frequent. Be sure to tell your friends about it!

Contact me and let me know if you want to read more about Connor and Electra!!

Like me on Facebook

Friend me on Facebook

Follow me on Twitter @DevonHartford

Follow me on WordPress at devonhartford.com

ABOUT THE AUTHOR

Devon Hartford spent most of his life in Southern California frequenting many of the locations in Stepbrother Obsessed. Devon is an artist and musician, and drew upon his experiences with both while writing his previous romance series The Story of Samantha Smith and The Story of Victory Payne.

OTHER BOOKS BY DEVON HARTFORD:

ROMANTIC COLLEGE COMEDY:
Fearless (The Story of Samantha Smith #1)
Reckless (The Story of Samantha Smith #2)
Painless (The Story of Samantha Smith #3)

ROMANTIC HIGH SCHOOL COMEDY
Stepbrother Obsessed

ROMANTIC NEW ADULT COMEDY
COVER MODEL

BILLIONAIRE ROMANCE:
ONE YEAR LOVE - Part One
ONE YEAR LOVE - Part Two
ONE YEAR LOVE - Part Three
ONE YEAR LOVE - Part Four

ROCKER ROMANCE:
Victory RUN 1 (The Story of Victory Payne)
Victory RUN 2 (The Story of Victory Payne)
Victory RUN 3 (The Story of Victory Payne)

ACKNOWLEDGMENTS

A HUGE thanks to all my passionate and fantastic beta readers:

Mylinda Abraham-Powell, Rosanne Triegaardt, Jackie Barnett, Tamara Clark, Mandy Jamerson, Mandy Karsa, Hayley Picknell, The REAL Julie England, Sandye, Neicy Cassidy, Her Highness Samantha Sheeley (Queen of All Typos), Sarah Lintott (The best Cowbag EVER!!), Megan C Christmas, Cyndi, Michelle Crane, Stephanie Svajgl, Maria Combee, Tania Clark, Steffini Walker Texas Ranger, Ratana Neth, Michele McKenzie, Sarah Frost, Wendy Boyer, and The Ever Special Mel Bushell for invaluable feedback and encouragement! You guys rock the typo sauce!

Hayley Picknell for slick Brit Pimpin' and awesome reviews everywhere!

Everybody's ever luvin' cowbag, Lindsey Melia for ghetto ghood pimpin'.

Chrissy Zent Sharp for awesome book pimpery via The Book Whore-der's Delights. Be sure to check them out if you're a Romance reader.

And last but not least, for last minute typo-snyping of the highest order and in the face of great personal danger, I award a Typo Heart to **Colonel Melanie Starr**, the one and only **Comma Bomber**, who saved this mission from certain disaster at the 11th hour, but not without significant personal sacrifice on her part. Colonel, I salute you!

Thanks to everybody else who has helped make this book a reality!